T0083125

Also by the Author:

The Trouble With Being Born, 2008

Peter: An (A) Historical Romance, 2006

S & M, 1997

The Peculiarity of Literature: An Allegorical Approach to Poe's Fiction, 1997

In Heaven Everything is Fine, 1991

Chick-Lit II: No Chick Vics, co-editor, 1996

Chick-Lit I: Postfeminist Fiction, co-editor, 1995

ARTHOUSE

a novel

Jeffrey DeShell

FC2
TUSCALOOSA

Copyright © 2011 by Jeffrey DeShell
The University of Alabama Press
Tuscaloosa, Alabama 35487-0380
All rights reserved
First edition

Published by FC2, an imprint of The University of Alabama Press,
with support provided by the Publishing Program at the University of
Houston–Victoria.

Address all editorial inquiries to: Fiction Collective Two, University of
Houston–Victoria, School of Arts and Sciences, Victoria, TX 77901-
5731

Cover and book design: Lou Robinson
Typefaces: Janson and Commerce
Produced and printed in the United States of America

The paper on which this book is printed meets the minimum
requirements of American National Standard for Information Sciences—
Permanence of Paper for Printed Library Materials, ANSI Z39.48–1984

Library of Congress Cataloging-in-Publication Data

DeShell, Jeffrey.
    Arthouse : a novel / Jeffrey Deshell. — 1st ed.
        p. cm.
    ISBN 978-1-57366-161-4 (pbk. : alk. paper) —ISBN 978-1-57366-825-5
(ebk.)
    1. College teachers—Fiction. 2. Film critics—Fiction. 3. Motion
pictures—Fiction. I. Title.
    PS3554.E8358A89 2011
    813'.54--dc22
                                                    2010041461

Contents

To Francis and Leo

Acknowledgments

I would very much like to thank the following for their support and help in the completion of this book: Dott. Alessia Rositani and the Giorgio Ronchi Foundation for allowing access to the *Casa Malaparte*; thanks also to Lucian Patraris at the Casa; Nik Morgano and Generro Cesarano of La Scalinatella; Cristiana Pasquarelli, of the *Palazzo dei Congressi*, for showing me the *Palazzo* and helping with my visit to the *Esposizione Universale Roma*; Giordano Al Zubi in Rome; the Committee for Research and Creative Work at the University of Colorado Boulder, who awarded me a Grant-in-Aid to help finance my trip to Rome and Capri; Todd Gleason, the Dean of the Arts and Sciences at the University of Colorado, as well as the School of Arts and Sciences and the University of Colorado for my sabbatical, which was invaluable in the completion of the book; and the Dean's Fund for Excellence at CU Boulder, which provided a number of hard-to-view DVD's. I would also like to thank a few of my colleagues: specifically Katherine Eggert, Bruce Kawin, Marcia Douglas, Emmanuel David, Stephen Graham Jones, Mark Winokur, John Stevenson, John-Michael Rivera, Jill Heydt-Stevenson and Sidney Goldfarb.

I would also like to thank Lynne Tillman, Robert Steiner, Marco Breuer and Lance Olsen.

Very special thanks are due to Patrick Greaney, who read and commented smartly on the manuscript, and who provided the title: he made the book much better.

Finally, I would like to thank Elisabeth Sheffield, who read and commented on early drafts, and whose fierce intelligence and love has made this book, and indeed all of my books, possible.

The Good, the Bad and the Ugly

Sergio Leone (1966)

He had better hurry, or he'd be late for his meeting with the Rodriguez Brothers. They weren't really brothers, just three guys all named Rodriguez. They probably weren't all named Rodriguez either, but what could you do? He sure as shit wasn't going to ask any questions.

He wanted to take the Grand Cherokee, but that was blocked by his F-150 in the driveway. As he searched in his pocket for his keys, he looked up toward the house, and noticed his mom's wheelchair, sitting on the porch, empty. That was unusual. His mother could walk some, but Liz kept her strapped in the chair because she was easier to manage that way. If she were inside with Liz, there was no reason the chair would be out on the porch. He looked around, past the house to the decrepit barn, then swiveled his gaze south and then east, to the hill, the driveway and the boys' trailer. No sign of her, or anyone else. Fuck. He hoped she hadn't wandered off. He did not want to be late for his meeting with the brothers.

He hurried across the driveway to the porch. Her chair was indeed empty, and the straps unbuckled, not broken. The wheels were locked and the chair was in the shade. A blue plastic cup was on its side on the floor. Maybe she was inside. He pushed the screen open and rushed to the kitchen door, where her could hear singing. Liz was working at the counter, singing to the radio, her back toward the door. She was wearing jeans shorts and a tube top. She was too old to wear a tube top. Too something.

"Hey Liz, have you seen my mother?"

She turned, placing her right hand on her heart. "Jesus, you scared me. I didn't hear you come in."

"Have you seen my mom?"

"She's outside on the front porch." She frowned. "I set her up in the shade and locked her wheels."

"She's not there."

"Oh no."

"Goddam it Liz, you can't do this. You can't just leave her." They both began to move from the kitchen out to the front door. "When did you put her out there?"

"Fifteen minutes ago. She can't hardly walk."

They were out on the porch now. "She must have walked somewhere. Where does she like to go?"

"She's always in her wheelchair. She don't go nowhere."

"Well, do you see her? You go north, and look in the garage and lab and around. If you see Jerry or Glow or anyone, get them to help. I'll go south and maybe check out the barn."

She stood on the porch, not moving. "I can't do this if she's going be wandering."

He turned and spoke over his shoulder. "It's a tough job."

"Yeah it's a tough job, cleaning up after your senile mom and watching that she don't fall out of that chair onto her face again. Not to mention making sure L'il Kevin remembers to put his dick INSIDE his pants when he gets dressed in the morning. Yeah it's a tough job, taking care of that near zucchini and a 'tard. So, unless you'd rather wipe your mother's ass yourself, leave me the fuck alone."

He stopped. "It beats working on Colfax for five bucks a hummer. Or did your new Trans Am slip your mind somehow?"

"Fuck you."

He started again, walking backwards and yelling, "Maybe when I go up to Denver I'll stop at Leroy's and say, 'remember Liz? She's now working the champagne room outside of Pueblo. She only has two customers, but they're real devoted.'"

"Fuck you."

"Her tits have gone and her ass has fallen, but she just bought a classic '91 Trani. Too bad she lives at the end of a fucking dirt road. With a bunch of tweakers. And that band she was always talking about starting? She just signed a four CD record deal with RCA. Going to do all her own songs, too."

"Fuck you asshole."

"She's a comet man. You gotta grab her coattails and fly."

Fucking Liz. It was too hot for his mother to be wandering out here in the desert. He walked up the hill on the dirt road, reasoning that the semi-paved road would be more inviting to his mother's sense of balance than the overgrown footpath by the barn. And the barn was scary. The opposite of picturesque, it was like a pimple on the face of a homely child. Nothing dramatic had happened to it: but the years first of indifference, then neglect and finally desertion, along with the wind, dust and snow, had taken their toll. When they first moved out, they had spent a couple of nights there, camping in the loft while they fixed up the house and arranged the Winnebagos (the mobile homes came later). They even had a Halloween party there one night, everyone X-ing out and grooving to Prince on L'il Kevin's box. But then Mace freaked, insisting the walls were too red, like blood, which got everyone thinking, and the party broke up. He and Jerry had returned a couple of days later, and some animal had crawled into something and died, aerating the entire structure with a decomposing funk. He wasn't going to go all *House of Usher* (the Epstein, not the Corman, although the Corman was cool too) here: nobody except for Kevin liked the barn. He reached the top of the mesa and noticed the dry wind kicking up dust and blowing a few tumbleweeds around. The light came low and direct from his left, and, coupled with the blowing dust, made him squint through his sunglasses.

This was ugly country. Oklahoma or Nebraska had nothing on this part of Colorado. Thirty, forty miles north, the truck farms of the Arkansas River Valley snaked along Colorado 50, offering some of the best cantaloupe and chilies in the world. Fifty miles west (as the crow flies, about a ninety mile drive), San Isabel National Forest marked the eastern frontier of the Rockies. But here was nowhere. And no matter how he tried, there was nothing he could do to make it engaging: it was too barren, too dry, too rocky and too monotonous to inspire feelings of awe, wonder, or the least bit of sympathy or connection. It wasn't a landscape, it was just land. Flat, dusty land with gorges and rocks. And harsh, glaring, unfiltered light. It wasn't beautiful, certainly, not like the deserts of New Mexico or the high plains of the western slope. It wasn't sublime, either, like the Arches or Badlands. It was just butt ugly, desolate, irredeemable, hopeless. Maybe he'd feel differently if he hadn't grown up here. Maybe he'd be able to see the stark severity as some kind of unspoiled purity. Maybe the pristine indifference could be recuperated as something meaningful: nature as timeless and inexplicable and humans as mortal and insignificant and all that bullshit. But he couldn't see it that way. He felt nothing for this topography other than a mild revulsion. And a sad exhaustion.

There she was, shuffling down the hill, just this side of the big overhanging rock and the large circular metal watering trough he called the pond. He liked to sit out under the rock sometimes and drink beer, and a few times at night he'd brought a bottle of scotch and looked at the stars. He thought about going back and getting the truck to give her a ride back, but he didn't want to lose sight of her, so he sighed and jogged after her.

"Mom, mom, wait up!"

She disappeared quickly behind the rock. There was shade there, and he could sit her down to rest if necessary. He wished he had a bottle of water or something. He looked at his watch: the Rodriguez brothers were going to be pissed. He finally cleared the big rock, and saw his mother, her right hand on the rim of the trough, circling slowly around the aluminum tank. He stood there and watched for a few seconds. "Mom! What are you doing out here, mother?" He walked to her quietly, gently. "If you want to come out here, I'll take you. We'll have a picnic sometime, a lunch." She was wearing her large brimmed hat—Glow called it her sombrero—and a grey velour warm-up jacket over a shapeless turquoise and pink housedress. She had once-blue fluffy slippers on her feet, now covered in dust.

She looked at him and smiled. She probably couldn't see much without her glasses. Her right eye-lash was clotted and her pale skin was red and blotchy. Her lips were dry and beginning to crack. They weren't taking good enough care of her, that was obvious. She moved past him, continuing on her way, clockwise around the trough. He took her arm and she allowed him to guide her to the shade, where she stood facing the rock. He thought he'd let her stay there for a few minutes before they walked back up the hill. He could even carry her part way if he had to. She didn't weigh much. The brothers would have to wait.

He heard them before he saw them. A loud guffaw, and then quieter murmuring. It could be Mace and Jerry, or Carlos and L'il Kevin, but he didn't think anyone else ever came out past the hill, at least on foot. Maybe they were being raided. No, the laughter was much too loud to be coming from slick wind-breakered Federales. Too loud even for hick Sheriff deputies or State Troopers in those failure-to-communicate sunglasses. He moved closer to the rock, between his mother and the road. He put his hand on the Glock in his back holster.

But if they weren't the police, who could they be? The Rodriguez Brothers would never come out here. And how many were there? And what the fuck were they doing out in the middle of nowhere like this? One voice was much louder than the others. They were talking about women. Pussy. One was saying how tight black pussy was. How he came in three strokes. And was ready for more in five minutes. A deeper, accented voice was saying although he preferred white meat, especially with brunette carpet and blonde drapes, at the end of the day, pussy was pussy. Ok.

If they got up past the top of the mesa, they'd likely trip the sensors that Glow had set up around the compound. That is, if things were working: they should have tripped something already. And if they got up there, somebody was on sentry duty. And that somebody would probably shoot them. With no hesitation, no compunction whatsoever. Mad dog white trash motherfuckers. Or brown trash, as the case may be. Rainbow trash. No, he probably should stop them before they reached the hill. He wished his mom were somewhere else, and not standing feebly next to him, staring at a rock.

When the voices were about ten feet away, he stepped out from the shade. They didn't stop immediately. There were two of them: a tall gangly white guy and a medium sized Mexican. The white guy had jean shorts, with a large translucent neon orange water bottle hooked to his belt, black high-top sneakers, a Dave Matthews tee shirt and wraparound shades. The Mexican was wearing a dirty white turquoise and white print shirt, sky blue Adidas workout pants cut-off at the knee, white Nikes and a Rockies baseball cap. The kid looked soft. The

Mexican was older, with a scruffy salt and pepper beard and a red and white do-rag. He didn't look soft.

The white kid had this goofy, default smile. His lips were think and full, and he looked like he found the world infinitely amusing, in a sort of spoiled, no-fucking-clue kind of way. His skin was pink, smooth and unlined, and his cheeks sported deep dimples. He was probably in his mid-twenties, although his posture, manner and features were those of an older teen. His shoulders and torso were cut, like he'd worked on them, but his legs were skinny, like he hadn't. The Mexican had those bushy, peasant eyebrows, and deeply tanned and deeply lined skin. He squinted, and raised his right hand to shade his eyes from the sun. He could be anywhere from thirty to fifty. They all looked at each other for a while, without speaking. He wondered if either of them had a gun.

Finally: "This is private property. You lost?"

"Yeah, we were turning around and our car got stuck in the ditch near your cattle guard. We saw fresh tire tracks, so we'd thought we'd follow this road until we saw a house. You have a cell phone we could borrow?"

"Folks live out here because they don't want to be bothered. Sometimes people aren't friendly when you trespass on their land." He wasn't sure where this dialogue was coming from.

"We don't mean nothing by it," the Mexican said. "Our car is stuck, maybe blocking your road. We just want to use a phone, man, nothing else." So their car didn't come all the way through the gate: maybe that's why they didn't trip the sensor.

He nodded, and stared at the Mexican. Even though he squinted his eyes were large in proportion to the rest of his darkened face. His lids were heavy, and the skin above his cheeks folded and leathery: they were the eyes of someone who worked without walls or ceilings, in vast open spaces, in panoramas with only land and horizon. He was hot, and could feel sweat on his brow. He looked at the kid, with his dark shades, the kind baseball players wore where the lens extended half-way around the cheek. He could see the Todd AO reflection of himself, his mother nearly hidden in the shade of the rock behind him, with the Mexican off to the side. He looked back to the Mexican. He grew up with Mexicans, Hispanics, Chicanos and Chicanas (who in Pueblo hadn't?) and while he loved the food and liked tequila, he'd never really gotten into the fiesta, siesta, languid senorita and leño scene. Too bad. He was no fan of Third Cinema either. When he thought about Mexicans, he thought about weddings, green chili, hanging around, smoking dope and talking in that whiny voice, hey, ese, she's really a virgin, eh. He'd steered clear of the Mexicans when he was in prison. He steered clear of everyone when he was in prison.

He looked again, from the Mexican to the kid, and then back. He didn't think they were packing. He wasn't sure what to do. He could try to get some help, but if Carlos heard, or Mace, they might come out here and cap them anyway. Just for kicks. And Jerry? He didn't know what Jerry would do. This had never happened before, strangers wandering across the three miles of desert prairie from the county road to make contact with the compound. There was nothing to hunt around here, and it was too far out of the way to be of much interest to snowmobilers or dirtbikers. Jerry liked plans: he tended toward violence when surprised. What Jerry would do would probably depend if he was sketching, crashing, pilling or smoking.

The kid shifted his weight and smiled stupidly. He wondered if they were high. The Mexican brought his hand to his face, and scratched his upper lip with his index finger. They stood there like that. Eventually, his mother made a small sound, and moved away from the rock. He kept his eyes on the Mexican as she shuffled past him, toward the kid. The kid laughed, and she adjusted her route and headed back toward the trough. He could see her eyes underneath the shade of her hat. She looked tired, confused. This was idiotic: he had to get her back to the house.

"Tell you what. You two stay here, right here, and I'll take my mom back to the house and get my truck and maybe we can get your car out of the ditch. What kind of car is it?"

"An old Toyota Corona."

"Corolla?"

"Corona. With an 'n.' Like the beer."

"Okay. We'll try to get your Corona out of the ditch and get you on your way. If not, I'll give you a lift into town."

"We could just call a tow truck. I got triple A."

"I like my idea better. It'll be a while, my mom doesn't move that well anymore. That sound okay to you?"

"Sure."

"If I were you, I'd stay right around the rock. My friends, the people who own this land, they like to hunt, and they might be out now."

The kid laughed. "Whatta they hunt around here?"

"Whatever they can find." He moved toward the trough, took his mom gently by the arm and led her toward the footpath.

Sátántangó

Belá Tarr (1984)

The Wind

The dust is everywhere, blurring lines and softening forms. Periods of calming and clearing occur, when the images sharpen and coalesce, but these are temporary, and soon the obscuring clouds return. The wind is always audible through a low oscillating drone or a high-pitched whistle (sometimes both). Windows rattle. It is a two-story farmhouse with many windows, a large rectangular cube, once painted white. On the western side, the paint has irregularly been eroded by the wind, dust and snow, leaving a textured and variegated surface, a plane of striated old grey wood upon which discolored paint curls and blotches. There are deep pockmarks and gouges throughout, and a football sized patch of wet rot where the wood appears on the verge of disintegrating. Three relatively new slats extend from the south corner of the wall, almost reaching the door. The new panels are whiter and smoother than those adjacent, but they are remarkable only in relation to the surrounding decay. A large rectangular window, set in the middle, with its frame peeling and fading beyond definite color identification, dominates the second story of the west wall. The three glass squares of the window (top, bottom and storm) are all intact, but a COOPER QUALITY GUARANTEED FEEDS sign backs the entire window, save for a six-inch wide strip of tar paper on top. The south wall is dominated by a low-sloped shed porch roof, which runs the half the length of the wall and is supported by three peeling white unfluted Doric columns. The south east corner of the porch roof sags badly. There are five rectangular windows on the first floor of the south wall, and a door in the middle of the porch. The windows seem in good repair, and all have curtains visible behind, except the middle one (to the east of the door), which is boarded up on the outside with rough planks. This wall, although somewhat whiter than the west, is still abraded and marked, with patches of variegated gray throughout. A pallid water stain, in the shape of a large steam iron, washes over the second floor directly above the boarded window. The door is steel and bright, with a rectangular window, and contrasts sharply against the dull paint of the frame and walls. A thick black metal screen door adds to the incongruity. A white Adirondack chair squats on the porch to the west of the door. Four small square windows placed at regular intervals mark the second story of the south wall. All are intact, although curtains can be seen only in numbers two, three and four, as the westernmost is boarded from the inside. The gable roof is simple and black. Gaps of missing shingles dot the slopes of the roof, and shredded tarpaper flaps ostentatiously near the south west corner. Two rectangular brick chimneys rise about six feet above the spine. One of the chimneys is slightly to the west of the front door, while the other extends flush with the western wall. The easternmost chimney shows a vertical zigzag line of black pitch separating lighter brick (below) from dark. A section of tin flashing remains only on the eastern side, and a few bricks are missing from the crown. A television antenna is bent against the western chimney. The east wall has no door, only four square windows—two top and two bottom—forming a regular grid. The top window on the southern side is broken, with a triangular jagged shard jutting from the bottom, and is boarded. The window just below is bereft of glass, and is also boarded. The other four windows are intact, with curtains noticeable. The brick foundation is visible on this east wall, rising almost a foot from the soil line. It has been patched in places with concrete, with the concrete often falling away, leaving a background of crumbling brick. There has been an attempt made to paint the foundation white, but the paint has not taken, leaving only thin pale streaks on a few dark bricks. A door with a window in its center rests on the foundation in the middle of the wall, a foot or so from the ground. There are no steps. Two grey satellite dishes are installed on the roof, one on either side of the spine, both pointing 114 degrees south east. The north wall features six square windows, three on the second story and three on the first. A jumble of rusted farm implements, including the bonnet, large spoked wheel and skeletal seat of an old tractor, haphazard platters of a decaying disk harrow, and threatening teeth of an upturned hay rake have reverted into abstraction about four feet beyond the north wall.

Directly north of the house stands a right triangular lean-to garage. The south wall is parallel to the north wall of the house, separated by approximately twelve feet. The north and south walls are made of old stone, and a sloping tin roof makes up most of the east wall, with a two-foot stone wall supporting beneath. There are two square windows, one set in the south wall, one in the north, both intact. The window of the south wall is backed by a fluttering black and white POW MIA flag. The stone is pitted and scarred, with the joining cement often crumbling. The opposite, or west wall (with the floor as the adjacent and the roof as the hypotenuse), is composed of three white metal garage doors. Two of these are open, and a large grey pickup truck is parked halfway inside the southernmost door. A black Hummer, a dark Jeep Cherokee, a white Trans Am and a black pick-up are arranged, on a black asphalt oval driveway, west, south west, and south south west to the entrance, with the black pick-up parked behind (south south west) the Trans Am. All vehicles point toward the garage. The driveway extends directly south from the garage, expanding in front of the western door to the house, and contracting again, stopping two feet south of an imaginary line extending directly from the house's southern wall. A dirt road runs south west from the driveway.

Two men are working underneath the grey pickup. The droning white noise has been replaced by a high pitched and insistent whistling. One man wears thick black military boots and a grey jumper, the other black high-top sneakers, jeans and opened flannel shirt with a dirty white sleeveless tee underneath. The soles of the military boots are worn badly at the heel. A third man, in stained white overalls, stands above, near the passenger side door. He holds two large nylon gym bags, one in either hand. Dust blows over the edge on the tin roof, which extends a foot past the top frame of the garage doors. A bright work light is hung near the rear axle underneath the truck. The man with the military boots removes a metal panel covering a sealed section of the gas tank. The other looks on and scratches his chin with his left hand. The man in the boots carefully sets the panel down on an old blanket he has spread out near his head. As he does so, the other man (flannel shirt) twists around and holds his right hand out from beneath the truck. The third man leans down and places the handle of one of the nylon bags into the hand of the second. He takes it and holds it to the first man, who carefully lifts it up and arranges it in the sealed compartment. He holds it in place with his right forearm, and nods to the second man, who twists again and holds his right hand out from beneath the truck. The third man bends down and places the handle of the remaining bag in the hand of the second man, and straightens and turns and walks south west, away from the garage, down the asphalt driveway. The second man hands the bag to the first, who turns the bag around and presses it into the remaining half of the sealed compartment of the gas tank. The second man leans and holds both bags in the compartment while the first man finds his wrench and sets it on his chest. He slowly lifts the panel he'd placed on the blanket by his head and, while the second man moves his arms and hands out of the way, carefully fits it into place covering the sealed compartment. He tightens one bolt, now another bolt, now a third and now a fourth. Each bolt requires between six and seven half-circle torque revolutions. The mechanical clicking of the ratchet is audible over the high-pitched wind. The second man watches the first and second bolts being tightened, and maneuvers himself out from underneath the truck and stands, brushing his hands. He hesitates, walks directly south, turns south east and steps onto the porch, opens the screen door and the metal door, and goes inside the house. The first man takes some grease from a small can he has placed near this left elbow and rubs it around the first bolt, now the second now the third and now the fourth. He looks at the bolts for some time, nods and maneuvers himself from beneath the carriage. He stands and wipes his hands on a rag he keeps in his right back pocket. He reaches up to a pocket near his chest on his left, unzips it, and removes a packet of cigarettes and a lighter. He takes a cigarette from the pack with his right hand and taps it twice on the hood of the truck. He places it in his mouth and takes the lighter from his left, and flicks the lighter once, twice, three times before a flame appears. He lights his cigarette, and returns the pack and lighter to his pocket. He zips the pocket. Simultaneously, two men emerge from the front door of the house, walking quickly toward the garage. Both are medium height, and both wear jeans. One of the men wears white high-top sneakers, and the other cowboy boots. Both have dark wrap-around sunglasses, and both carry hats in their hands. One has a long black braided ponytail that flaps around his neck, and the other a shaved head. The man with the ponytail wears a white Denver Broncos # 7 Elway jersey with dark letters and trim, and the other a dark windbreaker that puffs out in the wind. They walk slowly north east from the front of the house, now north into the garage. The man in the windbreaker crosses behind the truck, nods to the man smoking a cigarette and opens the door and climbs into the driver's seat, while the man with the ponytail hesitates at the passenger side door, places his John Deere baseball cap on his head, opens the door and climbs in. The windbreaker man closes the door, arranges his dark CR baseball cap on his head and pulls the bill down low, reaches back to grab his seat belt, dragging it across his body and buckling it. He adjusts the rearview mirror and the side mirror. As he is doing this, the ponytailed man reaches behind his right shoulder to his seatbelt, drags it down across his body and buckles it. He looks to the left and the right. The man in the windbreaker leans backward and extracts his keys from his pocket. He leans forward, inserts the key into the ignition, and starts the truck. He looks backward over his right shoulder, and using his side mirror, maneuvers the truck backwards and proceeds directly south until the southern edge of the house, where he arcs the rear of the truck gently north. He stops, changes gears, and drives south south west, off of the driveway and down the dirt road. The truck is soon swallowed by the dust.

Carlos

Carlos stands in the garage, smoking his cigarette, looking out into the dust. He inhales loudly, wetly. Two drops of sweat run, one following the path of the other, from his hairline down the middle of his short forehead to the bridge to the tip of his blunt nose. He wipes both of them away with the back of his right hand. His eyes are small and squint naturally, constantly. His hair is collar-length and unwashed, and tucked behind his right ear. His beard, streaked and flecked with grey, clings to his thick upper lip, chin, cheeks and throat. The Chinese characters for prosperity are visible beneath his beard on one side of his meaty neck. He sneers slightly and it's evident that he's missing two teeth (right premolars). He walks quickly to the south west corner of the garage, where he pushes a button (a mechanical grind replacing the high pitched whistle) and walks south west into the dust and onto the driveway, between the Hummer and the pickup. He continues down the driveway and onto the dirt road. He removes his cigarette with his right hand and flicks it away. After twenty feet down the dirt road, the road begins to slope upwards into a hill. He turns abruptly west, follows a short dirt path onto a cleared dirt porch and up two wooden stairs, where he carefully opens a light metal door and walks into the trailer, closing the door, with some difficulty, behind him. The drone changes to percussive rattling, shaking and creaking, as the gusts meet the walls and joints of tin and metal. Rock chords are faintly audible over the rhythm of the wind. Carlos stomps his feet to shake off, and wipes the dust from his lips with the back of his right hand.

The kitchen is small, about eight feet by ten, and against the west wall a row of six square wooden cabinet doors run eye level above the Formica counter, with a small black microwave oven set between the second and third door (south to north). The row of cabinets ends, as does the counter, with the black refrigerator at the north end. Four longer rectangular cabinet doors are underneath the counter, with a vertical row of three smaller utensil drawers and a single rectangular cabinet door next to the refrigerator. The sink is above the second pair (from the south) of the rectangular cabinet doors. The sink, and every inch of counter space, is piled high by a full and motley complement of soiled dishes, pots, pans, plastic and aluminum containers, silver and plastic ware and other and varied instruments and vessels for the storage, cooking, reheating, conveyance and distribution of food and beverage. There are crusts, films, stains and skins on nearly every available surface of the room: the tile floor near the refrigerator door is marked with a damp darkness the size and shape of a toddler's torso; the western wall decorated or desecrated, like a Pollock or a slaughterhouse, by once liquid pigment now fixed; a thickening white epidermal flap is coagulating near the rim of a saucepan and a fork and serving spoon seem fused to a chafing dish by a glob of furry grey paste. Crumbs crunch underfoot, adhere to handles and fester in corners.

Carlos stomps heavily south, to the doorway of the kitchen. "Danzig?"

"Yeah."

"First?"

"*How The Gods Kill.*"

A particularly loud creak and groan can be heard over the music. "Fucking wind."

"Fucking wind."

He turns and walks north, into a bedroom. The door closes behind him.

Liz

A dark room, with a vertical sliver of silver light visible to the right. The low rumble of the wind drones on just this side of aural perception. A brief cry is heard. The drone continues, as does the darkness and the sliver of light. Suddenly a loud, long wail breaks the silence, punctuated by a brief scream. "Christ!"

A lamp with a square, 60's shade suddenly illuminates a circle of a corner of the room, opposite the sliver to the right. A table supports the lamp, as well as an old analog clock, an empty water bottle, a plastic container for a dental appliance and half-empty pack of cigarettes and a highball glass used as an ashtray. The walls are grey and cracked, with fine spiderweb fractures emanating from the edge where wall meets ceiling. The Harris bed is small, with a white tube frame arcing high at the head. Thick dark hair is splayed against an off-white sheet. Another long moan is heard. "Ok, goddam it, ok." The head rises, and a thin pale arm sweeps the darkened blankets from the torso as hips rise and rotate. A woman sits in the middle of the bed, her head down in her arms and her thick dark hair shading her face. She's wearing a translucent white cotton tee shirt, dark panties and bright white ankle socks. She's very thin, and her collarbone protrudes obviously from the cotton of her shirt. Her flesh hangs loose off her arm, and her belly is distended, nearly touching, in this posture, her upper thighs. It's impossible to discern her age from this angle. She leans back abruptly and twists her torso to reach back to the nightstand, where she removes her appliance from the plastic container and places it in her mouth. She stands, and her hair falls to her shoulders, revealing two bright and restless eyes set in a lean, smooth face. Her mouth is crooked, the thin bottom lip belonging to a different mouth than the top. She smiles (grimaces), stretching her lips over her teeth, smiles (grimaces) again. She reaches up with her left hand and grasps her canine teeth with her index finger and thumb and adjusts. She smiles. The lines of her mouth now match. She brushes back her hair and sighs. It's still impossible to tell her age: her eyes are quick and her face unlined, but there's something older about her mouth and chin. Likewise, her limbs and torso are slender, but the flesh is lax and doughy. Her hair is thick, luxurious almost. Another sharp cry is audible over the background of the wind. "I'm coming,

I'm coming." She twists, leans back over the bed and turns out the light. The darkness and the sliver of light return. The bed creaks and something passes quickly in front of the light. Now only darkness, the thin slice of light, the drone of the wind.

L'il Kevin

A very large, well-built man plays with a small kitten on the wooden floor of an old barn. The roof of the barn is missing slats, every other one in places, and light streams in through the clouds of dust, creating a zebra pattern on the floor and in the air. The man is wearing camouflage pants, sneakers and a sleeveless grey tee shirt with the words "Pueblo's Pride" stenciled in black cursive letters across the chest. He has patches of dust on his knees and elbows, and the right side of his dark hair near his ear is powdered white. The cat is a gray tabby with white paws. The man is on his hands and knees, and he takes the cat underneath the arms with both hands and rolls left onto his back and holds the cat up over his chest. Dust rises into the air, the cat kicks its hind legs and purrs, and the man laughs. He rolls to the right onto his knees, keeping the cat cradled against his large chest. More dust rises, and the cat meows but makes no attempt to escape. The man laughs loudly, and both the laugh and the echoes can be heard clearly over noise of the wind in the large decaying building.

The eastern wall of the barn is nearly intact, save for the high window that has been boarded up. The wall is missing a few flinders here and there, and the light that shines through illuminates the motes of dust in the air. The outer side of the wood is rough and rutted, with assorted knots and nail heads pitting throughout. There are a few patches where the wood has weakened and split, but most of these are concentrated around the small door near the southern edge of the wall. The inner wall is slightly smoother and more regular with periodic splotches of dark paint. The door is not boarded, and shakes in the wind. A thin strip of light is visible around all four sides between the door and the frame.

The man and the cat continue to play together on the floor. In the center of the barn they are too far away from the west wall to notice the wind. With a meow, the cat quickly escapes from the man's arms and scurries west north west, through a maze of broken machinery and discarded tools, up a ladder and disappears into gloom. The man stops on his hands and knees and looks up to the top of the ladder where the cat has disappeared. He has a large swatch of dust on his right cheek, and a thin film of sweat is visible on his brow, as well as on his thick forearms. The expression on his face is curious, untroubled.

He slowly gets to his feet. He grins. "Lebron? Lebron? Come Lebron. Come on. I know where you are. Come back down." His voice is thin, tentative, inexperienced, and must come from someplace other than the large sculpted chest and throat. "Lebron, come! I don't want to go up to the loft."

He sighs, and moves toward the clutter of cracked and warped vegetable display racks, spreaders with dented barrels, a crate of black used workman shoes, a squat Coke vending machine (15¢) with the top missing, a wooden crate of broken hand-drills, drill bits and various files and rasps, a cast iron block and tackle set, a rusted steel chicken watering can, a pile of large cultivator tines partially protected with a grey tarp, and various other dust-covered farm and kitchen tools, old suitcases and other used and broken implements and detritus. He eventually makes his way to the bottom of the loft stairs. The light is weaker here, as the roof above is nearly undamaged. He looks up the stairs, and carefully and slowly picks cobwebs off of his face with the middle finger and the thumb of his right hand. "Lebron. Come down Lebron, come down." He stops picking at his face and moves quickly up the stairs, taking two at a time.

The roof covering the loft is largely intact, the slats continuous and integral, with only a few punctures and fissures. The light pattern is celestial, remarkably similar to that of the interior of a planetarium. The floor is bare, with only a thin covering of dust and hay particles. An ancient rocking chair sits facing a gap in the wall in near the far (north west) corner, and the large hayloft door has been boarded up with a patchwork of highway road signs, pieces from an old Chesterfield billboard with the word "Smells" in the bottom south corner, "Milder" upside down in the top south and half of a six foot Arthur Godfrey face (pointed down) in the center, and a collage of various license plates and the sides of wooden oil crates interspersed between. The wind blows fiercely through the various cracks and punctures of the wall.

L'il Kevin looks down and notices his pants have a six inch horizontal rip across the right knee, and there's a thin four-inch line of blood where his skin has been cut. He squats down and examines his knee, touching the blood with the forefinger of his right hand. The cut is not deep. "Lebron, Lebron. Look what you made me do, Lebron." He scans the room. "I see you, I see you. Come here and look what you made me do." He stands and quickly moves to the south west corner, where he stops, bends down and picks Lebron up gently with his right hand cradling the cat's chest. He carries him over to the north west corner, and sits in the chair, the cat in his lap.

He directs Lebron's head to the hole in his jeans and the cut on his knee. "Look what you made me do, Lebron. Look what you made me do." Lebron shakes his head and meows. "It doesn't hurt." He pets Lebron on the head. "I can do whatever I want to you. I'm stronger than you are." Lebron rolls on his back and playfully claws at L'il Kevin's arms. L'il Kevin rolls him back so his chest and stomach lie flat against this right thigh. "I'm so much stronger than you. I can do whatever I want." He leans forward and peers out the gap on the wall. He squints because of the wind. "Look Lebron, there's Carlos." He continues to pet Lebron on the head and shoulders. "Look at the wind, Lebron, look at the wind. There's a tumbleweed." He holds Lebron up so his head is even with the gap in the wall. The wind makes the cat close his eyes and squirm. A few moments pass. "I'm so much stronger than you. I can do anything I want to you." He puts Lebron back in his lap and continues to pet him.

Mace

The interior of the laboratory is bright white, and is lit by six strong fluorescent tubes. There are no windows, and no wind audible. A low electric hum can be heard constantly in the background. The room has the solid stillness of a bunker. Four sixteen inch square vents occupy each of the four corners of the ceiling, and an LED timer centers the far (north) wall. Against this wall stands a thick wooden counter, supported by four thick wooden legs. Four large silver metal cylindrical containers with thick walls (heating mantles) are set into the counter. Thin wires run from the bottom of these containers to four switch boxes on the floor. The switch boxes contain two switches and a potentiometer each. Inside these metal containers rest four 22 liter glass flasks, each three fourths full of a bubbling bright liquid. 80 mm glass reflux (distillation) tubes rise from the tops of the flask almost to the ceiling. One smaller (10mm) tube runs from a barb near the bottom and a similar tube from a barb near the top of each of the reflux tubes. There is a digital thermometer set above the top barb into each of the reflux tubes. The joints, tubes, flasks and corks are all connected cleanly and solidly. Five ring stands, with two or three attached clamps per stand, sit on the counter between each flask and mantle. Beneath the counter four 20-liter glass storage jars have been placed. On a chrome table pushed against the left wall sit a number of flasks (mostly Büchner and Erlenmeyer), as well as two separating funnels and three coils of plastic tubing. There is a large electronic scale on a chrome stand on the right wall. A bank of four analog gauges and four switches make up a panel on the right (east) wall, near the door. The room is clean and orderly.

A tall thin figure in a light colored level A hazmat suit with in-hood respirator moves stiffly, checking the thermometers near the ceiling, starting with the one on his left (west) and moving one by one to the right. He bends at the waist to look closely at the flasks of boiling liquid, now beginning with the one on his right (east) and moving one by one west. He is no hurry, his steel grey eyes peer intently through the clear PVC face shield. He straightens up and looks at the wall timer, moves down to the row of switchboxes on the floor, where he flicks one switch (the far west), moves to the next box and flicks the far west switch, to the next box (the far west switch) and to the eastern box, where he flicks the far west switch. He straightens, surveys the scene, and moves to a door to his right (east).

Jerry and The Professor

"Where's the truck?"

"I don't know. Where we park?"

"We parked over there by the dumpster. In that empty space there."

"Fuck."

"Did Glow take it?"

"Guess so."

"Did you have a fight or something?"

Jerry walks to the rim of the parking lot, and stands under an overhead light. Most of Avondale is dark, although a snake of weak streetlights is visible curving west on Santa Fe toward Vineland. He takes a lighter and a single cigarette from the top left pocket of his army jacket, puts the cigarette in his mouth, cups his left hand over the tip and lights up with his right. His face is smooth and youthful, and rather thin. His dark hair is cut short, a medium fade that allows him to style the top. He has the beginnings of a three-day beard on his chin, upper lip and jawline, but his cheeks and neck are clean. His bones are fine, and his mouth is curled into a mischievous but engaged smile. His eyes seem permanently narrowed, and belie the ingenuous promise of the rest of his face. His broad shoulders taper down quickly to a narrow waist, and his boot cut jeans ride low near his ass. He has a nice-fitting black silk polo shirt underneath his jacket, and pointed alligator cowboy boots with sharp silver toes. He looks west, down the empty street.

"So how we going to get home?"

"What time is it?"

"Quarter to two."

He shrugs, turns and looks east.

"Is she coming back?"

He takes a drag from the cigarette and begins to walk west down the sidewalk. His boots make a loud clicking sound on the concrete. A breeze blows from the east. The Professor shakes his head and follows. The Professor is thin and slightly round-shouldered, with dark curly hair starting to grey. He is clean-shaven, but needs a haircut, as a flop of salt and pepper hair extends haphazardly down over his forehead. His wrinkled eyes—visible through the clear lenses of his black horn-rim glasses—and lined brow—furrowed into a nearly permanent expression of apprehension—make him look older than his brother. He is wearing a dark long sleeved shirt, jeans and dark low top sneakers. He follows a few paces behind Jerry before catching up with him.

"Aren't we going the wrong way?"

"I thought we'd hit The Hangar for breakfast. Give Carlos and Mace a call to join us."

"It's a quarter to two."

"It'll be four thirty, five by the time we get there."

They walk two abreast down the sidewalk, reaching the second streetlight. The streetlight inscribes a circle of light with a circumference of about 12π (36.7) feet. The circle encloses sections of the street, sidewalk and dirt shoulder. A vacant lot lies beyond the shoulder, and further down Santa Fe the promise of darkened fields. They walk into the center of the light and move towards the edge. They are enveloped by darkness, and the light of Jerry's cigarette glows prominently against the black horizon. The breeze blows at their backs.

"Are you tweaking?"

The cigarette glow burns brighter, arcs gracefully down. "No." The boots click on the sidewalk. "You drunk?"

"A little."

The cigarette light lifts back up and glows brighter for a moment. The boots continue clicking on the sidewalk and they reach the third streetlight. Here the sidewalk ends, replaced by a beaten dirt path. Weeds encroach on the path from the fields. Jerry moves onto the street, and the clicking from his boots modulates, without breaking rhythm, into a softer, less obtrusive footfall. They walk into the light, and continue out of it.

"Those boots hurt your feet?"

"Not yet."

The night is silent except for the rhythm of boots on the asphalt: the street is deserted, there are no crickets or other insects, and their breathing is somehow muffled, soundless. Only the quiet contact of boot leather and night blacktop, continuing, marking, propelling. They pass in and out of a streetlight's illumination.

"How's mom?"

"Not so good. You should pay more attention."

They walk. Down the street, into the darkness, into the light and into the darkness. They walk.

Mother

She sits at the window in her wheelchair and stares east. East into the seemingly endless plain.

Glow

She hurries down the two steps from the door of the trailer she shares with Jerry, and walks directly east. The wind, which is at her back, howls loudly as it blows her fine light hair around her face. She is wearing gold aviator sunglasses, desert shorts, a white tank top and low white boat sneakers without socks. Her legs are long and dark, with the tattoo of a cobra rising up onto her calf from her right foot. She reaches the entrance to the lab, and descends the four stairs to the door, which she opens. Keeping the door open, she sticks her head in for a moment, closes the door and runs south east to the garage. She cups her hands and looks into the garage door windows, the north, the middle and the south. She turns to see a dust devil rise up twenty feet high just south of the Professor's trailer, spin west for a few yards and then disappear. She turns back and runs south down the driveway until she clears the western wall of the house. She quickly turns east and hops onto the porch, where two strides bring her to the screen door, which she opens, and the front door, which she also opens and enters. She closes both doors behind her. A few moments pass and door opens and the screen and she's out, walking directly west, against the wind, across the driveway, until she reaches the dirt road. She follows it south west until she reaches the path, which she follows west up to the door of the trailer of Carlos, Mace and L'il Kevin. She knocks. She waits. The wind blows. She waits for a few moments more and then moves east on the path. She doesn't wait to reach the dirt road, but turns directly north as soon as she clears the east side of Mace's trailer. She runs directly north until she reaches the Professor's door, which she knocks on and waits. The door opens, and she stands there talking to the Professor. The door closes, and she walks west until she clears the trailer, then north west until she reaches her door, back where she started.

Tango

The barroom is rectangular, with the east and west three times the longer walls. The bar extends almost the entire length of the west wall, but only the northern half is used. The swinging door leading to the hall of restrooms sits in the middle of the north wall, and a cd jukebox is to the east of the door. The walls are dull dark wood, and feature various posters of topless women and motorcycles, interspersed with neon beer signs. The base and sides of the bar are dark stained wood, and the top is made of lighter wood that has been heavily lacquered and polished. Coins have been imbedded in the lacquer, mostly pennies and nickels. Three shelves, which are mirror-backed, run the entire length of the bar. In the northern half of the bar, the bottom two shelves are sporadically stocked with bottles of various hues and shapes. This stock begins to thin as it moves south, and is replaced completely by stacks of paper goods, various dust-covered file boxes and ancient glassware (some in boxes) before the shelves reach the southern half. On the top shelf sit various vintage whisky decanters, all covered in dust, and they, like the bottles, stop about halfway south.

There are four polished metal picnic-size tables in the northern half of the room: two are arranged east west and jut against the east wall (the southernmost, #1, near the center of the room, the other, #2, six feet north); the third table is arranged north south (parallel to the bar and between the two east west tables and the bar) and the fourth, the northernmost table, also arranged north south and perpendicular to the northernmost east west table (between the northernmost east west table and the northern wall). The southern half of the room is occupied by a pool table and, north of that, a foosball table. In the center of the room, between the foosball table and the metal picnic tables, is a vacant space of about ten feet north south. There is a dartboard on the eastern wall here, but the clearing is mostly used for dancing and standing.

Liz has pushed the mother against the wall, just north of the dartboard, where she holds a juicebox and a straw. The mother is wearing dark velour sweatpants with a wide white stripe and matching jacket over a simple thick white cotton blouse and puffy slippers. Liz sits at the southernmost table (#1), in the south east corner, wearing a plaid print western shirt, a thick silver necklace with large chunky stones and dark jeans with high heel boots. North is Carlos, in a dark sleeveless tee shirt and a silver necklace, with dark jeans and pointy boots. West of Carlos is Mace, in a dark ratty suit jacket and matching vest with dark jeans with thick black boots, and west of Mace is Jerry. South of Jerry sits Glow, in a light grey sweater, tight dark jeans, high top sneakers and big hoop earrings. West of Glow, at the southern edge of the westernmost north south table (Table #3) sits the Professor, with L'il Kevin in a tight tee shirt and jean shorts with expensive basketball shoes north. There is an empty space between Glow and Liz. Two thin cowboys play pool while two cowgirls lean against a southern strip of bar and watch them. One of the cowgirls is remarkably overweight. Two Mexican couples of twenty-five or thirty years of age occupy the table (#2) directly north of Jerry, Mace and Carlos, and the northernmost table (#4, near the juke box) is occupied by four older white men and two younger women. One of the men has a cane, and they talk in low whispers by themselves, ignoring the women who are silent. The bartender is a bald, heavyset man with a dirty white shirt underneath a dirty full-length apron. He's assisted by a scrawny cocktail waitress who looks to be about twelve, with bad skin and a pearl stud emerging from beneath her lower lip.

There are three clear glass pitchers of beer on the table in front of Liz, Mace and the empty seat. A half empty beer glass sits to Jerry's left (east), and an empty highball glass, as well as a half full tall shot glass, rest near the north east corner by Glow. Mace holds a full glass of beer by the base in his right hand and talks to Carlos. Carlos has a half-full shot tall glass to his right (east), directly north of an empty tall shot glass. A three-quarters full beer glass sits north of the empty shot glass, and a half-full bottle of tequila is west of that. Liz brings a tall glass of gin and tonic to her mouth. The Professor, his back toward Glow et al, stares into a rocks glass filled three-quarters full with ice and scotch. L'il Kevin is sitting backwards on his chair, facing Mace and Carlos, his legs splayed around either side of the back, and is holding a nearly empty beer glass in his left hand. An empty tall shot glass is on the table, west of L'il Kevin's back. A plate with three lemon slices and seven lemon rinds sits on the table directly south of Mace.

"Our defense sucks."

"It's sucked for years. It's always sucked. Long as I can re-member."

"You ain't got no memory."

"It sucked when we went in country, it sucked when we got out. Tell me when it didn't suck."

"You all doing all right here? More lemons?"

"Yeah, we're ok. Jerry, didn't our defense always suck? I mean always?"

"Leave Jerry alone, man, he's talking to his woman."

"I don't know, man, I don't know. I don't think so."

"I have a name, Carlos."

"You have a lot of names."

"Fuck off."

"Want me to tell you a couple?"

"How fucked up are you?"

"You need some pussy Carlos. Lack of pussy make you mean."

"And stupid."

"Pretty soon, we're going to have to hide Jerry's mom away. Be finding the wheelchair all bent up in Carlos' room."

"That's not funny."

"Couple of skid marks on the ceiling."

"Hey dickhead, talk about your own mother."

"My moms is dead."

"Killed herself when she first saw your ass."

"G and R man, G and R! Welcome to the fucking jungle. C'mon Liz, get your ass up. She'll be all right. Where's she going to go?"

"Hey Mr. Juan. Turn it up. The music. Crank it."

Mace drains his beer, moves the pitchers to the east and hops on the table crouching, now hops down between Glow and Liz, nearly falling to his right. He backs into the center of the clearing, where he begins this spastic shimmy. Liz sets her drink down, looks at the mother, and stands. She follows Mace's lead south west and, holding her glass, begins to sway back and forth on her toes. Jerry rises abruptly, and holds his right hand south across the table to Glow. She shakes her head twice and then stands, taking his hand with her right. He wheels 190 degrees around the western edge of the table and proceeds (sidesteps) due south. Glow pivots, and, facing Jerry (west), also sidesteps south, until they are clear of the southern edge of table #3. They begin to dance in a western swing style, with Jerry stationed as the axis around which Glow spins and revolves. Glow stumbles and smiles. L'il Kevin empties his beer glass while staring at her. The Professor continues to look down into his rocks glass in front of him. Carlos gazes at the dances, an ugly smile on his face. He leans over and carefully fills his tall shot glass from the tequila bottle. He then abruptly tilts his head back and swallows the shot, wiping his mouth with his left hand. The mother begins to laugh, and drums the fingers of her left hand against the armrest of the wheelchair in time to the music.

L'il Kevin stands and walks east to the table, where he leans over, takes a beer pitcher with his right hand and fills the glass in his left. He straightens and looks at the dancers, and begins to stomp his right foot and nod his head. The Professor takes a drink from his glass and turns around so he's now facing east south east. He looks at Carlos and L'il Kevin. To the north, one of the Mexican women at table #2 stands and holds her hand out to one of the men, who shakes his head no and folds his arms in front of his chest. The other man, sitting directly south of him, looks away. The woman leans over the table and tries to prod the first man up by nudging him in the left shoulder with her right hand, but he remains still. The woman shrugs, and turns to the north west. She motions to the other woman with a nod of her head, and the other woman smiles and stands, moves quickly around the western edge of the table where they both proceed south, past tables # 3 and #1, and then shift direction to south south west. They avoid Glow and Jerry and find space near the bar, where they arrange themselves in a line running south west to south east, and begin to dance. The easternmost woman does a butterchurn motion with her hands revolving in front of her, and the other shoulder shimmies back and forth right and left.

Jerry allows Glow to orbit him, then turns east and faces Liz, with whom he begins to twist. Glow, left without a sun, turns north east, towards Mace, who, with his eyes squeezed shut and mouth moving, seems oblivious to all. She turns again, directly north, where her gaze meets L'il Kevin's nodding and stomping bulk. She smiles, holds both hands out, palms upturned. He smiles and drops his eyes, moves south toward her. She begins moving her hands up and down in front of her torso, and he begins moving his head, right hand and right foot up and down in time to the music.

Carlos carefully pours another drink from the bottle into his tall shot glass, lifts it quickly to his lips and again drains it. He stands and stretches, looks around, then walks around the table (west, south, east) until he faces Jerry's mother. He pulls her chair out from the wall and moves north until he's standing behind it. The Professor stands. Carlos leans over and pushes her slowly south west, cutting between Jerry and Liz and between Mace and the back (south) of Glow. They reach the back of the northern most Mexican women, and he rotates the wheelchair south and north west until it cuts between them. They stop dancing and stare at him and at the mother in the wheelchair. He turns the chair north east and begins to slowly walk back the way they came.

Jerry moves south past Liz and takes Glow's right hand in his left and spins her around south west to west to south, where she stumbles and falls to her left knee, her shoulder crashing against Mace's left leg. Mace opens his eyes and shimmies backwards, south west. Carlos and the mother reach the middle of the room and continue on their way north east, swerving just slightly to avoid the genuflecting Glow. The mother has a big smile on her face. She drops her juicebox near Glow's right foot and continues to grin. Carlos begins to turn her west as they reach the north east corner. The music stops.

Thunder Road

Arthur Ripley (1958)

He never liked the Pueblo run. He liked driving up to Denver and Boulder (Shamu was fun and easy to sell), and although Springs (guns and God) gave him the willies, it was still better than the Pueblo. A couple of times a year he and Jerry would drive down to Taos and Albuquerque: Jerry would hot rail and crank the tunes, usually Arrowsmith or Zeppelin, and insist on driving. And Jerry wouldn't shut up, and then they'd argue because he wouldn't want to stop to eat because he was railing, so they'd both be exhausted and irritable by the time they got to Raton pass, but somehow it was still cool. Just the two of them. Family. But he hated going into Pueblo. For anything, but especially to sell drugs.

First stop, the Silver Saddle. Charlie Pride once played here. Stuck in the middle of the prairie, right on Pueblo Boulevard, there used to be nothing around except various pickups and semis scattered akimbo on both shoulders of the darkened road. Now progress—in the form of PrairieView liquor, a Shell Mini-Mart, Woody Woodstove and a shared hardscrabble parking lot with a couple of streetlights—had landed across the street. Behind the Saddle, he could see the darkened silhouette of a cheap subdivision about three blocks into the background. The pickups and semis of old had thinned, replaced by beat-up Broncos and Tahoes. Progress had, if anything, made the place even more depressing. The vibe was still honky-tonk: mullets, chained wallets and shitkickers, only now the dive and its denizens were older and more decrepit by three or four decades, so that the Marlboro-throated yee-ha's, the bloody-knuckle dialogues and the sleeper-cab screwing that seemed so essential (at least to its participants) in the seventies was now only a tired, sad parody, like an old-timers ball game or a Sinatra concert when Blue-Eyes'd forgotten the words. Getting hammered on plastic pitchers of Coors Banquet was one thing at twenty and something belonging to a different, infinitely more pathetic universe, at fifty.

The parking lot to this particular, infinitely more pathetic universe was three-quarters full. He pulled around to the back. Billy was supposed to save him a parking space near the dumpster, and, yes he did. Billy was ok. They had gone to high school together, or rather, they had both attended the same white brick building for roughly two school years, Billy being a mediocre but popular athlete from one of the mediocre but popular Pueblo families, and he being a lonely, studious masturbator, jacking off nightly to mental images of mini-skirted pom pom girls while Billy received real head from the captain of the girl's basketball team in the back seat of his sky blue Cougar. Twenty three years later here they were: the meth dealer and the honky-tonk manager, ready to do business. Billy. It was always Billy, always Danny or Sammy or Jenny or Lorie or Marty or Tony. Fucking children, high school kids forever. Billy was ok, he supposed. Billy was ok. For a tweaker.

He rolled down the window and shut off the truck. The night was warm and windy. It was only a little after eleven. He'd be out of here by eleven-thirty, and have plenty of time to make the other stops before two. He checked his Glock. Second nature. He put his windbreaker on over the pistol, looked around, then got out of the truck.

The dumpster stunk of cowboy puke and French fry grease. This was his life. He looked up: quarter moon, no stars. He could hear the one-two one-two of the country bass through the walls. He pounded on the kitchen door, and when nothing happened, he pounded again. The wind kicked up and blew dust in his eyes. The music stopped just as the door opened. A figure in a cowboy hat, a button-down cowboy shirt with the sleeves cut off, long shimmery athletic shorts over bright white kicks filled the doorway, blocking out much of the backlight from the kitchen. Skinny legs, cut guns, massive gut. It was Boobs, Billy's cousin. Legend had it that Boobs was so stupid, he misspelled his own name, Bob. Hence the nickname. He wasn't L'il Kevin stupid, but still.

"Hey."

"Hey. Billy around?"

"I don't know. Probably. I think he's out front."

"Can I come in?"

"He expecting you?"

"What the fuck you think? Yeah he's expecting me."

Boobs didn't move. "He's probably out front."

He waited a couple of beats, then gave a little shrug with his head and right shoulder. "That's cool. I'm taking off. A couple miles down the road I'm going to give Billy a call and tell him I tried to see him, but couldn't get in. Tell him his cuz wouldn't let me in the back door. Later."

They stood there looking at each other for a moment. How did one grow a belly like that? He looked like the Kool-Aid man. Boobs was no tweaker: he was an eater. Fuck this. He didn't need this crap. He could get rid of Billy's order with Victor or the Klamm Shell. Let Billy start twitching, let him twitch all fucking week. He was tired of dealing with morons.

"Kay." Boobs backed up into the doorway, tried to flatten himself against the wall. Like that would work. He turned sideways and maneuvered himself into the kitchen. It was empty, and it smelled like disinfectant, green chili and grease. He noticed small muffled laughter and the low murmur of indistinguishable conversation from the barroom in front, and he heard Boobs slam and lock the door behind him. The Silver Saddle usually served burgers and burritos until one-thirty, and so the abandoned kitchen was unexpected.

"Why's the kitchen closed?"

"Close at ten now. Wasn't worth it," Boobs grunted past him.

Billy sold some of his product to the staff to keep the plates clean and the burritos folded, so this probably meant that he would either cut back on his order or ramp up his personal consumption. If he had to bet he would bet on the latter. He would always bet on the crank. He followed Boobs out of the deserted kitchen, through a heavy swinging wooden door and into a short hallway. The laughter and talking were louder, but still indistinct. The smell of disinfectant and ammonia suddenly spiked, and then leveled off as a restroom door opened and closed, disgorging a short bowlegged dude with slicked-back hair and a La Raza Unida leather jacket who quickly brushed past. He didn't want to search out Billy in the bar. He didn't want to be seen either by the cops (fat chance) or by some skanky bag-chaser looking for a ten-dollar bump (although the skanky bag-chasers tended to frequent Maria Maria's in Salt Creek). Let Billy do retail if he wanted: he'd stick to wholesale. "Boobs. Boobs." The gut swiveled in his direction. "Get him for me?"

Boobs stared and his eyes narrowed, like it was taking him time to translate. "Sure thing." The pay phone on the wall rang once, then abruptly cut off mid-second ring.

Billy came scurrying around the corner, looking like, well,

looking like the meth-head manager of a shitty country bar. His eyes were bright, his skin sallow and he kept his lips closed over his exploded teeth. His once barrel-chest was sunken (looking like something structural had collapsed), his once buffed biceps were flaccid (like all the muscle and bone had been surgically removed) and his waist looked like it had been hijacked from a twelve year old boy. He wore navy blue track pants with a matching jacket over a dirty Denver Broncos Super Bowl Champions XXIX San Diego tee shirt. "Let's go into my office," he mumbled, and unlocked the door next to one of the toilets.

He had learned early not to feel either sympathy or disdain for his customers. Lately (always?) he had started to veer pretty hard toward disdain (except for Nish). Not because they used, he could understand that: most of his customers, hell, most of the people on planet earth, led fairly shitty lives, and whatever got you through the night was ok by him. He even didn't mind selling his Shamu to Boulder party tweakers, as their lives would probably nosedive soon enough. His did. No, his contempt was aesthetic, having to do more with rotting teeth, feral lies and unholy body odor than any algebra of need. Anyone believing ice glamorous should hang a while with old Billy here, in his closet of an office off the toilets, accessorized tastefully with a ratty naugahyde loveseat, a Depression era filing cabinet and two wooden chair/desks from some forgotten middle school. Or if you wanted real glam, then go back to the Village, to a place called Slingshot, where pretty boy sketch pads would booty bump in the basement, suspended in rows of hammocks, pants to knees and asses over teacups, while an 'attendant' with clean syringes in the right-hand bucket and dirty in the left would methodically and detachedly insert a solution of Tina and water into the maws of waiting nethermouths, like some hellish and humorless parody of communion. He hadn't seen any booty bumping in Colorado. He was glad he only did

B to B these days: no under the streetlight passing to teenagers, no back alley handshakes, no four a.m. strangers in the living room, and no lesion-lipped skitzgirls (and boys) begging to blow him for a quarter. No, he sold nothing less than ozzies to people he knew.

"Hey Professor. What'cha got for me?"

"Same as last week. Same as the week before. And the week before that."

"How much?"

"Same price as last week. Same price as the week before. And the week before that."

"Any discount for repeat customers?"

"Same answer as last week. And the week before. And the week before that. You want discounts, go to Wal-mart."

"What's your damage?" Billy was sitting on the top of one of the middle school desks, looking up at him. He looked even sicker than usual. He bent down to scratch an ankle and his greasy blond hair cascaded over his face as the music started again in the saloon. He wondered if Billy had already ramped up his consumption. He wondered how long Billy would last. At least he wasn't a slammer: the skin on his stick arms and the top of his hands looked clean and he'd always been a smoker. Besides, he had a position in the community to maintain: a job to go to, a wife (no kids) to support, and that Pueblo family he didn't want to shame. But he didn't look good: he looked even skinnier than before, he needed a shave and he wouldn't make eye-contact. He was probably twitching and tweaking. But he was definitely twitching.

He thought briefly about cutting him a break, pretending he wasn't carrying as much, selling him three ozzies instead of four. He could easily make it up later. A dope dealer with a conscience, how fucking sweet: although purchase limits weren't unheard of as it was good business practice to keep your costumers alive. It wouldn't make any difference to anybody whether he sold it to Billy or to Rosie or to Miguel or Nish or Jimbo or Victor or Elizondo. It was all packed in eight balls anyway. He had twenty-five ozzies in the truck and tonight he was going to sell twenty-five ozzies. That was the bottom line.

"So, you close the kitchen at ten?" Billy didn't look up from his ankle. The music was loud. He leaned forward and repeated, "YOU CLOSE THE KITCHEN AT TEN?"

Billy looked up, but didn't look him in the face. He nodded and smiled weakly.

"I can give you three ozzies for $5000."

"What?"

Fuck this, he wasn't going to shout. He took a pen from his pocket and looked around for a piece of paper, a bar napkin or something. He couldn't see anything. The room was decrepit, but, like many a tweaker's domain, cleaned to within an inch of its life. There was probably something to write on in the file cabinet, but he wasn't going to snoop around in another man's business. He grabbed the other school desk, swiveled it over until it faced Billy, and sat down on the top. The boom boom of the bass was going right through his head. "Look at me. LOOK AT ME." He moved closer so he was right up in Billy's grill. Billy wouldn't make eye contact. His breath stank from rotten teeth and dehydration. Tina breath. "No kitchen staff. You still want the four? I'll give you three for five."

There was no hesitation. "I still want the four." Fine. He wasn't going to pretend he didn't have it and he wasn't going to ask again. He nodded. "Sixty-six dude. Sixty-six." Billy stood quickly, reached in his jacket and pulled out a thick white envelope. The music stopped, and he could hear muffled applause coming through the walls.

He was pissed all the way to the Green Light. He should just mind his own fucking business. Billy, notwithstanding his name, was a big boy, and could take care of himself. He felt both embarrassed and rebuked: his too-obvious concern had suggested an intimacy that neither he nor Billy desired or knew what to do with. He felt foul. And stupid. He'd lost the upper hand. And for what? So Billy-boy wouldn't smoke himself into a stroke? What an asshole.

It had rained briefly while he had been in the Silver Saddle, and the streets had taken on a slick bluish glow. For some reason, he'd decided to take Pueblo Boulevard to Prairie to Northern to Thatcher to Lincoln/4ᵗʰ Street instead of the quicker I-25 to Santa Fe route. With the Friday night traffic, the stoplights and other bullshit annoyances this would probably add at least fifteen minutes to his night.

His mother used to be afraid of the highway, so she would always take this route whenever she drove downtown. Even staying off I-25, it wasn't the quickest way: if you stayed on Pueblo Boulevard north you'd hit Thatcher directly, right before City Park, avoiding both Northern and Prairie. Street names were funny. The words "Orman," "Abriendo" and "Thatcher" didn't have much meaning outside the peculiar context of driving, walking or living in Pueblo Colorado. They have might have some vague denotations—Orman was a governor, Abriendo was Spanish for 'open up' and Thatcher started Pueblo's first bank—but they possessed connotation, significance really, only as the untranslatable names of streets. Abriendo signified a particular street, a specific place, distinct if ambivalent feelings—a hot dustiness, Chuck's Texaco, the way to his Aunt Virginia's— a cluster of half submerged memories and sensations he could never begin to comprehend or to communicate to anyone else. Not that he wanted to.

Before Thatcher turned to Lincoln he made a quick right on Veta Avenue. There was a small park on the left, and he slowed to a stop. There it was, his first home, the house he and his parents lived in until he was six. He remembered snow up to his chin, burning his foot on the heat register, and falling off the top of the slide in the park. Home sweet home. He had no idea why the fuck he was doing this. The house was dark and people were asleep. He looked at his watch. It was almost midnight: time to sell more crystal meth. He hated this fucking town. He drove away slowly.

The Green Light was deserted for a Friday night. A couple of middle-aged guys in white Grand Prix Restaurant softball uni's sat playing dice with the bartender, and that was about it. Downtown was often dead, but not this bad. He spotted Nish in a dark corner booth. "Bud, and a Jack with ice." Nish was his favorite customer, almost a friend, as close to a friend as he had in Pueblo anyway. He was slightly older, maybe about fifty-five, and possessed a definite gravitas: he smoked crystal, had fought in Vietnam, and was a lawyer. In short, he was much too interesting a character for Pueblo Colorado.

"What's up, Nish?"

"Hello my young friend. Please sit."

"I'm forty-two. Not so young."

"Young at heart, young at heart."

He swung around into the booth, facing the door, Nish on his right. Nish slid a bowl of pretzels in his direction. It was dark in the corner: Nish's long hair was haloed by a white neon Miller sign, and the faint glow of the ambient light penetrated only to the middle of the table. He popped a pretzel into his mouth as the bartender brought the drinks, setting Nish's Jack next to a nearly full one. They had a routine, a ritual almost. He'd order a Jack for Nish and a Bud for himself and they'd sit in a corner booth, quiet for a while, two to three sips of the Jack, and then Nish would suggest a topic in that bass voice of his—movies, which judge was getting blown by the DA, the fucked-up state of the world and country—and then they'd proceed down that conversational path, branching off, taking their time, until he'd finished his beer and then another, which was a signal for Nish to smile and press a roll of 33 Franklins into his hand, after which they'd both go back to the truck for the two ozzies.

"I'm going to be boring tonight I'm afraid, and for that I apologize in advance. But if you can't talk to your dealer, who can you talk to? Can I be any more melodramatic? I feel like Garbo. But I have a story to tell you. Bear with me: it won't cost you much, maybe a half an hour, and I'll still buy at the end."

"*Grand Hotel* or *Flesh and the Devil*?"

"Oh, *Flesh and the Devil*, certainly. I don't want to be alone." Nish looked down at his drinks. His face was dark, surrounded by the white aura, with not enough detail to read. Nish's hand moved down to one of the glasses, grasped it, and then moved up. The ice clinked, and the hand moved back down. "So, anyway. Do you know Bryan Brill?"

"No."

"He's a big macher in Denver, in the Denver 'gay community,' if 'gay community' isn't a contradiction in terms. He started Access Systems and is now filthy. He's famous for his spectacular parties. I'll get you invited if you'd like: I'm sure you could do some business."

"You know I don't work like that."

"Yes of course. It is wise to be particular, to limit your client base to buyers you can trust. But sometimes, trust is misplaced. You were married, yes?"

"Yes."

"And what happened?"

"Prison happened. Go on with your story."

"I didn't know you'd 'done time.' How very interesting. Where?"

"Bayside. Southwest New Jersey. Go on with your story."

"You'll have to tell me about prison sometime. Have you read Genet?"

"You'll have to tell me about Vietnam sometime. Go on

with your story."

"I expect there were not too many PhD's in Film Studies from New York University at Bayside prison. What was it like?"

"I made license plates. Go on with your story."

"Really?"

"Go on with your story."

One of the men at the bar laughed. Nish took another drink: he could hear the ice cubes tinkle in the glass and Nish's throat swallowing. "Oh yes, my story," he began again, presently. "Somehow, I don't feel the urgency to tell it anymore. I've been waiting for you all evening, but I don't know if I want to tell you now. I don't know why I thought you'd care. It's funny the things we fixate on. This afternoon when I got up, it was the first thing I thought of, telling you my story. But now I'd much rather hear about prison. And your marriage."

"Go on with your story."

"No."

"Why not?"

"Because it's an old story. And I'm an old storyteller. Let's talk about something else."

"You don't look old. You look good."

"It's dark. I look okay in the dark. Like Gloria Swanson."

"But you're still big."

"You've heard of Tina dick. I take Viagra."

He didn't know what to do with that. It wasn't exactly too much information, because he didn't know if Nish was kidding or not. His face was too dark to read. Suddenly, "Gloria Swanson or Greta Garbo?"

"Swanson."

"Swanson or Crawford."

"Crawford."

"Crawford or Bacall?"

"Crawford."

"Crawford or Kim Novak?"

"Kim Novak? I'll take Monica Vitti."

"Monica Vitti?" Nish guffawed, took a drink of his Jack. "You and your Europeans."

"I like Kim Novak. Polly the Pistol. And that look she gives Kirk Douglas in *Strangers When We Meet* when he tells her she isn't that pretty, that's great."

"Don't forget *Vertigo*."

"I never dug *Vertigo*. I can never tell where Hitchcock is, if he *is* his fucked-up characters or if there's some ironic distance there."

"Ah yes, *Vertigo*. Where Scotty overcomes his fear of heights, his desire for the other and even death itself, all in a single moment of absolute cinema. Where he remakes the world according to his own image, like a perfect Hegelian master, and then has nothing left to do except regret and remember. To Bach if memory serves."

"Bach and Barbara Bel Geddes."

"Yes, Bach and Barbara Bel Geddes. *The Goldberg Variations* and Miss Ellie. You'd take Novak over Crawford?"

He took a sip of his beer, and held it in his hand. "I guess. What about you?"

"Crawford or Hepburn?"

"Katharine or Audrey?"

"Katharine."

"Katharine."

"Hepburn or Davis?"

"Davis."

"Really?"

"Really. I think Bette Davis is *the* very best actor. American, European or Asian. Anything. Bar none."

"Early or late?"

"All. Not *Whales of August* late. I can't watch her in color. It's not right."

"*Dark Victory* or *Mr. Skeffington*?"

"*Skeffington*. "Trippy dear. . .' in that near falsetto. *Victory* has the better lines . . . 'I'll have a large order of prognosis negative'. . . but I could never buy that praying scene at the end. Who was she praying to? And then there was Bogie's Irish accent. And the Tree."

"The Tree?"

"George Brent. And when she finds out she's going to die, she leaves the restaurant and gets drunk with Ronald Reagan. Finding out you'll be dead in six months, confronting George Brent and then Ronald Reagan on the rebound . . . no wonder she was praying."

"So you didn't mind a blind Claude Rains? So he couldn't see how hideous she turned out?"

"*We* could see. No one did ugly like Bette. That was part of her charm. Maybe most of it. She was truly enchanting, in the real sense of the word. I always felt she convinced people she was actually pretty, made them see what she wanted them to see. It was all magic, cigarette smoke and mirrors, gesture and diction, and if you could somehow see her as she actually was, you'd be faced with Jane Hudson, not Maggie Cutler. That was acting."

"You never thought she was pretty?"

"Not naturally, like Ava Gardner or Lana Turner. Or Carole Lombard. It was all pure expression. She acted beautiful, and so she was. Or she acted ugly, and so she was. I got the feeling there was nothing there until she acted. This isn't a criticism: I don't think she was superficial, or shallow or vacant . . . far from it. She was just always acting, never not acting, always playing a part, and there was nothing there except those parts she played. There was the truth. She was nothing except acting, and she showed how we are nothing except acting too.

"What about Margo Channing?"

"Her greatest role. It's just as difficult to imagine Bette without Margo as it is to imagine Margo without Bette. Margo certainly colors Fanny Trellis and Elizabeth Vale, not to mention Leslie Crosbie and Henriette Deluzy-Desportes. The parallels might be there, but they go two ways."

"So she was only a temperament?"

"No, she's the greatest actor of all time. And somehow the sexiest."

"Carrying a torch?"

"No one ever handled a cigarette like Bette. That Paul Henried cigarette trick: fuck that. It's obvious Bette could smoke and drink him under the table. Margo Channing tapping and then lighting up at the awards ceremony, pouring herself a drink and then waiving away the mixer, that's a sublime 20 seconds of art. Or Miss Elliot torching up at the party, staring off into space after her failed screen test in *The Star*, or when she's tromping around in her fuck-you mode in that riding outfit, cigarette holder, jodhpurs and dominatrix boots when she's in the horse club in *Dark Victory*. Nothing is cooler than Bette Davis smoking."

"They airbrushed her cigarette out of her postage stamp."

"You're kidding."

"Nope."

It was silent for a few moments.

"And I loved the way she spoke too, enunciating each syllable, almost as if it were italicized. I loved the way that mid-Atlantic diction would cut through the surrounding miasma and gauze right to the quick, to the quick. Listen to how she pronounces the last syllable in 'But you are Blanche, you are in that chair.' Or the poetry of 'We're all busy little bees, full of stings, making honey day and night. Aren't we, honey' where she refuses to modulate the pitch or rhythm of the 'full of stings making honey day and night' until she finally pauses, and the 'aren't we honey' isn't a question. It's beautiful."

"So you are in love."

"Remember, I was married. I know the difference. There'll never be another actor like her. Not Streep, not that *Titanic* chick, not Kidman, not Moore. We're not even in the same neighborhood here."

He paused for a moment, and took a drink of his beer. He stared at the label, and heard the ice clinking in Nish's drink. He didn't look up.

After a while he started again. "It's weird: you asked me about actresses and that's part of what I really love about film, how we can name these films and talk about scenes, and we visualize right away the setting and the acting, and if we re- cite lines we can remember them immediately, the way they sounded and what they meant. 'I could've been a contender, and not a bum.' But there's another part, and this may be the part I like best, when there's an filmed image that I can't attach to a content, that I can't attach to the larger narrative, that I can't tell you what film it's from. It's these images that float to my consciousness unannounced, sort of like a cinematic déjà vu. Do you know what I mean?"

"A little bit. For me it's Pasolini's hats, or Bresson's staircases."

"Yeah, but the fact that you can name them disqualifies them. These are more like dream images . . . they've become part of my subconscious so I think they belong to me, I think I've lived them. But I know they're from film: I just can't tell you which film. And if I could identify them, I'd fix them in my memory, and that would ruin them. They need to be ephemeral. The closest example I can give is Dreyer, especially *Vampyr*. But that's not it, because I named it, identified it. . A man in a fedora walking by a brick building . . . A rotund man yelling through the door at his German Shepherd . . . A young girl looking up at a withered tree . . . Ah fuck it, I'm not making any sense."

He had one more stop to make. And then home. Victor, from Belmont. Victor was Jerry's friend, not his: he couldn't stand the show-off motherfucker. Victor was way into being a dealer—the thug-life fantasy of fancy cars, women, big-ass house, even some gaudy bling—he was just asking to get picked (this was, after all, Pueblo, not Miami). And if he got picked and talked, their ass was grass. Fortunately, the Rodriguez brothers knew about Victor and would, he imagined, take the appropriate steps to protect their investment. Even more fortunately, Victor knew that the Rodriguez brothers knew about Victor, and was, at least until now, sufficiently impressed. In any case, he didn't think Victor long for this world.

Someone, it might have been Jerry, had convinced the dude to do late night car transfers, instead of public buys where his outfits and entourage were all too easy to observe. So he had to drive up, or rather down to Salt Creek, to this unnamed dirt road behind a junkyard at two-thirty-five to meet Victor and friends in his Denali and accompanying Beemer. And since Victor was deprived of his public performance, he became even more insufferable in the privacy of his SUV, where his audience was limited. He could do this. He didn't want to piss off Victor, or anybody else. He just wanted to get home, have a scotch and get to bed. He killed his lights and coasted down the hill. He looked at his watch: two-thirty-five . . . now. Four headlights in front of him to the right flashed quickly. He checked his Glock and got out of the truck. A pair of headlights flashed again. That would be Victor. He walked quickly to where those headlights had flared. He stopped at the door: it looked too big for his old ride. He heard a noise at his feet, and watched as a lit running board deployed from the side of the vehicle. The back door opened.

"How you like me now, Professor, how you like me now?"

"Hey Victor. I see you got a new ride."

"Come on in, come on in." He smiled as he climbed into the cavernous back seat. There was only Victor, slouched in the far back corner and a driver: no women or posse. The new car smell was obvious. He closed the door, but the light stayed on. "You like the leather, man? It's fine, fine. Glove quality. Cooled seats, even here in back. I tell you man, this Navigator got it going on. Hummer can't touch this shit, man. It's got a phat V8, 300 ponies, twenty-inch rims and a THX audio system. You like movies, we could watch a movie back here, some Johnny Wad, or *Scarface*. Benny, give us some AC back here. You know Benny." He made eye contact in the rearview mirror with the driver, both nodding. "Those kicks of yours looking a little shabby, Professor. You gotta get yourself some new threads, you look like you work at Sears or something, dude. Seriously. Big time player like yourself, you need to look the part. Gap Outlet ain't gonna make it. How old's your Ford?"

"Two thousand."

"What the fuck? You ain't making no dollar bill at the gold mine? Shit, you gotta live it up while you can. I ain't saying you gotta burn up all your profit, like your bro if you know what I mean, but damn, treat yourself to some new Keds at least. You must have a bank account the size of Nebraska. Look at me: this jacket set me back two grand, the kicks a G and a half, this earring a cool five. I hate to be the one to break it to you, but Benny's looking like he carries more *ferria* than you. You look like you Benny's driver. Give me a call, we go to my man up in Cherry Creek, he does all the Broncos and Nuggets, at least the ones worth doing. I tell him who you are, he do you for free, you know what I'm saying. Armani, Hugo Boss, Elevee, he got it all. Life's too short, especially for *vatos* in our business, eh."

"You done?"

"I'm just saying. We could be gone tomorrow, you know. I don't believe in any of that life after death horseshit: you sell what you sell you're an accident waiting to happen. You know what I'm saying. You gotta live for today, spend the green, new car new clothes, some bling, MSB, money sex and bitches and all that. That's my philosophy."

Ah, so you're an Epicurean, I see, familiar with the *Ta Kuria*.
He didn't particularly care to talk philosophy with Victor.

"Look at your bro, he was where, Iran? Iraq?"

"Kuwait."

"Kuwait. He probably saw dudes getting whacked out there, right, out there in the desert. He don't cry, he don't mope, he learn from it, and comes back and parties like it's nineteen ninety-nine, you know what I'm saying. You could take something from that, from your brother. He always liked to have a good time, was always a playa, but now man, he's a fucking inspiration. He goes too far sometimes, I dig that, but the baller's fun to be around. You could take some of that, that's all I'm saying."

"I know what you're saying. Thanks for your concern. Tell Benny to turn out the light so we can do some business."

Branded to Kill

Seijun Suzuki (1967)

Cooking always wired his ass he'd been up almost twenty hours but was as far from sleep as Pueblo was from Paris he'd never been to Paris except in the movies *Elevator to the Gallows* Jeanne Moreau walking from zinc bar to zinc bar Miles Davis in the background looking for her Julien Julien or those seedy chic Montmartre cafés in *Bob le Flambeur* frosted glass black and white checkerboard floors Gitanes Pernod with water he'd been to London Berlin and Rome but only to France once with Connie on the train from Spain to Italy maybe it was time for a holiday springtime in Paris maybe a permanent vacation maybe it was time.

He brushed the snow off his legs and chest and stomped his feet quietly didn't want to wake his mom or Liz it was a bitch outside windy snowing like a motherfucker he could smell red sauce his mother's recipe Liz must have made spaghetti for dinner the smell of home he smiled like George Bailey took his coat off hung it on the hook and went into the kitchen careful to close the door behind him before he turned on the light he filled a large glass with ice quietly then headed for the TV room he always drank after a cook until he slowed he'd down a few drinks pop a couple of Ambien and crash for twelve or so once out of laziness he'd done a couple of shots of Histenex that put him out for almost thirty and made him stupid for six more but tonight he'd stick with the Johnny Black maybe a little porn then back to his place for a flick he hadn't been to town to pick up his mail so he didn't have anything new but that was cool he could always find something to hold his interest maybe a double feature until dawn something like *The Petrified Forest* and *Story of a Love Affair* Lucia Bosé was hot better than porn but first whisky We can stop in Avignon and go down to Nice and Maybe Cannes I don't want to stop in Avignon I want to get to Milan it'll be the middle of the night anyway We could see Le Côte d'Azur he smiled you can be the Barefoot Contessa she took a drink of her wine a black Spanish Rioja and looked at him coolly it was loud the club car air thick with talking laughing and smoke I want to get to Italy if you wanted to stop in France you should have told me before I got the sleeper she attempted to pour wine into her glass but the small bottle was empty her thick lips were darkened by the Rioja contrasting sharply against the pale thinness of her face You want another drink You going to have one Might as well Sure he turned to look out the window it was nearly dark and he found himself staring back at his reflection and the reflection of the brightly lit bar car behind him.

Dude You startled me what are you doing up Watching a little pussy you just finish he could see his brother's silhouette illuminated by the 50 inch plasma in the darkened room Yeah he didn't know why he was surprised to see Jerry his brother couldn't be described as exactly having sleep patterns and he and Glow didn't keep a television he closed the door moved to the liquor cabinet and filled his pint glass halfway the ice crackling and popping Jerry turned his head Jesus you got enough ice there cutting good whisky's a waste might as well be drinking Ballantine I can see a little water maybe but you got a slushy there You learn how to drink in Kuwait or was it Saudi Arabia because when I left for school you didn't know shit That's one thing the army taught me bro how to get high I'm a trained expert on anything to get you off he sat down on the couch and put his feet up on the coffee table careful to avoid the dirty plate and tumbler in front of him they were all slobs leaving their crap everywhere Liz couldn't keep up his moms was trouble enough the room smelled like garlic he pushed the plate away with his foot and took a sip of his scotch perfect looked over at his brother You're in the right business Jerry laughed Fucking-A right.

He looked up at the screen to see a thirty inch dick penetrating the Grand Canyon of a reddened asshole christ What're we watching You can see what we're watching Yeah I see this tube of man-meat burrowing into skanky pus-hole lit up by 2-3 thousand watts of HMI or blondes not exactly a turn-on It's snowing man there's no dish We have other DVD's this is nasty You don't dig the backdoor seen enough of that in prison huh You're funny This remind you of when you bent over some Rahway cot while Adebisi put it in your *culo* It was Bayside not Rahway and I kept my *culo* to myself Whatever dude I'm just saying you could use a little fish taco it's been a while Can we just find something else to watch look at her she looks like she had her brains fucked out in 1998 You're tense man uptight you don't even visit the ho's no more What the fuck business is it of yours You got money bro go up to Springs if you bored with Pueblo pussy Put something else on Or even Denver if you don't use it you're gonna lose it people are talking man the Professor ain't getting none 'cept off the internet What are you on tonight I ain't high just trying to help a brother out Well thanks but no thanks You never dug the hardcore did you bro Whatya you mean I ain't checking your manhood dude I'm just saying he watched the purplish red shaft ram deep into the red rimmed asshole over-lit over-sized over-exposed No he admitted I don't dig the hardcore sex fucking it's not like that Sure it is bro it's exactly like that that's all it is in and out in and out no wonder you staying at home I knew guys like you in the desert guys who thought we were doing something important guys who needed their illusions I'm not following You know what I'm saying guys who couldn't say to themselves ok we're here to kill the towelheads cuz we need their oil or ok we're here to kill the towelheads cuz they trying to kill us you the same when it comes to pussy you can't say ok I need to fuck cuz I need to fuck you gotta attach it to all that other shit that's ok bro it's part of your charm but it's also why you at home at night So it doesn't matter to you whether it's Glow or Liz or some Salt Crick cooch a hole's a hole huh Naw man I ain't sayin that at all some holes are better others What do you mean by better Tighter he chuckled Tighter huh a hand removed the cock from the ass and thumped the swollen glans against asscrack here comes the money shot the thirty inch dick began to shoot thick milky ropes of stringy cum into the inflamed gaping asshole Can we please watch something else Jerry killed the picture and the screen went black.

They sat there in the dark awhile he took another sip of scotch wondered what Jerry was on about the wind whistled outside maybe it was time to head to his trailer Top or bottom You don't want to move all the stuff to the top do you it's heavy We might have more room on the bottom It's cold in here I opened a window do you want me to close it That's ok her nipples were poking through her thin white tank and he could see goose pimples on her arms I'll close the window a little you climb on up he turned to push the sash down leaving an inch or so opened then the shade and as he turned back he saw her bikinied ass full and round eye level as she clambered into the top bunk he smiled he'd always wanted to fuck on a train he started up after her Lock the door please and don't forget my wine he quickly turned the lock grabbed her wine bottle and plastic glass from the small shelf and hurried up the ladder banging his knee on the edge of the top bunk he was already hard his erection poking through his pajamas leading him up under the covers Look who's horny she took the bottle and unscrewed the cap as he maneuvered himself between her legs and began to hump through her panties the silk smooth against his tip and shaft he kissed her shoulder and reached down to squeeze her ass as she raised up on her elbow her head and neck twisted to take a drink from the bottle the plastic glass discarded he was fast losing his restraint the rhythm of the train rushing through his veins into his penis Wait a second she said and he couldn't tell if she was irritated or not her body neither responsive nor inert neither opening up or pushing him off You wanna smoke a bowl peacepipe bro Thought you said you weren't high I ain't yet he shrugged Sure why not as he felt his brother shift forward on the couch and fool with something on the table he caught another whiff of garlic and took another sip of his drink why don't you turn something else on what's loaded My guess would be porn Where's the remote Somewhere on the table I just had it here it is That's the TV remote where's the other one Fuck I dunno you wanna do a pipe or a bong Pipe Wuss he leaned over and pawed along the coffee table until he found the other remote clicked it on Turn the screen on Hold your horses I'm loading the bowl I'll do it where's the remote By that empty glass there a quick thumb flick energized the plasma a chubby young latino woman licking a large black uncircumcised penis Next a skanky dyke with blonde skanky hair with her mouth in the ass of another skanky dyke with blonde skanky hair next Nah wait Next No I like this I like me the hardcore the harder the better titties and lingerie and shit that don't cut it this is the stuff I like tongue in asshole finger in pussy or tongue in pussy finger in asshole I ain't particular cocks balls cunts and cum This is disgusting boring I wouldn't touch those chicks with your dick All right all right tell me something first when you jerk off do you think of cunt you know or cunt you don't tonight when you go chicken choke you gonna think of these two blondes here or your ex-wife I never think about my ex Still you probably think of real life women right pussy you know you never lick totally strange cunt like these women here right you go chat em up on the net first right Fuck you So what you'd do in prison surrounded by all those guys What did you do in Kuwait Lemme tell you a secret bro Kuwait was a lot like Pueblo heat sand wind brown people and getting high Change it please a brunette felching cum out of a blotched red ass we just saw this jesus the image of a young female Asian face filled the screen from bangs to chin red lips grimacing too white forehead painted Noh eyebrows scrunched in pain or pleasure it was hard to tell reverse zoom the hair and neck entering the frame then slender white shoulders a pan up from the neck to the spine and gently writhing shoulder blades now the slightly undulating small of the back the camera stopped the white almost luminous flesh rhythmically rippling to one of Satie's *Divertissements* her skin glowed nearly incandescent under the softlights This is nice he muttered keep it here the camera resuming down her back to the cleft an unhurried zoom focusing on the knob of her slowly gyrating coccyx you think she' got some sumo doing it from the back Nah she's flying solo I seen this before you know who this belongs to don't you Carlos he digs the slants Ugh his stomach turned Here bro take the edge off he took a toke from the lit pipe and passed it back I wish you hadn't told me about Carlos Oh yeah man he likes feeding the kleenex to the sloped twat Jesus that's the trouble with this shit that's why I don't like hookers or tittie bars there's always other guys around seeing what you're seeing fucking what you're fucking You do it in front of other guys I don't mean physically retard I mean they're there in my mind with sweaty backs unclipped toenails and bellies hanging over their cocks I can't get that shit out of my head not to mention some other dude's money shot the camera moved from her tailbone up to the cleft of her ass an abrupt cut to an overhead the entire body centered and white nearly overexposed balanced on knees and left elbow right arm underneath hand between legs left arm extended breathing mixed with soft moans noticeable now over the Satie in spite of Carlos and his kleenex his balls began to tingle Jerry inhaled loudly the pipe's cherry glowed brightly So you only tap virgins huh so Connie never had dick before she met you what are you talking about And what was that chick's name in high school you used to poke on all the time Katrina Kristina Karina It was Kira Yeah Kira so you bloodied her sheets too huh Jerry passed him the pipe he took another pull the smoke harsh and dry he swallowed back a cough What the fuck are you on about I mean when you were tapping your wife you didn't think about the dudes who visited before you No it's different I'm guessing there were a few pure speculation you understand no first-hand knowledge involved Completely different not the same thing at all I mean even Kira was no nookie rookie was she bro she was a senior when you hooked up What's your point All I'm saying is that everyone got a past dude you can't be think about who was where and what did who and who did what and who did who you know what I'm saying you gotta get back in the game bro get your helmet buffed your shaft oiled your dick smoked cook up a little Shamu take it up to Vail or Aspen go to a couple bars we know and I guarantee you'll have those skinny *fresas* on your tip in no time bro all the pink taco you can eat you'll be picking blonde pubes outta your teeth for a week Yeah just what I need to cut myself up on some crank whore's spine and catch myself a dose of Ninja Use a rubber bro don't make everything so goddam complicated he took another small sip of scotch turned his attention to the writhing figure on the screen the undulating rhythm increasing slightly the skin turning from a translucent white to a bright almost taxi-cab yellow he looked closer the color wasn't from the light or post production it was body paint looked thick brushed on he'd have to borrow this dvd take it back to his trailer One hundred an hour three hundred a night no kissing on the mouth no backdooring no barebacking no sixty nine I'll go down but you wear a raincoat this shit ain't negotiable if this ain't cool then you turn around get yourself to the Mystic on Elizabeth or Aloha Glorya's on Main maybe some skanks accommodate you there we cool Cool All right then sorry to be such a buzz-kill but I like to make everything clear from the beginning any-way she gave him her first smile I'm a good deal I got my own rubbers I don't drink the desk clerk's taken care of and I work flextime we can start with an hour I do what I do and then if that ain't enough and maybe it is maybe it isn't we extend the session two hours or a whole night I even take Visa and Mas-terCard no Amex and no Discover I'll start with an hour One hundred I have cash That's good that's good these rooms are nice Pueblo finally got some class Where are you from Walsen-burg you know where that is Yeah I know where it is You don't seem like you from around here can I take my coat off I'm sorry of course let me hang it up for you he'd only looked at her face her high forehead long black hair smart brown eyes and busy red mouth but as he took her coat a long white poofy goose-down thing he let his eyes pan down her dog-collared neck to the tight black lowcut spandex pushing her bubble breasts to-gether into conspicuous décolletage the stretch material was not as flattering to her slightly convex belly which was pinched by the large silver script Candy belt buckle her fleshy hips were sheathed in tight denim shorts that ended too early her thickish fishnetted flanks tapered quickly to Wal-Mart wedgies she was more substantial more compact denser than he usually liked she looked too much like a Midwestern hooker he wondered if this was a mistake Checking out the merchandise huh what do you think she turned around pointed her ass in his direction it was smaller and tighter than the rest of her body suggested and as the denim rode up he could see a bright turquoise thong through the black netting of the fishnets he hoped she didn't have one of those lower back tattoos she twisted her head and pushed his face away from her clavicle Ouch when was the last time you shaved Couple days ago It's not comfortable to me he moved his hands to the mattress and pushed himself up until his head brushed the top of the car the rhythm of the train still pulsing in his dick Do you want me to shave now he breathed heavily No she said simply shaking her head she turned back and took another drink he waited as she brought the bottle down from her mouth licked her dark lips then dragged her lower lip against the rim of the bottle this wasn't for him he knew that she wanted more wine she looked up at him appraising weighing questioning touched his cheek with the fingertips of her right hand he wondered what she was registering it was almost as if she were trying to remember who he was the train slowed her thumb moved down to his lips his brother belched You want another hit I'm good you see mom today Yeah at dinner How's she doing I dunno 'bout the same What do you mean did she eat I guess What do you mean you guess she's your mom too I know she's my moms too Liz is feeding her in the kitchen these days I'm aware of that She puts folks off their feed what with the dribbling and drooling and gacking and shit no one wants to watch that while they eat You need to check up on her she's your responsibility too I checked up on her she was eating fine what the fuck else you want me to do we got Liz Yeah we got Liz how did we get Liz I forget wasn't she fired from some clinic or something some hospice she was fired from a hospice the Sangre de Cristo Hospice and why was she fired huh Jerry why was she fired why was she fired from the Sangre de Cristo Hospice for stealing drugs stealing drugs from hospice patients bro and who goes to a hospice exactly who are these hospice patients hospice patients are those who are getting ready to die that's who she stole drugs from Jerry people who were getting ready to die that's who we have watching our mom Jerry that's who we have watching our mom jesus fucking christ Check this out here's her friend the camera dropped and panned right away from the undulating yellow figure to a medium shot of a very tall blue backlit female silhouette then tracked out the frame expanding to a long shot including both figures yellow focused or otherwise unaware of blue's presence the moaning constant but the Satie fading in to something from Mozart blue began to step camera right toward yellow she's tall for a gook look at those legs You've seen this before A few times yeah he could see Jerry firing up again out of the corner of his eye she *was* tall for an Asian barefoot and backlit so details nipples pubes mouth eyes undefined he felt his cock stiffen took a drink and swirled an ice cube around in his cheek spitting it back in the glass So what happens now Jerry chuckled Whattya think happens they make green she straightened turned her head toward him You like he nodded wished she'd take off those cheap shoes she stood there he stood there a single loud voice passed in the hall from left to right then abruptly stopped he could feel himself breathing So you want to get started Yeah she pivoted and tossed her head clumsily her hair swishing around to the front of her face a gesture studied from some televised reality talent and practiced for insufficient hours in front of the mirror he caught a whiff of inexpensive shampoo and hoped that was not her best move they faced each other for a while until she shrugged I usually get paid in advance Of course he pulled out his money clip from his jeans counted out five twenties and held them out thought of George C. Scott and those thick black plastic eyeglasses she drew the fingernail of her index finger lightly down his wrist up his palm and to his ring fingertip as she grasped the bills with her thumb and pinkie she smiled as she leaned back to stuff the money into the right front pocket of her cut-offs Now we can get down to business you can tell me what you want or you can just relax and let mamma drive he didn't know what to say closed his hand around his money clip what's the matter honey pussy got your tongue Take off your shoes So bro I think I'm going to bug leave you with your two friends Jerry stood up you want me to leave the leño No thanks You need some kleenex lotion paper towel you know while I'm up I'm good asshole why don't you take this plate and glass to the kitchen Ain't mine dude ain't mine Lazy fuck Later bro the stench of sulfur and garlic overpowered the sweet dope scent You're a fucking pig you know that Something to remember me by he buried his nose in his shirt the vague odor of acetone a welcome relief to his brother's miasma he paused the dvd a close up of yellow's face in focused grimace in the background over her right shoulder the suggestion of blurred blue and listened attentively for his brother's footsteps down the hall followed by the rustling of his coat and finally the opening and closing of the door he set his glass on the table and moved his right hand down to his crotch and squeezed his shaft through his jeans he probably should close the door but his mother wouldn't be coming out here to fix herself a snack or make a late night bathroom run and he didn't really give a fuck if Liz caught him jerking off besides she had her own bathroom so the odds were pretty good he could squirt this in peace he gently bit the tip of her thumb her eyes remained locked on his with that same inscrutable expression he pulled her right hip toward him and forced his knee between her legs she turned and fell back on the bed her shoulder blades and head flat on the mattress her chin pointed toward the ceiling her hands suspended in midair the left still holding her wine bottle he might have heard her sigh over the rhythm of train her legs pelvis and belly still motionless immobile unreadable the train began to speed up his own cadence began again quickening with the tempo of the tracks he began to gently suck the knob of her collarbone what did she want her breath unaffected her body unimpressed what did she want what did it matter he suddenly wanted to fuck her more than anything he moved his hands down to her ass and buried his face between her shoulder and throat more than anything in the world she sharply turned her shoulder and face away Your whiskers are scratching my neck he raised up on his elbow his rhythm immediately arrested his cock already shrinking she twisted away and brought her wine bottle to her lips the rhythm of the train continued mocking he reached over and reanimated the images onscreen the yellow face tipped forward straight black bangs covered the eyes and face blue breasts arms and head came into deep focus over the writhing yellow shoulder she was tall for an Asian looked a lot like Makiko Esumi he rubbed his shaft and tip harder through his jeans he'd never fucked an Oriental or Asian or whatever never had the opportunity maybe he'd follow his bro's advice go up to Aspen and drag some glass through the classy clubs get himself something clean and tasty like Makiko here although he really dug Setsuka Hara loved that smile she must be what now eighty-five at least and probably dead blue Makiko moved closer to yellow as the camera tracked backward and up a medium crane shot with yellow struggling in the center of the frame blue centered in the background still backlit still walking slowly toward forward the Mozart ended abruptly and for a few seconds only yellow's heavy breathing and moaning audible before some bouncy Frank De Vol number kicked in he unbuttoned his jeans and slid his right hand under the boxers to his cock the video as if sensing his intention switched quickly to a medium shot from beneath yellow up through the glass bed then a slow zoom and pan focusing on the toes of her left foot then a slow slow pan up the foot to the ankle he extricated his cock from his underwear and held the tip gingerly between his thumb and forefinger thought of the open mouth on the palm of Cocteau's poet Air air up to her knee then lower thigh You want me to take off everything or just my shoes he sat down on the bed Everything Lights on or off he lay back put his hands under his head noticed the faint odor of cigarette smoke from the bedspread stared at a sprinkler nozzle on the ceiling too many decisions he looked around wondered if there were any more sprinklers or if that single would cover the entire room he heard a shoe fall to the floor and her clothes rustling around You're not a talker huh that's ok by me so I got ten-twenty-nine so we go till eleven-thirty if we still going then we stop and renegotiate you want some help with your jeans he kept his eyes on the ceiling I'm fine You fine huh ok so here I am ready to roll you need anything a drink he didn't answer didn't take his eyes off the ceiling you want to put on some On-Command maybe get you in the mood there was probably another nozzle in the hallway to cover the hall and bathroom he pointed his chin down to check out the hall ceiling the top of her head entered the bottom of his peripheral vision the hall was dark and he couldn't see very far into it I was in a couple of pornos for the internet good money but what if my cousins or something saw me I don't want to do this forever he returned his gaze to the ceiling above closed his eyes maybe when he opened them she'd be gone is that what he wanted he opened his eyes looked up at the nozzle again wondered if there was a camera inserted inside wide angle or fish-eye if you wanted the entire room but the you didn't need the room just the bed something fast so the low light wouldn't matter you'd also want to be able to zoom in on different parts he wondered if anyone was watching he wondered what he would look like now You asleep he didn't want to be cruel might as well get this over with opened his eyes sat up with his back against the pillows and headboard looked at her a small bird with a nail though its neck who was more ridiculous she or he now what he wasn't sure of the script here train or no train he wasn't going to beg he was tired of dry-humping her underwear and she seemed more interested in her wine than anything he had to offer he sighed heavily began to extricate himself from her legs but she wouldn't move her thighs clenching What are you doing he noticed a slight quiver from her back and shoulders c'mon let me up she wouldn't budge was she playing with him turned her head she was laughing her eyes sparkling Why are you acting the fool Just wanted to see what you'd do How about if I do this he pulled her tee shirt over her head and kissed her mouth hard through the thin cloth her mouth opened and tongue sought his pressing against the now damp cotton she slid under him as he reached down and pulled her panties to the side she guided him into her wet cunt he felt the rhythm of train knot at the base of his cock he thrust deeper and deeper into her he heard the wine bottle clatter to the floor he leaned back the camera panned up past the knee to the upper thigh and crotch the spasms of her arms legs and shoulders belying the delicacy by which the tip of her index finger tickled the very top of her shaved pussy he stroked himself once twice three times then put his feet on the coffee table he clattering the dish and cup the garlic tomato and basil scent of red sauce filled his nostrils god she was hot he should stop didn't want to shoot all over his jeans he didn't want to stop a slow zoom into her glistening twat he eased up didn't want to come too quickly suddenly shockingly a thin blue finger appeared burying itself deep inside the yellow pussy the camera zoomed jesus christ she stood there in front of his bed looking small and young he could see her shivering slightly it wasn't from desire he'd probably come pretty quickly if she blew him and she wouldn't have to fake orgasm and he wouldn't have to worry if she were faking it or not he could remain relatively uninvolved stare up at the ceiling stroke her head moan a little while she sucked his cock I could use a blow job she looked relieved Ok but you wear a rubber he nodded she moved with her knees on the bed to unbuckle his jeans he was in rhythm now his thrusts in time with the tempo of the train she responded biting his ear through the cotton of her shirt he tweaked her right nipple with his left thumb and forefinger she gave a little gasp and bit his ear harder the train started slowing down and with it his own rhythm he tried to compensate faster faster but couldn't she gave a little laugh he tried harder but both he and the train ground to a halt and he started to slip out the image inverted the blue finger now yellow the background labia now blue the finger withdrew leaving streaks of pink which inverted again to yellow blue and green and then to bright white and dark black reverse zoom to belly then to torso then head to toe dark figure standing behind supine white jump cut to overhead dolly shot open aperture white figure almost invisible against the luminous bed rotating her hips slowly toward dark hundred of butterflies and moths pinned against the bare walls two pistols on a small dark table he had never used a condom for a blowjob before she had removed his jeans and boxers in no time and was now unwrapping the rubber she had thrown the bedspread over her shoulders and had finally stopped shivering although he could see her hardened nipples and gooseflesh on her arms she placed the condom between her teeth and lips gave his cock a few pumps and leaned over this would be quite a trick she caressed and nosed his balls and then placed the condom on his shaft her tongue darting down to moisten his shaft then with her lips and tongue forced the rubber over his glans he felt the warmth of her mouth through the latex and in spite of himself he arched his back and let a moan escape from his throat So what do we do now wait for the train to start I guess he moved his mouth down to her breast and began to lip and kiss her nipple Ouch goddam it I told you your whiskers hurt my skin Sorry sorry Christ the train lurched forward again just in time a siren began to shriek was that from the film and four grainy black and white views of a badly lit snow-covered prairie and vague variously shaped buildings appeared on screen what the fuck he stopped in mid stroke what was going on was that his trailer yes it was and there the hill by the barn this was the compound why vid the compound and what the fuck was that siren shit he shoved himself back in his pants it must be that alarm Glow was fucking with all last summer didn't think it worked Liz's door opened What's going on she yelled from the hall The alarm What alarm he didn't answer saw Jerry and Glow hurry past his trailer from right to left on the bottom screen across then appear quickly on the upper right screen Glow had a backpack and a coat Jerry in shirt sleeves they were both carrying rifles jesus he heard the front door open and turned as Jerry and Glow hurried into the TV room from the hall What the fuck neither responded as Glow quickly remove a laptop from her back pack and powered it up so why the guns Alarm Something tripped the sensor at the gate So why the guns Who knows Could it just be an animal a deer or something or some malfunction Two sensors tripped one at the cattle guard set at five hundred pounds the other twenty feet down the road at a K no deer would do Maybe the snow What Maybe the snow could you turn that fucking siren off thanks maybe it was the snow One maybe but not both Not the snow a vehicle We being raided A single vehicle no other sensors tripped Fuck who'd be driving around on a night like this That's what we're trying to find out Glow tapped the keyboard the cameras shifted angles and she brought them up to full size cycled through his trailer the road into camp from the abandoned barn the main house and garage from the lab and the lab and garage from Glow and Jerry's trailer nothing just a dimly lit snowy prairie and now lit driveway in the center of the compound Help me help me help me Liz can you check on my mom please they wouldn't raid us with one vehicle would they his voice hung in the air Glow clicked and the image changed from dimly lit b&w to weird sci-fi green Pretty clear said Jerry These are gen 3's Nice where'd you get 'em Where do you think I got 'em You down with o p p yeah you know me you down with o p p yeah you know me Jerry's phone Hello Glow's alarm just one vehicle as far as we can tell no I dunno I don't think it's a raid huh the Rodriguez Brothers why would they come out here on a night like this Check it Hold it Carlos they all leaned forward he could clearly see two headlights coming up the hill it was having some trouble in the snow but was making steady progress a quick zoom Whose Range Rover anyone we know drive a Range Rover So what do we do Maybe it's a mistake someone made a wrong turn Bullshit it passed the barn and crested the hill Glow switched cameras to the view from Carlos' and took off the night vision to grainy black and white We'd better get out there Yeah you coming No Don't touch anything the camera will follow automatically the Range Rover pulled even to the camera then passed he couldn't see any shadows indicating the number of passengers now just blurry taillights he heard the front door open and close the lab camera would give him a better view but had no idea how to switch the Rover entered the lit perimeter of the driveway and stopped the camera catching the driver's side in three quarter view he wondered where Jerry and Glow were or Carlos or Mace or L'il Kevin who the fuck was that some lost cowboy or something the snow was starting to pick up big wet flakes Christmasy like a Budweiser commercial without the horses still he reached down on the table and took a sip of his watery whisky a couple of minutes ago he was getting ready to money shoot to digital Asian pussy now he was watching a snow-globe scene out of a Range Rover ad maybe those two Japanese hootchies would climb out of the Rover and lambada over to his trailer or maybe the DEA had added carbombing to its war on drugs this was pretty weird spooky *Invaders from Mars* or *War of the Worlds* Haskin's not Spielberg's spooky it was quiet now still his mother calmed the house hushed outside silent and motionless except for the snow black and white static camera endless long shots no action here he was in a Wenders film *Kings of the Road* slow tracking shots and all he didn't think they'd have to wait long and he was right the driver's side door opened and this young dude maybe college age popped out in a rasta tam and one of those down vests from the seventies definitely not DEA and definitely not one of the Rodriguez Brothers without closing the Rover's door he moved toward the lab and stood there looking around blowing on his hands he still couldn't see Mace or Jerry or anyone and didn't look like the kid could either he turned back toward the Rover and shrugged his shoulders get in dude get back in your vehicle and turn it around and go back from where you came he walked slowly toward the door of the Rover and then like he made a decision or something he moved quickly toward the front of the vehicle he heard a loud bark as the dude's shoulder twitched and then another as the mushroom shape of his head deflated and his body fell backwards into the snow part of him knew exactly what he was seeing part of him didn't believe that they had just killed a guy another bark and then another but the figure didn't move he sat there mesmerized he probably should get out there but what could he do the tip of the passenger door moved and two hands raised up quickly over the roof and then just as quickly disappeared did they kill someone else he didn't hear anything jesus Carlos rushed into the light of the driveway from the direction of the garage his rifle pointing at the passenger side he stopped at the door and stuck his head and gun inside the Rover then waved his right arm over his head before leaning down what the fuck was going on his view blocked by the Rover's chassis Carlos could be cutting some guy's throat for all he knew he saw Glow emerge from the shadows of the house rifle pointed at the figure body corpse of the passenger then Jerry his weapon relaxed but not shouldered stuck his head in the SUV walked around to the driver's side and without glancing down stepped over the body and ducked into the driver's side door he rooted around for a few seconds then stood up and waved his rifle over his head a white circle appeared on the rear driver-side window

Jerry jerked around then another just below on the rear door then another on the windshield Jerry shouldered his weapon scooped snow off of the hood and fired a snowball into the darkness someone Mace and or L'il Kevin returned fire one two in rapid succession in trying to dodge Jerry tripped over the body in the snow and had to catch himself with an extended hand to the ground Carlos and then a blonde head rose above the chassis of the Rover and slowly moved toward the front door of the house Glow lobbed a couple of snowballs in support of Jerry who had moved to the rear of the Rover and was building and throwing as fast as he could Carlos and the blonde disappeared into the shadows as Jerry took a snowball to the head staggering back for a moment he heard the front door open and what sounded like a sob.

Grand Illusion

Jean Renoir (1937)

*T*here was really no other place to put her. They could have kept her in the house, but they had all but abandoned the three upstairs bedrooms, using one as a junkroom and leaving the others stripped, both without furniture and one without even a door, and had wintersealed the oak door in front of the stairs. His mother and Liz occupied the ground floor. The TV room was suggested and immediately discounted, as Nintendo and porn took precedence over hostage parking. The basement was unheated and out of the question, as was the storage room, even though it had a lock. Mace volunteered their trailer, but Glow gave him The Look, and he didn't press. Glow's and Jerry's trailer was small and fully occupied, and so the honor fell to him: he had the largest trailer and lived alone, with the only spare habitable bedroom in the compound. The room had a thin, cheap door, and a lock that Jerry, with some difficulty, turned around. The flimsiness of the mobile home door was a concern, and so Glow quickly fetched a pair of sex handcuffs with black leather padding. He didn't argue, although he thought that the combination of her injury, the meds he had given her, the lock and the facts that it was snowing and that Liz had removed her boots was probably enough to keep her from escaping. Everyone was jumpy. It was wise to err on the side of safety.

It was Jerry, naturally, who articulated the question that was floating around in everyone's thought balloon, after he turned the lock. "What are we going to do with her?"

"We'll keep her here for awhile. See what she knows."

"She knows we capped her boyfriend."

"So what are you saying?"

"We can't keep her here forever."

"So what are you saying?"

"We can't keep her here forever. That's all I'm saying." He yawned, packed up his toolbox, and left.

L'il Kevin carried her in, like some sort of Pietà, Liz following, with Glow and Carlos stopping at the threshold. "Watch her right leg, L'il Kevin, watch her right leg." She was doped, unconscious, her lips open and her eyes closed. L'il Kevin set her gently on the couch, and stood looming over, puzzled and excited. She was probably the finest thing he had ever seen, especially at such a close distance, and he was in no hurry to quit the charmed circle. "She's going to need some blankets."

"Right here."

He looked around, and snapped Glow's handcuffs on her left wrist. Now what? He couldn't see anything to attach the other end to. There was no brass bed like in Almodóvar, whom he hated (and Banderas was embarrassing), just a small room in a shabby mobile home with a newish leather couch, a floor lamp, and a couple of large metal bookcases (with DVD's and books spilling out) that didn't quite block the picture window completely. It smelled of bodies and wet boots.

Glow, attuned to such logistics, offered, "If you turn her around, you can snap the other end on the bookcase." L'il Kevin gracefully and gently turned her around on the couch, but her arm wouldn't stretch far enough to reach the gray metal. "We'll have to move the couch. So it's at an angle." There wasn't enough space in the small room. "L'il Kevin, why don't you step out? Liz and I can take it from here." L'il Kevin reluctantly backed out toward the door, his eyes never leaving the supine figure. They pushed the couch away from the wall so that they could fasten the other end of the handcuffs to one of the bookcases. Liz departed, and the crowd at the door dispersed. The girl was a mess.

The right arm of her brown suede jacket was streaked with blood, and she had a smudge of blood on her forehead above her left eye. Her dark blue jeans were ripped at the seam on the right ankle, and there was a dark stain on the right knee. She moaned softly as he placed a scratchy wool blanket over her torso and legs.

No, they couldn't keep her here forever, that was true. But after what had happened to her boyfriend, well, he didn't know what to do. She was young, and very good-looking. It was complicated. He turned out the light, closed the door and pushed the lock in, and carefully placed the key to the handcuffs in his wallet. She'd probably be out for another four or five hours, and maybe he could get some sleep.

He yawned and looked at the clock. Eight-thirty. He'd slept fitfully, alert to every sound and creak: the trailer, never quiet under the best of circumstances, seemed last night a nocturnal symphony. He had thought about the girl. And her boyfriend. Whom they had murdered.

The light filtered through the curtains, illuminating clearly the bottom edge of his bed and reflecting off the mirrored closet door, creating the illusion of light and spaciousness in what was really a small dark cheap cell, too flimsy and earthbound to qualify as a garret, too shoddy to suggest a crypt. It was a small room in a cheap trailer. The girl was next door, hopefully still sleeping. She'd clouded his dreams all night, like an unexpected and strange succubus, a creature from another movie, a demon from a mis-aimed curse. This was bad, but he had more of a general sense of foreboding and dread than specific feelings of guilt, regret or ideas about what to do next. He didn't feel at all sorry for the punk (you don't surprise people like that at three-thirty in the am) as any sort of sympathy he might have felt was overwhelmed by feelings of anger, resentment and annoyance his death and the subsequent necessary actions and decisions to cover up his death required. Actions and decisions he hadn't yet even started to consider. If he did feel guilt, it was guilt for the fact that somehow *he* had caused the kid to return. He had finally recognized the kid from the summer, when he had helped him and the Mexican with their car. For some reason the kid had returned in the middle of the night, five months later, and had gotten himself shot up and killed. Kilt. He needed to find out why the kid had returned.

He'd have to speak to the girl. She was the biggest problem, in all sorts of ways. The dead kid was no longer the main concern: burying a body so it wouldn't be found wouldn't be difficult in this desolate prairie, although the ground was currently frozen (*Shallow Grave* without the cash). No, she was much more troublesome. What did she know? And would she tell? No one was that anxious to kill her, at least he didn't think so. They were running a business, and killing was gratuitous. They weren't murderers anyway. "I want reliable people, people that aren't going to be carried away. I mean we're not murderers." Fucking Marlon. Not even gangsters or mafioso. Just more or less desperate people trying to get by. Ouch. He'd have to talk to her and find out what she knew, and what kind of person she was. And then they'd have to make some decisions. He got up from the bed, took a piss and brushed his teeth. First he'd get dressed, and then look at her backpack. And then he'd talk to her. He needed some coffee.

He started to put on some old gray sweat pants he liked to wear around the house, but thought better of it. If he was going to talk to her, he should wear something more intimidating, something that screamed Cagney or Tony Montana I will fuck you up or something. Maybe he could get Jerry in here to play the bad cop, and then when she was reduced to tears, certain her life was over, he'd come in and save the day. She'd collapse in his arms and tell him everything, her lips moistened and her perky nipples pushing through her blouse, like Lizabeth Scott or Veronica Lake. Not the Scott of *Too Late for Tears* or *Dead Reckoning*, more the Scott of *Easy Living*. Well, maybe not Scott at all, although he did like that lisp. He'd have to wear something a little more stylish and ominous than gray sweatpants with the flared cuffs.

His black jeans were mostly in good shape, and he had some beautiful grey slacks he seldom wore. He stood in front of his dresser: his three or four pair of black 501's, along with twenty or thirty tee shirts, mostly from Old Navy or the Gap, mostly black, were folded and stashed in his chest of drawers. He had a few other dress shirts and slacks in the back of his closet, but he couldn't remember the last time he had worn anything but jeans or sweatpants and a tee shirt: whenever he did manage to leave the compound the places he went to didn't really invite dressing for dinner. He turned and looked out the window: it had clouded up again and had begun to snow. He wasn't going to wear Timberlands and a polar fleece long sleeve, and he hated the desert camo everyone else seemed to favor. He had better hurry: she was bound to wake up, notice the pain in her leg and the handcuffs on her wrist, remember the bloody corpse of her boyfriend, and start screaming or something. She'd probably be hungry as well.

Maybe he should get some coffee first. He wandered out to the living room. Place was a mess. He remembered all of the people gathered in his spare bedroom, and that smell, that

musty odor of bodies and footwear, the great and literal unwashed, and he cringed a little. He wasn't used to having company and he couldn't remember ever having a woman inside
his trailer. He looked down. Who was on the turntable? Dino.
Reprise Hits. Perfect. Fucker laid some serious pipe. Didn't care
about *any*thing else. This might wake her up, but he needed
some music to help him think. He switched the amp on and then
placed the stylus carefully down on the first track. He loved the
swirling string intro, followed by the drunken sounding chorus,
"Everybody loves somebody sometime," the honky-tonk piano
rhythm, and Dino's suave motherfucking voice, *Something in
your kiss just told me*, backed by the *ooh ooh oohs* of the chorus,
man that was cool. Ok. His black jeans and a nicer black tee shirt
with his newly polished half boots. He wouldn't need to wear
the Glock, it would be too much like a cop show or something.
He hurried back to his bedroom and dressed quickly.

Jerry had rifled through her backpack and suitcase. He unzipped it slowly, cautiously, and although he was alone, secre-
tively. A Nokia cell phone with the battery removed, a makeup
kit (Chanel), a small water bottle, a newish iPod player with
headphones, some expensive looking body lotion, Ice Tech
sunglasses, keys (including a Saab key) on a key ring, a couple
of pens, a couple of loose tampons, some assorted change, an
old eyeliner pencil, loose Q-tips, a small toiletry bag with a
tooth brush, tooth paste, a travel bottle of Listerine, a stick
of deodorant and two condoms, a passport and a nice leather
wallet. He opened the wallet. Her name was Shelby. She was
twenty-two, and a student at Arizona State. Her driver's license
showed an Evergreen Drive address in Scottsdale Arizona. She
carried two Platinum Visas and a Gold American Express card,
along with credit cards from Shell, Nordstrom and Tocca. In
the money fold of her wallet he found two hundred dollars in
cash, an address scrawled on a small piece of paper, three credit
card receipts (one from a gas station and two from restaurants),

her contact lens prescription and another condom. Shelby Palmer. What a waspy name. He looked at the passport: seven or eight indecipherable visa stamps on four pages. He put the phone in his pocket and rezipped the bag. He decided he'd try to hide the fact that he'd gone through her stuff.

He cleaned out his bathroom of anything that might tempt, specifically his razor and the few meds he kept in the cabinet, then snuck up to the office door and leaned his ear toward it, but couldn't hear anything. He heard the chorus hit the high note on *Sometime* and the orchestra fade out. Not a peep from behind the door. He unlocked the door and went inside. The swinging horns started, and as he closed the door, Dino's voice echoed through the room, *Please release me, let me go*. He smiled. Maybe he should have turned the music off.

The girl, Shelby, opened her eyes and stared at him. She looked afraid and yet defiant, spoiled, used to getting her way like the girls he used to teach at Hunter (it had been quite a while since they had drifted back into his consciousness). She was pretty, beautiful even, in that pampered, athletic, fuckable way. She had dirty blond hair, dark eyebrows and clear skin. Her thin lips were drawn into a frown, but her brow remained unfurrowed, although bloodied slightly above the left eye. Her eyes were light brown, hazel really, and the right was slightly bloodshot. She reminded him a lot of Sandrine Bonnaire. She had seen her boyfriend shot and killed, had sprained her ankle trying to avoid the gunfire, had been drugged and then handcuffed to a bookcase and awakened by Dean Martin in some strange house, but she still looked good.

"Hi." It occurred to him that she might need to use the bathroom. "Do you need to use the restroom?" She looked at him, and then slowly looked away. He didn't want to loom over her, drooling like L'il Kevin, but the only chair in the room was covered with books and crap that used to be on the couch. So he stood there. "Are you hungry?" She looked back up at him, closed her eyes. "Do you want me to undo the handcuffs? You can't be very comfortable." She opened her eyes, and turned away from him on her side.

Now what? Maybe he should get some coffee and some breakfast, see how his mom was doing, and then come back. She was going to have to pee soon. "We need to talk. We need to talk about what happened last night."

"Fuck you," she said to the couch.

"Suit yourself." He turned and walked out of the room, closing and locking the door. He kept the stereo on, put his leather coat on and snow boots over his shoes, deadbolted the front door to the mobile home, and trudged through the snow to the farmhouse.

He was grateful that he didn't have to answer any questions about her at breakfast: Jerry, the boys and Glow were elsewhere, tweaking, sleeping or some combination. His mom was fine. She was dutifully eating her breakfast, bacon and scrambled eggs, and dry toast, as Liz no longer gave her jam or butter because she would smear it all over her face and arms. Well, actually, she wasn't that fine: she kept trying to pour her milk into her juice, spilled egg all down her bib and on the floor, kept her left arm bent crookedly at the wrist (maybe she slept on it and it was sore), and mumbled "bingo, bingo, bingo" and "Jesus my friends, Jesus my friend, Jesus my friend" all the time he was there. He wasn't sure she recognized him. It was shaping up to be a bad day for her, and they couldn't take her outside because of the snow. Liz was grumpy. "I can't handle her, you're going to have to take her someplace. I can't handle her anymore, you're going to have to put her in a home." Yeah right. He gave her a couple of Ambien with her juice to keep Liz happy. He took a plate of bacon and eggs with some coffee back for the girl.

He carried the plate and coffee cup into her room. He had turned Dino down, but not off. *Return to me* . . . "You want to try it again?" No answer. She was in the same position as when he left her. "I brought you some food. And I'll take your cuffs off, so you can go to the bathroom. Please? We need to know what happened. Who this guy was. Who you are. Please? Tell me what happened. Slowly. Take your time. Don't leave anything out."

"Why should I tell you anything?"

"Because you have to go to the bathroom. Because you're hungry. Because your leg is going to start hurting pretty soon and I'll give you something to make it stop." He hesitated. "And because I'm your best friend here." Cheesy dialogue.

She turned around suddenly and sat up. "What are you doing to me? What have I done to you? I haven't done a goddam thing to you. Why won't you take me to a doctor? Why don't you take me to the emergency? Who are you? Who the fuck *are* you? I'm not going to tell you a fucking thing." He set the plate and cup on the floor and walked out into the living room, closing and locking the door behind him.

He flicked the stereo off and sat down on his Lazy-Boy. It was a comfortable chair, an expensive chair, and fairly new. It was a bit nicer than most of the other furniture in the mobile home, except for the stereo and the television, and the leather couch in the study.

The couch Shelby was going to soil if she didn't start cooperating. She was a real problem, a real headache. They could keep her here for a while, but not indefinitely, Jerry was right about that. He'd go in soon and try again, at least undo the handcuffs and show her where the bathroom was. Cute as she was, she was beginning to get on his nerves. Spoiled bitch.

Maybe she was a sign, an omen, a warning to cool it for a while. They all could use a little time off, especially after what happened last night, although he wasn't sure how the Rodriguez brothers would react if he split. Actually he was sure how they would react: they'd be angry. But how angry? They could bring their own cooks in any time. He had always liked Walsenburg, and there were plenty of out of the way nooks and crannies in Huerfano where they could go. Some excellent dope came from Huerfano County: maybe it was time to look into changing businesses, move from manufacturing to farming. Geanetta and his cousins might not dig the competition, but they'd start small, stay small, and they had enough cash to set something up.

Or maybe it was time to chuck the whole fucking thing. Tell the gang *au revoir* and move to France or something. Or Tuscany. Or back to his grandfather's village in Molise (and then what? His French wasn't that great, his Italian non-existent). Or not tell them anything and just leave. Two problems with that: one, what would he do with his mother? and two, he had about a million, which, even if he were careful, might not last him long. He'd put a bullet in his head before he went back to Pueblo to live. And he wasn't sure how Jerry would react to his departure. He was the only person the Rodriguez Brothers trusted, and if he left, well, no cushy jobs at the meth lab. Three problems, maybe four. This was complicated. First things first: he had to find out what was going on with Shelby.

She was sitting up, staring at her hands (or handcuffs), her breakfast plate and coffee cup untouched. Without saying a word, he walked over to the chair, cleared the books off onto the floor, and sat down, facing her. Until he spoke, he wasn't sure how he was going to play this: rough macho gangster or concerned possible pal. "We have a problem here. And by 'we,' I mean you, me, and the rest of us. A shared problem. And to solve the problem, we need to know how you got here."

"Fuck you."

"Yeah, fuck me. Look, I didn't ask you to come here. I didn't ask your boyfriend to drive three miles down a private road looking for trouble. I didn't ask him to come barreling down our driveway, unannounced, at three o'clock in the fucking morning, now did I?"

"And you didn't ask him to stop all those bullets either."

"No, I didn't ask him to stop all those bullets. We overreacted, I admit. But we need to know what happened. We need you to talk. How did you get here? Why did you come?"

She hesitated for a moment, her brow furrowed. "Okay, okay. I'll talk to you. But first I need to piss." She looked up at him boldly, pleased with her expletive.

"Yeah." He stood up and gathered his wallet out of his pocket, opened it, and extracted the key. He held it up. "If you look outside, you'll see it's still snowing. We took your heavy coat and your boots, and it's cold. There's nothing around here, and the road is three miles away. Plus you have a sprained ankle. Even though you wouldn't get very far, I don't want to have to come looking for you in the snow." He undid the cuffs, and she rubbed her wrists, just like in the movies. She started to stand, then with a little noise she stumbled back to the couch. "Your leg hurts, huh? Your ankle's not broken as far as I can tell. I'll give you some percodan after we talk. Come on." He held his arm out to her. "I'll help you."

They shuffled into the living room. It wasn't quite to the level of "What a dump!" but it was close, with a couple of dirty plates and accompanying silverware on the coffee table and a few papers and books strewn around on the scruffy polyester covered sofa from his mother's house. It featured that sort of thickened smell of masculine space. For the first time he noticed that all of the walls were completely bare. "I'm sorry for the clutter, I wasn't expecting company." She grunted and limped along beside him.

"Is that my pack?" she asked hoarsely.

"Yeah. Do you want it?" She nodded. He left her perched on one leg. "Here."

"Thanks," she said, as she hobbled into the bathroom. He

decided to put the music back on.

"So, what do you want to know?" She was sitting up on the couch, a pillow under her ankle, a blanket around her legs and her jacket around her shoulders. The smear of blood on her forehead turned out to be a shallow scratch. He'd offered to swab the cut with peroxide, she insisted on doing that, and applied the band-aid herself. Dean sang "The One I Love Belongs to Somebody Else" in the background (Frank's version was a downer: Dean sang as if he were relieved).

"How about your name?"

"Didn't you go through my bag?"

"No."

She leaned forward and rubber her swollen ankle. "Where are my boots? Don't you know you're not supposed to take the boots off of somebody when they hurt their ankle?" She looked at him with what probably was intended to be a fierce expression. "You might not get the boots back on. Don't you know that?"

"We wanted to see if your ankle was broken."

"If you're so interested in my health, why don't you take me to emergency? You're not a doctor, are you?"

"No."

"I thought I heard someone calling you doctor. Before you knocked me out. What did you give me, anyway?"

"I gave you a shot of ketamine to relax you. And then Ambien to help you sleep."

"Special K huh? I've done that before."

"What's your name?"

"You didn't go through my bag? Or my suitcase?"

"I told you, no."

"Shelby. Shelby Palmer."

"And your boyfriend's name is Dylan Samuels? Was."

"Yeah, but he wasn't my boyfriend. He was just some guy I hung out with sometimes." She shrugged, looked up at the ceiling. "I didn't know him very well."

Was she telling the truth?

"I need a nicotine. Is there a cigarette in this trailer?"

It was the way she said "trailer." She thought he was one of them, thought he was like them. To her there was no difference between him and Carlos, or him and Liz or L'il Kevin. He was just an ice cook, a gangster who had killed her friend and was holding her against her will. He looked at her. For some reason it was important that she understood that he was different, that in fact he had more in common with her than he did his fellow cooks. He wanted her to see that he was educated, that he could have a conversation, that he could treat women with respect. He wasn't at all like any of them: they shared a job and nothing more. He was as alone there as she was. He managed to speak, "I don't smoke. So what's your story?"

She looked at him. "My story? Let's see: I'm twenty-two years old, and I go to Arizona State. I'm an undeclared major. I have a 3.2 GPA . . . And I'm being held hostage by a bunch of fucking cowboy glass cookers. That's my fucking story!"

What could he say? What could he do to indicate they were alike, like Masons in *Exterminating Angel* or Jews in *The Garden of the Fitzi-Continis*? *It's tough to be alone on a shelf/It's worse to be in love by yourself.* He stood up. He had no uniform, secret handshake or special tattoo. What was he going to do? Let Jerry handle everything? He couldn't deal with two bodies. He closed his eyes, opened them again. He should have brought the Glock to scare some sense into her, although that would probably just reinforce her impression. Guns and trailers. "Look at me. We have to be careful here. Look at me. This is real. Your boyfriend is really dead. We have to know what he knew before we can let you go. You have to talk to me. You saw what they can do. Believe me, I want you out of here just as badly as you do. But you're going to have to talk to me. I'm your best chance." It was a weak speech.

But it seemed to have some effect. She hesitated, then shrugged. "Ok. I was bumming at school, February blues or something, and I needed some Aspen powder. My family owns a condo in Dolomite Villas, so I thought I'd bop up there and surprise them." Surprise them? So they don't know you're coming? "My Saab's in the shop. It's always in the shop. So Dylan heard that I needed a ride, said he was going up to Snowmass, and I could ride with him."

"Why didn't you fly?"

"My cards got maxed at Christmas."

"So how do you know Dylan?"

She chuckled. "Everybody at ASU knows Dylan. He's a dude who gets stuff, you know? X, pot, H, peyote, shrooms, opium: he's a one-man party. He used to organize raves. He's been to Burning Man five or six times. He likes having fun, and he likes getting people together."

He was only half listening. He thought back to the smell of wet boots, and the dirty dishes in his sink. He usually kept his bathroom pretty clean. What difference did it make? He sat down. "Is he a student?"

"No. I don't know. He's a party dude, that's his job."

"He was going to give you a ride for free?"

She scowled. "What's that supposed to mean? I was going to pay for gas. I ain't no ho."

"I didn't mean anything. I just want to know how close you were to him."

"He was around, that's all. I never fucked him and I didn't owe him shit. Satisfied?"

"Go on." Jesus, he felt like Edward G. Robinson questioning Paulette Goddard.

"We get started late. I thought it was a bit weird, but Dylan said he liked driving at night. He picks me up at four, and says he's got to make a stop in Flagstaff. I said that's cool. It's his ride, you know. We burn a joint, listen to some Snoop, it's all good. Anyway, we get to Flagstaff and we go up in the hills. We're about forty-five minutes off the highway when we come to this little shack in the woods. Dylan tells me to hang tight, so I hang tight, burn another joint, crank the tunes. He's only gone for ten minutes or so, and when he gets back, he's pissed. Something torqued him off big time. He has a little fit, pounds the steering wheel and shit, motherfucker this and motherfucker that, until I say dude, chill, or something like that, and then he mutters under his breath, starts the Rover, and we tear down the mountain."

He looked at her intently. She was no Einstein, but she did have the ability to tell a coherent story and speak in complete sentences. Was he that starved for meaningful conversation that this spoiled coed actually sounded intelligent? She really reminded him of Suzanne in *A Nos Amours*, although he liked the older Bonnaire of *Monsieur Hire* slightly better (both images made him feel creepy). "What do you think happened?"

"Something pissed him off. I don't know. Maybe he was supposed to meet somebody out there or something. Anyway, he keeps bitching, all the way through Arizona and into New Mexico, muttering under his breath and just being generally nasty, you know, until we get to Gallup. It's already been dark for a couple of hours, and I'm getting hungry and I need to use the bathroom, so we stop at Wendy's. I get out of the john, and suddenly he's all happy and shit, like he's x-ing or something. He's got ketchup on his face and chattering, you know, something about how two years ago he did an ice buy in Boulder from this guy who looked like a college professor, not like a gangster or a biker at all, and then this summer when he and his friend Ramon were tripping near Pueblo, they drove their car into a ditch, and they walked up to a barn or something, and who should help them but that very same schoolteacher. And the teacher didn't recognize him, Dylan was sure of that, but he was acting all weird, like he was trying to hide something, and

Dylan just knew that he was holding, and so all he had to do was find that schoolteacher's barn and all his problems would be solved. And even when fucked up, he, Dylan, always had a great memory for direction, so not to worry, he never got lost, and he'd called up Ramon too, so he had a pretty good idea of where to go, it might take a while, but he'd find the place. So we should hurry and get on the road, because we had another stop to make blah blah blah. So I basically figured out why we'd stopped in Flagstaff, and why he was going to Snowmass."

"That's why he came here."

"That's why he came here." She looked at him with an arrogant smile. "I figure you're the school teacher."

So that was it, plain and simple. A twist of fate, a chance meeting, a missed connection, and now one dead dude. Even though he knew rationally that this wasn't his fault, part of him felt slightly guilty. If he hadn't helped tow their car out of the ditch, maybe the kid wouldn't have seen him enough to jar his tripping memory. But if he hadn't intercepted them that day last July, they might have made it all the way to the house, and so the outcome, at least for the kid, would have been ultimately the same. He tried to think about meeting the kid in Boulder, but he didn't remember.

The small fragment of guilt was accompanied, dwarfed by a larger, more insistent (and more pleasant) feeling of interest and intrigue. Other than Nish, and sometimes Jerry, almost all of his conversations were monosyllabic exchanges focusing on commercial, technical or other mundane concerns: he seldom spoke with people who spoke in full sentences, let alone coherent paragraphs. His discussions with women had been exclusively mercantile for quite a while, although, truth be told, in the last year or so even those brief negotiations of fees charged and services obtained were few and far between. Glow and Liz he mostly gave orders, or in Glow's case, suggestions. It was nice listening to someone who had been to college, who knew how to tell a story. And it didn't hurt she was good looking. Classy, as Dean would say, classy. At least compared to his current entourage.

"Why are you looking at me like that?"

He shrugged his shoulders. "I'm trying to figure out what to do."

She looked around, and leaned forward on the couch. "Get me out of this trailer and to some town. I swear I won't say a word. Scout's honor."

You want me to help you escape? This was stupid. He sighed. He couldn't imagine a way this would end well, the two of them embracing in front of some alpine farmhouse. No matter how this turned out, things would never the same for either of them. And yet. He needed some time to think. He stood up. "We'll see."

The Texas Chainsaw Massacre

Tobe Hooper (1974)

"**H**ey. Shelby." She was in that familiar posture, her face buried in the couch with her back facing the door. He flicked on the light. The room smelled a little close. "Shelby." He didn't think she was asleep but he wasn't sure. "It's my mother's and Glow's birthdays, and we're having a little celebration in the house. You might as well join us." No answer, no movement. He shrugged. "Cool. I'll bring you some cake."

She turned to look at the ceiling. He had taken the cuffs off before he'd gone to bed. "Spare me your tweaker ball. Where's Dylan? Let me see Dylan."

"I thought you might want to get out of here for awhile. Get the blood circulating, stretch your legs. How's your ankle, by the way?" He thought about explaining that he didn't use what he made, that only Jerry and Carlos tweaked, and Glow sometimes, and Mace only smoked dope, and Liz just drank and smoked dope, but said nothing.

"Hurts like hell. What are you going to do with me?"

"I don't know." He smiled, didn't want to freak her out. "Snow's too deep to get to take you anywhere now. It'll melt soon enough. This is Colorado: if you don't like the weather, wait a few minutes." He smiled and felt stupid.

She sat up and looked at him, straight in the eye. "My father's got bucks."

"We're not kidnappers." We're not killers either, but look at us. "C'mon. If you come to the party, I'll go get your suitcase: you can shower and change clothes. I'll even buy you a beer."

"I'd rather have a percodan."

"Deal."

He handcuffed her to the bookcase while he went to the house to find her suitcase. The big dining room table, seldom used (everyone except his mom usually took their plates to the TV room) was set—with the good plates, a white table cloth and mismatched cloth napkins—but abandoned. He glanced to his left. Liz was at the stove and his mom was parked in the corner snoring lightly in the warm kitchen, a bright pink Mylar balloon floating above her chair. He heard the television loud from the playroom. He walked around the table and opened the door part way: Mace, Li'l Kevin and Glow were all drinking beer and watching a basketball game. Carlos was probably working in the garage. He wondered where Jerry was.

They had quietly tidied up the day before, although he wasn't sure how they had disposed of the body and didn't want to ask. Carlos had probably taken care of it, although he wasn't sure what "taken care of it" meant. Carlos the Cleaner. "So pretty please, with sugar on top, clean the fucking car." No, that was the Wolf, not the Cleaner. L'il Kevin and Mace had tossed Dylan's and Shelby's suitcases down the basement stairs. What would they do with of all that? He'd think about it later.

This was hers, the expensive looking leather one. He wondered if anyone had gone through Dylan's bag yet. What would be the point? It was probably best not to know, best to keep him anonymous. If they were lucky, if things worked out the way everyone wanted (well, everyone except Shelby), no one would ever know what had happened to Dylan. He would simply and completely disappear. Milk-cartoned. He wondered if Dylan had a family, a mother and a father, siblings. Probably: even Arizona party boys had to come from somewhere. He didn't want to know, he didn't want the dude in his consciousness *at all*. He'd bury or burn his things as soon as he could.

He carried her suitcase up the stairs. Jerry'd already gone though it. He should probably check it out again, give it a quick once-over. He didn't think she had a gun, but she might have a pocket-knife or something like that. He felt a little uncomfortable as he set the suitcase on the dining room floor and opened it. Yeah, Jerry had gone through it all right. Either that or she had just stuffed a bunch of underwear, clothes and shoes randomly into the bag and let a grenade go off inside, and he didn't think many women packed like that. He heard the television sound get louder as the playroom door opened.

"What are you doing?"

"You went through this right? No guns or knives?"

"What are you doing?"

"I'm going to give her some clothes."

"Why?"

"Why do you think?" He stood in order to look into Jerry's eyes, see if he was high, tweaking, twitching, doped or hammered. He could even be sober. He also didn't want to have Jerry looming above him. "So she'll have something to wear." Jerry was wearing sunglasses, which didn't necessarily mean anything.

Jerry turned, walked back to the basketball game. "Be careful, bro. Don't get involved."

He moved his Lay-Z Boy around so it faced the door and sat down while she showered and cleaned up. He heard the shower through the door. What the fuck was he doing? Maybe if they could get to know her, see how pretty and human she was, she would be harder to, well, dispose of. But what choice did they have? If they let her go, she would talk, and they all would be fucked, from both the police and the Rodriguez Brothers (he'd prefer the police). They could keep her around, but how long until she got hold of a telephone, or car keys, or some other goddam thing? Maybe even a gun? He could keep her doped and locked up, but the Buffalo Bill it rubs the lotion on its skin it does whatever it is told image was too repulsive: whatever happened he simply wouldn't allow himself to go there. Carlos or Jerry would take care of her, probably sooner than later. He assumed they knew what they were doing, assumed they could do it quickly and painlessly, assumed the army had taught them something. Who was he kidding? Carlos was a hard, pipe-hitting fuck who'd do some *thangs* to Shelby: he'd have to keep her away from Carlos. This was a disaster.

Maybe bringing her to the party was a mistake. Maybe he should keep her hidden, out of sight out of mind, and then give her too much of something in the next couple of days. She wouldn't get used and abused, à la *Irreversible* or *Salò*. He didn't have any morphine, K was hard to OD and a meth overdose was anything but painless: he didn't want her to have a stroke and spazz out, he just wanted her to go to sleep and not wake up. The percodan would be almost impossible to administer, as it was difficult to force someone to OD on pills if they didn't want to and he didn't want to cook it up into a shot. He thought there might be some liquid Lorcet around from his mother's bladder operation. That would be the easiest for both of them. A shot to ease the pain of her ankle, and then goodnight, goodnight, sleep well, and when you dream, dream of me. He wasn't sure he had the balls to kill anyone.

Especially anyone he knew. His brother was right. Maybe that was what this was about, getting to know her. In order to be able to do her a favor, kill her nicely, he'd have to be detached, which meant no party and no interaction. He'd handcuff her in her room, then go to the house and have some cake and some drinks, think about anything else, and tomorrow, cool as Cool Hand Luke, actually more like Hud, fix her a shot. But who'd Hud ever kill? By getting to know her, by taking her to this party, he was going to make it impossible to kill her himself, which meant Jerry and/or Carlos would do it, which meant that probably it wouldn't be very pleasant. On the other hand, it might be nice to give her a last waltz, and he'd talk to Jerry about making sure, when the time came, that it was quick and painless. Hell, maybe he could fix the shot and have Jerry give it to her: that might be the way to go. He'd check for the Lorcet in his mother's room.

He heard the water shut off. Did she suspect anything? Could she guess the ending? If she could, she'd probably do anything to avoid her fate. She was an undeclared major, which probably meant she wasn't the sharpest tool in the shed: maybe she honestly thought that, after having made a solemn promise not tell *anyone* of her excellent adventure, she'd be released. Could she really believe that? What kind of person could possibly believe that they'd let her go, just like that? She was innocent, okay: all she wanted was a ride to Aspen and she ends up in some prairie trailer cleaning up for her last party with a bunch of meth chefs. But could anybody be that innocent? She must have some inkling, some suspicion.

He had written a paper way back in graduate school on the necessity for dramatic irony in contemporary film, on how, depending on the genre and advance publicity, the audience already knew the ending before the film even started, and this was one fine example: the heroine didn't know shit and went on with her life like she was all that while everyone in the audience understood that she has going to get Kruegered in the next room. Perhaps they'd even seen it in the previews. Shelby would make the perfect splatter victim: blonde hair, nice white teeth, a body to die for and a sassy 'tude . . . what else could happen but mutilation and a slow death, like Phyllis in *The Last House on the Left* (except for the hair color and 'tude). *Last Trailer on the Left.* "It's only a movie, it's only a movie." He'd try to make sure she died offscreen, like that blonde Norwegian fox in *Friday 13ᵗʰ II*, Kirsten Baker. He was pathetic. The bathroom door opened and she limped out.

She cleaned up well. She had changed into faded jeans that hung low on her hips, and had replaced her thin sweater with a thick, pale green pullover that looked good and expensive. Her hair was damp and hung heavily, and it seemed darker than before. likely because it was wet. She'd scrubbed her face and put on pale red lipstick. She was wearing a black high top sneaker on one foot and a grey thick ski sock on the favored. He got up out of his chair. It has been a while since he had seen anything so attractive in the flesh.

"You look nice."

"Hey, it's a party. I couldn't get my shoe on: you got anything for the swelling? And it hurts like hell."

"Let me get you a percodan now. It's anti-inflammatory."

"How do you know so much? You a pharmacist?"

"No."

"I saw all those DVD's, movie books and stuff. Are you really a schoolteacher or something? A professor?"

"No."

She waited from him to continue, and when he didn't she shrugged. "I'm going to need some help through the snow."

"Let me get that percodan first."

The snow was about a foot deep, and it was difficult maneuvering through it with her bad wheel. He carried a two hundred dollar of red wine (Burgundy) for Glow by the neck with his right hand, and pressed a small rectangle box with white down slippers for his mother against his hip with that elbow.

He had spent twice the money on Glow's present compared to his mother's. He didn't think his mother could understand birthdays or gifts anymore, although she might notice her feet were warm and cozy. Shelby leaned on his left arm lightly and only when absolutely necessary. The wind was swirling, and it was almost dark, and this was a bad idea. He wished he'd lent her a coat. She slipped down just before they reached the door and, quickly twisting away on her left elbow, she struggled awkwardly to her feet, ignoring his outstretched hand. She brushed the snow off her knees and arms without looking at him.

The talking and laughing they had heard just outside stopped abruptly when they opened the door. Five or six pink, red and blue Mylar balloons floated randomly against the ceiling, looking like fat shiny insects. There was a bright red paper and tissue accordion Valentine heart in the center of the table, along with a couple of thick red and pink unlit candles on a tray. A few wine bottles and beer cans were scattered about. It should have looked more festive than it did. Jerry was at the head of the table, facing the front door, sunglasses in place. His mother was on Jerry's left, her hair slightly disheveled and eyes bright at the plate of food in front of her. Glow was on his right, hair pulled back in a tight pony tail, a bottle of Johnny Black in front of her, a small plate of food pushed away to her left. Mace was next to her, in fatigues and a black stocking cap, and Li'l Kevin was next to him, by the kitchen door, tearing into a piece of fried chicken. Carlos was across the table from Kevin, leaving a space next to Mom for Liz on his right, and another place across L'il Kevin for him. They weren't expecting Shelby.

"We'll need another chair." His words reflected and ricocheted about the room, unabsorbed. He was wondering if Jerry would give him shit, but he just turned the lenses of the shades toward him and said nothing. Glow looked at Jerry, then at him, her face a mask. Mace took a drink of beer and swallowing loudly, returned to his mashed potatoes. Carlos glanced at him, a loose but foul smile on his face. Liz scurried in, carrying a bowl of something green and steaming and sat down next to his mom. Li'l Kevin looked up from his chicken, saw Shelby, and smiled. L'il Kevin wasn't that dumb, even he could see she was the shiniest thing in the room. His mother didn't do anything. What a crew. *Pink* fucking *Flamingos*. He turned and gestured toward the empty chair. "Have a seat. I'll drag a chair out of the TV room. Is there another place setting?" "If she needs a seat, my face is available," from Carlos. He didn't want to fight Carlos. "I'll get her a coke," said Li'l Kevin. "Does she want a coke?"

"Thanks Li'l Kevin. I'll get her a drink. I guess I should introduce you. That's my brother Jerry, with the shades. Next to him is my mother, it's her birthday today, a robust eighty-two, and across from her is Glow, whose birthday was last Wednesday. Glow's not telling how old she is. Next to her is Mace, and Liz is next to my mother, and Carlos is next to Liz. The polite young man who so graciously offered you a soft drink is Li'l Kevin. Everyone, this is Shelby."

Her scratchy "hello" drew a few nods and grunts. Dead man walking.

The slippers, while not heavy, were slipping off of his hip. He grabbed the box with his free hand. "Are we opening presents yet?"

"What do you mean, 'opening'? You ain't wrapped shit." Thanks Carlos. He needed to change the vibe. He moved around to behind his mother, leaned over her right shoulder and set the bottle of wine on the table. "Glow, this is for you. Happy birthday." She leaned forward and picked it up, read the label. "A Richebourg, from Denis Mugneret. 1995. I'll save it. Thanks." She seemed pleased in spite of herself. He pulled his mother away from the table and set the box of slippers down on her lap. His mother, startled by the sudden movement, gripped her armrests tightly. He kneeled down and spoke to her gently. "Mother. Mother. Happy birthday, mother." Her eyes fastened on the plate from which Liz had been feeding her. "Mother, look at me please, mother, look at me." He was aware that everyone else was looking at him, everyone except his mother, who kept her gaze locked on the food in front of her. "Mother, it's me, your oldest son. Please look at me. It's your birthday, mom, and I bought you a present." He opened the box and rumpled the paper, hoping to distract her. "Mother, look." He put his hand on her chin and gently tried to turn her face toward him; she resisted, keeping her eyes on the table. He increased the pressure ever so slightly. Her eyes showed panic. She made a noise, "Eeh, eeh, eeh."

"Leave her alone, she's eating." He dropped his hand to her arm and squeezed it. The noise continued, "Eeh, eeh, eeh, eeh." He whispered in her ear, "Jerry's right mom. I'm sorry." She didn't even recognize him. He took the package from her lap and set it behind him on the floor next to the wall. "Happy birthday." "Eeh, eeh, eeh, eeh." He stood and swung her back toward the table, locking her right wheel. "Eeh, eeh, eeh, eeh." Liz quickly brought a forkful of chicken with potatoes up to her mouth. The noise stopped as she opened wide to admit the food. He patted her on the shoulder and turned and walked to the TV room, closing the door behind him. That went well.

Thoughts came separate and disconnected, like his mind was dropping frames. The television was on with the sound off. Another basketball game. He'd made a fool of himself in front of everyone. His mother was deteriorating badly. There was no escaping that. He didn't know how long she could remain out here with Liz. He'd have to talk to Jerry. Thank God he'd set up a trust with Nish. He couldn't leave Shelby out there amongst the wolves. He gathered himself, grabbed a thin chair from against the wall and brought it back to the dining room table.

Shelby was standing there by the door, ignored, looking frightened but cool. He moved quickly. "Here, take this seat.

I'll squeeze in here, next to L'il Kevin" (he wasn't going near Carlos). "Let me get you a drink. What'll you have? We have beer, wine, tequila, vodka, and I think Glow will share her scotch. Anything you want. We're having fried chicken, mashed potatoes and green beans, and there's a big chocolate cake for dessert. Let me get you a drink, and you can fix yourself a plate. What'll it be? What'll it be?" He was aware he was talking too fast and sounding the fool. He was nervous.

"Will a drink be ok with the percodan?"

"One or two drinks won't hurt. It's not like you'll be driving anywhere."

"I'll have a little vodka. With tonic if you have it and with soda if you don't."

"Vodka tonic it is. An excellent choice, I might add, excellent choice."

"We got no tonic. Someone finished it up last night."

"Vodka soda then. Do you want a lime?"

"We got no lime either," said Liz, and she poked another forkful of food into his mother's eager mouth.

"So, vodka soda then." He waited a beat to see if the availability of vodka and/or soda deserved mention. It didn't. He didn't want to leave her out here by herself. "That sounds good to me too. I think we have a Smirnoff's and Grey Goose, why don't you come with me to see what we can find?" He felt stupid, like a sit-com husband using an all-too-conspicuous remark to steer his sit-com wife into the kitchen for a private conversation about the hostess's sex life or canapés. He was grateful when Shelby limped after him without hesitation or comment.

The kitchen wasn't big, and the door was stopped open to provide easy access and egress for Liz to carry the dishes to and fro. He opened the cabinet next the fridge and looked inside. "Grey Goose, Smirnoff's *and* Stoli Citron. What's your pleasure?"

"Stoly sounds good." He heard conversation and Mace's big

laugh in the next room.

"Having fun?" he asked, as he pulled the Stoly bottle down.

"Chuckles galore," she answered, with surprising poise. "You should probably take me back to your trailer."

He set the bottle on the counter and took a couple of tall glasses from a cabinet to the left and filled them with ice from the refrigerator door. The roar of the ice dispenser ceased, and he heard ". . . fuck her" from the next room, followed by Mace's laugh booming over the others'. He smiled. "And have you miss all the laughs? Nonsense." He was trying to be reassuring, like John Wayne in *The Cowboys*, but feared he was coming across more like the *Life-is-Beautiful* Roberto Benigni.

She moved closer to him, and said in a low voice, "What's going to happen to me?"

He turned away from her and opened the refrigerator door, looking for a lemon and the soda. He found the soda quickly, but, since he could see the produce drawer was empty, he had to stoop down and push a few jars and bottles around before he located the net bag of yellow fruit. He hadn't expected the question so soon, or so directly. He stood up quickly and set the lemons and the soda bottle on the counter next to the glasses. He took a knife from the drawer at his waist and cut one of the lemons carefully into fourths, not wanting to mark the counter. He smiled, concentrating on his task. "Nothing's going to happen to you. When the snow clears, we'll give you a lift into town. You'll have to promise to keep your mouth shut. We have your address, and we have some very nasty friends. If anything happened to us, they'd retaliate. You'll have to trust me on that."

He wondered if she believed him, or if it was beginning to dawn on her that she probably wasn't going to make it out. He poured vodka, then the soda in the two glasses, the squeezed a quarter of lemon into each. He swirled one glass a round and handed it to Shelby, then picked up the other to taste it. It was strong and good.

"I hope it's not too strong."

"No. It's fine."

"Anyway, we're not the ones you have to worry about."

She looked at him. "So there's a gang that's more trippin' than this one, huh?"

"Hard to believe, isn't it?" He looked at her. Her hair had dried into a dark, dishwater blond, setting off her eyes nicely. He was slightly surprised to see that her eyes were a darker color than he had originally supposed, almost brown. He looked away, down at his drink. "We should get you some utensils and then get back to the party." He took a butter knife with a serrated edge, a fork and a spoon from the drawer, grabbed one of the good plates (pink Fiestaware from his mother) out of the cabinet and followed her out of the kitchen. He sat her down next to L'il Kevin, who grinned from ear to ear. He took another drink as he sat down. He wasn't hungry at all. He tried to catch the conversation at the other end of the table, but quickly gave up when he couldn't hear or follow very well. He had a guest to feed, a guest he was trying to forget. "Please pass the chicken."

"Would you like something to eat? You can have some of my food."

"No, no thank you."

"Look at L'il Kevin, trying to get him some with a plate of fried chicken and lettuce salad. Go for it boy." Mace chuckled loudly. Carlos continued. "That shit never work for me, chicken and salad. I always had to throw in a joint or two, or a lude or some x or something."

"Or a roofie."

Carlos laughed, "Yeah, or a roofie. Never got nothing with chicken and lettuce salad. Taco Bell's another story." Mace, Jerry and even Glow and L'il Kevin started to laugh. "It wasn't at all difficult to have the bitches give it up for a Chalupa or a

Nachos Bellgrande. Nothing off the value menu. I ain't fucking cheap. But the pussy was always easy with a Chalupa." The laughter crescendoed.

This is it, this is who I fucking live with, this is my life. *The Friends of Eddie Coyle.* You think you got problems. He looked over at her. She was hunched over, staring down at the empty plate in front of her, her hair hanging down like curtains over the sides of her face.

Carlos was digging it. "By the way, Shelby, or Missy, or whatever your name is. Don't be too nice to our boy here," he gestured across the table with his fork. "We call him L'il Kevin, but that refers only to what's above his shoulders, if you catch my drift." He shrugged. "You probably find out soon enough." More laughter. Mace snorted numerous times and pounded the table, unable to catch his breath.

"I don't get it. What's so funny? Whatcha laughing about? What's so funny?"

He looked over at her, still in the same position. He resisted the urge to touch her shoulder or comfort her verbally. He resisted the urge to say something to curb or deflect the taunting as well.

"We should change your name to Large Kevin."

"Kevin Bellgrande."

"Whatcha laughing at?" asked Kevin between mystified giggles. "C'mon, tell me. What's so funny?"

"Kevin. Kevin," from Carlos. "Kevin." He waited until Mace calmed, and the general laughter diminished. Diminished in volume, but not in cruelty. "Kevin. I won't call you 'L'il' no more. Kevin, tell me, what do you like most about our new girl here? What is it exactly that tickles your pickle?"

"Tickles my pickle? That's funny."

"Kevin, Kevin! Pay attention here. I'd like you to tell our studio audience what it is that you like about our guest here. Now granted, we don't get no visitors out here, but I ain't never seen you offer food to anyone else, and I've known you for what, three, four years? C'mon. You can tell your Uncle Carlos. What do you like about this *puta*?"

"That's enough."

"*Puta*? What's that?"

"Scuse me. You're right, you're right, please forgive me. I'm sorry, I'm sorry, Miss . . . what is your name again?"

"Her name is Shelby. Would you please pass the chicken? Did you get the 150 fixed Mace?"

"Shelby, Shelby. So Kevin, what is it you like about Shelby? What do you dig? Don't be shy. Her legs? Her smile? Her eyes? Her butt? You a tit man, Kevin? Huh? Or is it her long, beautiful anglo hair?" Carlos stood up and reached across the table to touch Shelby's hair. He smacked Carlos' hand away and rose quickly. The room got quiet. Man with no name. Showdown.

"What the fuck you doing? You might want to sit back down and reconsider, know what I'm saying? I know you all important and shit, but I still cut you."

"What the fuck are *you* doing? Why don't you leave her alone?"

"Why?"

That was the million dollar question, wasn't it? Why, if she would be killed, shouldn't they have a little fun first? Take their pleasure where they found it? "Honey, we all got to go sometime, reason or no reason. Dyin's as natural as livin.'" *The Misfits*. We're all fucking dog food. He didn't particularly want Gable's role, what was his name? Oh yeah, Gay. Gay. The older dude who puttered around, did the chores and protected the sweet young thing. And got to tap Marilyn at the end. Nice work if you could get it. Or believe it. Both dead within a year. Well, were they going to fight? He had no doubt Carlos would cut him if sufficiently provoked. They stared at each other for a while. Carlos' eyes were red and dilated. He wore a mean little unconcerned smile. Now what?

"Why don't you chill?"

"Mind your own goddam business."

"Sit down, both of you. This is supposed to be a party. Give my brother and the girl some food. Carlos, be cool. Now ain't the time." The next sentence, the "Later, perhaps, but not now," went unspoken. Although everyone heard it. Even Shelby.

Thank you Jerry. On the one hand, he was grateful for the fact that he wouldn't have to fight a wired and always nasty Carlos. He could take care of himself pretty good, but Carlos, Carlos was the type that would give the blade that extra twist to cause you some bonus pain. Two eyes, and maybe a finger too for an eye, a couple of teeth and maybe your right nut for a tooth. Cool, but he took things personally. He knew hard-ons at Bayside like that, even in medium, guys you glanced away from immediately, motherfuckers who'd sooner rape or cut you than talk to you. On the other hand, he wished Jerry hadn't voiced what everyone was thinking, what everyone knew: Shelby would be killed soon, sometime between 48 and 72 hours, if he had to guess.

Liz stood up and carried the plate of chicken down the table and set it in front of Shelby, then continued into the kitchen. As Carlos sat down slowly, still with that mean little smile, Mace tipped his beer can in salute and Carlos nodded in response. Glow slid the platter of potatoes down the table with the back of her hand. He relaxed his shoulders and turned back toward the girl. She remained still with her head down and her hair protecting her face. With the tongs lifted a chicken wing above the platter and held it suspended. "White meat or dark?" Shelby didn't move. "This is pretty good. Liz knows what she's doing." Nothing. "C'mon, you must be hungry." Still nothing. "I'll give you some of both then." He set the wing and a half breast on her plate, and then took a drumstick and another half breast for himself. His mouth watered, although his stomach felt queasy and tight. He pulled the potatoes toward him and spooned some on to her plate. The thick mass stuck to the spoon, and he tried to shake it off, cracking it loudly against the plate. Shelby jumped. He served himself a dollop, then sighed and sat. There were green beans up by his mom, and the salad bowl was next to Jerry, but he was ok for now. The rolls were to Carlos' right.

Fuck him. "Hey Carlos, pass the rolls."

Carlos looked at him, guffawed. "What?"

"I'm sorry. Carlos, would you *please* pass the rolls?"

Carlos took the bread, moved it from his right to his left hand, and set it down between them. "What's with her? She praying? Hey, you praying?"

"Leave her alone."

"No, I'm not praying." She looked up, directly at Carlos, her hair falling away from her face, her eyes narrowed and flashing. "And if I were praying, I certainly wouldn't pray for an asshole like you. You," she said slowly, still looking directly at Carlos, "can go to hell."

Carlos shrugged, leaned forward slightly. "I'll see you around, you know what I'm saying? I'll see you around."

Shelby moved her hand to her glass to take a drink, but lost her grip, the glass falling to the floor and shattering. "Fuck." Before he could stop her, she had dropped to her knees to pick up the shards. Predictably, she was cut within seconds, the bright red blood appearing absurdly quickly.

He kneeled down with her. "You're cut."

"You're observant."

"Let's take you to the bathroom. We have band-aids and disinfectant, and we'll wash it out."

She stood up, holding the index and ring fingers of her right hand. "Leave that alone Lil' Kevin: Liz will get it with the broom." He stood up, hesitated. The closest bathroom belonged to his mother, and he didn't want Shelby to see the various piss shields, diapers and other invalid paraphernalia that adorned the space. Liz was not the most fastidious of house-keepers, and although she might have cleaned things up for the party, there was the real possibility they'd find the lavatory an embarrassing mess. Liz's bathroom, however, was on the other side of the TV room, and everyone would know why he'd go to his right, to the further bathroom, rather than to his left and the more immediate facilities. Especially since she was bleeding and they were somewhat in a hurry. Why should he care what Shelby would think? Why should he care what anyone would think? Fuck it. He'd take his chances with his mother's john. He took Shelby's elbow and pointed her to their left. "We'll turn left into the hallway and then a quick right." He could see blood oozing down her fingers. He took a red and white checked napkin from the table and handed it to her. Liz shot him a look. She limped toward the hallway, and he followed.

Only one of the lights above the sink was working, and a bare 75 watt ceiling bulb provided unfiltered illumination. He had to blink. It wasn't too bad. The bathroom was turn of the century, and had been redone sometime, he guessed, in the fifties. They'd ripped up the skanky green carpet when they moved in, installed rails around the tub and replaced the window, but hadn't really done much more. The pale yellow porcelain fixtures were in pretty good shape, but once green tile around the tub was faded and moldy, and a few tiles had crumbled completely away near the showerhead. The ceiling boasted a large crack from the door to just above the sink, and paint was chipped and peeling from the moisture. They could at least give it a new coat of paint, patch the ceiling. But his mother probably wouldn't notice, and he wondered how much longer she'd be using it anyway. There was an acrylic urine shield on the floor around the toilet bowl, and a few towels hung on the railings around the tub, surrounding a small sad white plastic stool in the center. Liz was having more and more trouble maneuvering his mother into the tub, and as a result she was bathed less and less often. He wondered if she had gotten a bath recently. The yellow shelves to the left were stocked with Depends and other assorted toiletries (rubber gloves, personal cleansing wipes, hydrocolloid patches for bedsores, baby powder and various medicated lotions for her dry skin). He opened the cabinet above the sink to get some antibiotics and a band-aid or two. The bottom shelf held her Alzheimer's meds, the useless siblings, memantine and galantamine, as well as donepezil and . . . there it was, a vial of Lorcet. He fumbled around the top two shelves, amongst the bottles of Ambien, Oxycodone, and Temazepam and Lorazepam, until he found the antibiotic cream and band-aids.

"Quite a collection."

"One pill makes you bigger, and one pill makes you smaller. Here, put your fingers under the water to wash them off." He took her hand. She was shaking a little bit. Her well-lit blood ran bright under the water, where it swirled around the sink and disappeared down the drain. Ok Norman. He thought about saying more, like "don't let Carlos get to you," or "everything's going to be fine" but didn't.

When they returned, the glass had been swept and removed, but much of the liquid and a few pieces of nearly melted ice remained. He could smell the lemon and vodka. He wondered if she wanted another drink. They both took their seats. He picked up his drumstick and absently gnawed at it. She took a forkful of mashed potatoes and set her fork down. Carlos, Mace and Glow were discussing basketball, Liz was feeding his Mom, and Jerry had taken off his shades and was looking in his general direction. He dropped his half-eaten drumstick back on his plate. He didn't meet his brother's gaze, instead turned his attention toward his mother. Liz was cleaning off her face with a handi-wipe (he could smell it from where he sat or maybe it was the spilled drink). His mother closed her eyes and scrunched up her face: he was startled by how much she looked like an infant. But unlike an infant, whose confusion was limited to the admixture of various unordered sense-stimuli, his mother's mind must be a chaos of impressions, perceptions and feelings not only of the present, but also of the distant and recent past: anything thought or perceived or remembered—no matter how dim or shadow-like—in the eighty some years of consciousness might be a piece in that stew. It was unimaginable.

"Are we ready for cake?"

"Sure."

"Let's go for it. Get this party started."

"I like cake."

Liz started for the kitchen. "Lil' Kevin, you want to give me a hand?"

He turned to Shelby. "You should eat something. Have some chicken."

"I'd like another drink."

"We're about to have cake."

"How about a beer?"

"What kind?"

She looked at him, shook her head. "I don't fucking care."

He shouted behind her into the kitchen, "Lil' Kevin, you grab me a beer? For Shelby here?"

"What, Professor?" He poked his head out of the kitchen.

"Grab me a beer? For Shelby?"

He smiled. "Sure, sure thing."

"Make sure it's cold."

Lil' Kevin scurried quickly in, set a beer down in front of Shelby, then ducked back into the kitchen. Liz yelled out, "Glow, would you light the candles please?" and Mace waited, then reached up and killed the lights.

The glimmer of the cake candles entered the room, followed by Liz and Lil' Kevin. "Happy birthday to you, happy birthday to you." Voices joined. He turned to look at see how his mother was reacting, but her eyes were hidden in shadow. Someone (Jerry?) had produced a cone shaped party hat, and she feebly scratched at the elastic cutting into her chin. "Happy birthday dear Mom and Glow, Happy birthday to you." Liz set the cake down in front of his mother, and he could see that she was perplexed, frightened but also interested. She recognized the cake at any rate. Jerry stood up and then leaned over. "Blow out the candles, mom. Here, Glow will help you." She continued to work the band on her chin. "Make a wish, mom, make a wish."

"I bet she wishes she could take that hat off."

"Make a wish. Glow, why don't you help her out?" Just put your lips together and blow. Glow leaned over and did the honors.

"Yay!"

"Let's have cake!"

"Anyone want ice cream?"

"I do."

"What about presents?"

"She didn't get much. You gave her those slippers and your brother and Glow bought her a new tracksuit. It's in her closet. I ordered her some earrings, but I couldn't pick 'em up because of the snow. Lil' Kevin drew her some pictures."

"How about you Glow?"

"Jerry gave me some wine." She shrugged.

Liz began to serve the cake. Shelby took a long swig of her beer, which reminded him to take a pull from his vodka. They should leave. It was early, but the drugs would come out as soon as Liz put his mom to bed, after the cake. He went to the kitchen and took a piece of tin foil, and put the vodka and the lemons (he had mixers and beer at home) into a plastic shopping bag. While the cake and ice cream was being passed around, he wrapped the chicken from their plates in the foil, and placed them in the shopping bag. Two large pieces of cake were also wrapped and packed. He went to kiss his mother happy birthday. Her face was covered with smears of chocolate frosting. He could taste it on her cheek.

About halfway down the path to his trailer, they heard music and turned around. Carlos' large silhouette pirouetted gracefully in the window near the door.

Shoah

Claude Lanzmann (1985)

nd they both returned together?

David Gomez (age 57, neighbor)

They didn't come back together, not exactly. They just happened to arrive back on Driftwood at the same time, or around the same time. Right after their mom had the stroke.

Melinda Gomez (age 55)

I think Jerry came back first, and then his brother a week later. The mother had the stroke right around Easter, maybe Holy Saturday. I brought the old man some homemade bread and cookies the next weekend, and Jerry was already there: he answered the door. I think we saw John the middle of the next week.

David Gomez

It could have been that Friday.

And how did they seem to you, Jerry and John?

David Gomez

They were upset, I'm sure.

Melinda Gomez

We didn't talk to them much. The father, he never liked people coming around. He was always giving everybody dirty looks and mumbling under his breath. The boys were always nice and polite, friendly enough. Well John was. It was funny. I would have guessed that Jerry would have been the one to go to prison, not John. John was always so smart, the smart one. Jerry wasn't dumb, but he didn't seem to care. They both seemed concerned about their mother though, seemed close to her. I'm sure it bothered them, saddened them. They took her in after the hospital.

David Gomez

That's right, they took her to live with them. Some place out in Blende, I think.

Melinda Gomez

I thought it was Avondale.

How long have you known them?

David Gomez

We've been here on Driftwood twenty-eight years last July. They moved here three or four years after we did.

Would you say you know them well?

David Gomez

No.

Melinda Gomez (shakes her head)

A four-lane road, past a gentle curve. Strip malls and various nondescript retail outlets dot both sides of the road. The sun is bright. Traffic is steady, but not too heavy. Coming up on the right a brick restaurant with its entrance pointing west, toward the parking lot shared with four or five other stores. A small neon sign glows in the window: Max's Mexican Food. On the left a low stone and concrete wall. The wall continues for a while, then a gate and a sign: Mountain View Cemetery.

What were they like as children?

Randy Thornton (40, friend)

Jerry was always high, that's what he was like. I didn't know his brother that well, he ran with a different crowd. Me and Jerry used to always go smoke in the cemetery. Before class, after class, free period, we'd go to the cemetery and burn one. And then we'd get the Visine. Gets the red out (laughs).

And John never went with you?

No, like I said, John ran with a different crowd. He was older, and didn't dig the *leño* as much. He was in the band or something. I remember once, after a football game, everyone used to go to Sam's Pizzeria, you know? Right across from the cemetery. It's a Mexican food joint now. Anyway, we all used to go to Sam's, and then go across the street, climb the wall, and hang, get high, get laid, get drunk, whatever. And Jerry was already higher than a fucking kite, and for a kick or something he asks John if he wants to party with us. There was Jerry, me, Rick Teel, Jon Addair, Charlie Dazzio and probably some other dudes. And John, he looks like he's not sure, you know, but he shrugs his shoulders and says why not and we split from Sam's and go across to the cemetery, to one of our favorite places, near the Bassettis's crypt. You know the Bassettis? Good people. They got this big crypt, size of a U-Haul trailer, and then a bunch of gravestones for the individuals around it. There're tons of trees around too. Or at least there were, I ain't been back there since high school.

Addair has King Bong, and we had some good Lumbo man, not as good as you get today, but some good shit for middle school back then, and we're ready for takeoff. First Addair, then me, then Jerry, we go down the line, and then John, who starts to hack like he's losing a lung, but pretty soon man, we're all flying. We're laughing at farts, at rocks, just laughing man. And suddenly John gets up, looks around, and says "What the fuck?" And someone says, "What the fuck you mean, what the fuck?" And John says, "I can't see any mountains." "So what?"

"Well this is Mountain View Cemetery, isn't it? Where are the mountains?" "It's dark, you stupid motherfucker." "I know it's dark, but you can't the mountains in the day. You can never see the goddam mountains from here." "What the fuck you mean?" "Mountain View cemetery faces north/south, fewer than three blocks of it face west. And the mountains are west, right? From Pueblo, the mountains are in the west. So look west, that way. What do you see?" "Nothing, it's dark." "What would you see if it were day?" "I don't know." "The bank building. And the projects. You can't fucking see the mountains from here. If you look west, all you see is the bank building and the projects. No way you see the mountains from here. It's a fucking lie." And he goes on and on. About how Pueblo's so stupid, you can't even be buried right. And you know what Jerry does? He finally stands up, walks over to John, and drops him with one punch. "Shut the fuck up." We were cracking up for days. "Shut the fuck up."

This was in high school?

Middle school. John was in high school but we were in eighth grade.

Stopped at a light behind an old purple Vega, with a large jacked-up black Titan V-8 with tinted windows blaring Mexican music to the right. Green arrow, then a left turn with a fenced snow-covered athletic field (football goalposts and baseball backstops on two corners) on the right, then an empty parking lot, and then a large low slung white brick building with a ten foot statue of a horseshoe and the words South High Colts in large letters at the base.

Can you give us a clinical diagnosis of the mother?
Dr. Samuel Robida (age 57)
Dementia is the clinical diagnosis. She did suffer an ischemic

stroke on Saturday, March 26th, 2005. It was determined, using the TOAST criteria, that the patient suffered a small vessel occlusion, perhaps more than one.

Dr. Sanjay Banerjee (age 39)

We cannot be certain, however, that this single event is the sole determining factor in her condition. It is a possibility that symptoms of the dementia were experienced before the vascular event. In fact, given her response to treatment, I would guess that the stroke of 2005 is simply one contributing factor.

And if her condition wasn't caused by the stroke, what did cause it?

Dr. Sanjay Banerjee

We're just not sure. She could very well indeed have vascular dementia, but she could have suffered a stroke, or series of small strokes, months or even years before the event of March 2005. Alzheimer's disease is definitely a possibility, as is Lewy Bodies dementia. We did discount a B-12 deficiency.

If you don't know exactly what you are treating, then treatment must be difficult. What is her prognosis?

Dr. Samuel Robida

We are treating her with Namenda and Aricept. Given her reactions to these drugs, I don't think we're anticipating a complete recovery of her cognitive and mnemonic functions.

Dr. Sanjay Banerjee

No. We're just trying to slow the deterioration down.

Could other factors possibly be involved? Environmental factors say?

Dr. Samuel Robida

A trauma could cause similar symptoms. A blow to the head. A brain tumor or encephalitis.

Dr. Sanjay Banerjee

Mad cow disease.

Dr. Samuel Robida

But these other factors were ruled out during examinations and interviews.

The same stoplight, but no snow. The sun is at a different angle, and the turn left discloses a vista of green grass and numerous students of both sexes in grey gym clothes running track and playing touch football to suggest early Fall. Next comes a parking lot full of late model trucks and SUV's (and a few cars), with a couple of skateboarders weaving in and out of the parked vehicles. Several students are milling around the main entrance to the building, loudly talking and laughing, and one is sitting on the base of the South High Colts statue, swinging her bare legs.

Were Jerry and John good students?

Duane Thomas (73, Music teacher, retired)

I didn't know Jerry, but I remember John very well. He had a good head on his shoulders. Was clever, you know, funny. Used to make everyone laugh.

Mrs. Gradishar (Language Arts, 70, retired)

I remember John better than Jerry. John was very bright. Jerry wasn't stupid, but he didn't apply himself. He got in with a questionable crowd. John loved to read, that I remember. He was one of my best readers. Jerry never seemed to take to reading.

Dr. Simon Fajt (47, principal)

This was before my time, you realize, but their South High academic transcripts support Mr. Thomas and Mrs. Gradishar: John was an excellent student, a GPA of 3.7 on a 4 point scale, taking mostly upper level courses, Band and college prep English and Biology. Graduate Gold Cord senior, ranked 46th in his graduating class of 305. A National Merit Scholar. Went to the University of Colorado, if I'm not mistaken.

Let's see . . . Jerry, on the other hand, was not so diligent. I see a GPA of 1.7 on a 4 point scale, with notations for absenteeism and truantism. I see two expulsions for marijuana possession, and indications that the police were notified both times. There are mostly basic courses listed here, although he did seem to do fairly well in Spanish.

Can you say more about the marijuana arrests?

Dr. Simon Fajt

I don't know that they *were* arrests. I only see here that the police were notified.

So we don't know if the expulsions were for selling marijuana, or just using the drug, smoking it?

Dr. Simon Fajt

No, we do not. And because he was a juvenile at the time of these incidents, I'm guessing his police record will be sealed. I don't know what South High policy was, what, twenty years ago. I know now South High School has a zero tolerance policy for all drug and alcohol offenses: in fact, the penalties are extra severe for infractions on school property. But as I've said, I don't know what the policy was in late 70's/early 80's. Jerry did manage to graduate with his class. And without summer school.

Rosalinda Vaca (77, Spanish and French, retired)

Jerry wasn't dumb, and he didn't sell drugs. At least I don't think so. He maybe had the wrong friends. The girls used to like him. He was handsome, and had a good vibe. I had no problems with Jerry. *Un chicano.*

A snow covered street, with modest bungalows on both sides. A couple of men are shoveling snow, but the scene is silent, tranquil. A slow right turn onto Surfwood, a block and then a left onto Driftwood. Both street signs are prominent. The sun is strong, the visor above the windshield pulled down. The truck pulls into the unshoveled driveway of a small red brick house in the middle of the block.

Did your brother and his wife have a happy marriage?

Michael "Babe" DeJoy (79, Uncle)

My brother was not a particular happy person to begin with. Our mother died when he was seven or eight, and he took that very hard, and never got over it, never got over it. He had a few career setbacks, and financial difficulties, they didn't help his disposition any.

Virginia DeJoy (80, Aunt)

He was a bastard. He cheated on her for years.

Michael DeJoy

We don't know that for certain.

Virginia DeJoy

He was mean. He was mean to her and he was mean to the boys.

Dolores Badovinic (82, Aunt)

Everyone has trouble, don't they? My brother, he doesn't have a good attitude, but things haven't gone too good for him, you know? The boys got into drugs, and Johnny went to prison. That hurt my brother bad, you know? It was all in the papers, in the *Star-Journal* and even in the *Denver Post*. How'd you like to open your morning paper and read your eldest son's been arrested for selling drugs? And then his wife got sick. This family, it's been unlucky.

Virginia DeJoy

He was mean before that. He always thought he was owed something, and nothing was ever his fault. I pity his wife and I always have. And those kids and drugs. Johnny was a good boy. I blame the drugs, I don't blame Johnny.

Do you think he ever abused his wife?

Michael DeJoy

No, he never knocked her around. I don't think he was like that.

Virginia DeJoy

Who knows?

Dolores Badovinic

No, my brother wouldn't do that. No.

The interior of a house. Two bunk beds are pushed in the corner of a very small bedroom, with posters of Terrell Davis, The Sex Pistols, Blade Runner and Casablanca tacked on the walls. There are piles of clothes on the lower bunk, some neatly folded, some haphazardly arranged, and a too-large bookcase full of books pushed against the wall opposite the beds.

Another room, with a single mattress centered on the dark carpeted floor. The two windows are small and high, suggesting a basement or garden level. A green, yellow and red Bob Marley flag covers the entire far wall, and two large black stereo speakers protrude, almost to the edge of the mattress in the center of the room. Cartons of record albums are stacked against the right wall, and three or four bicycles—including a ten-speed with taped ram handlebars and an old Stingray with a leopard print banana seat—are crammed in the near corner, close to the door.

You were John's dissertation director, is that correct?
Professor Rudolph Mengert (60, Professor of Film Studies)
Yes, I was. He wrote a very fine dissertation on film noir, the *Nouvelle Vague* and Greek myth. It was extremely smart and well written, and, I thought at the time, eminently publishable.
Did he publish it?
No.
Why not?
Well, it did need some revision. After he received his degree, for whatever reason, he never worked on it. A shame.
Did you communicate after he graduated?
For a while. We corresponded when he first started teaching at Hunter, and I updated my letter of recommendation for three or four years after. But then, well, he stopped asking me about the letter, and I went to Italy for a couple of years, and we lost touch. I was saddened to hear he was imprisoned.

What did he teach at Hunter?

Introductory film courses I imagine. He was an adjunct, not regular faculty. And he was struggling financially, he did tell me that. He applied to a number of jobs every year, but never got very far in the interview process. That was a real shame. He had a fine mind. A scientist's mind and a film lover's eye. He was chemistry major as an undergraduate. I remember that very well.

Why do you think he had such a difficult time finding an academic position?

Almost all of our graduate students have a difficult time finding academic positions. Unfortunately, there are far more applicants than there are lines. Our department grants between five and seven PhD's each year, and we place one, maybe two in tenure track lines. Rarely two. If he had published his book, that would have helped.

The mother sits in her wheelchair in the kitchen of the main house. Her eyes are open, and her breathing regular. She stares straight ahead, and her mouth twitches slightly. Liz moves in front of her to the sink, and the sounds of water running and dishes being washed begin. The mother continues to stare straight ahead, her chest rising and falling.

What about more abstract environmental causes? Like abuse?

Dr. Samuel Robida

As I've indicated, a trauma to the head can cause similar symptoms. But there was no indication of physical abuse noted anywhere in her chart. Dr. Banerjee and I performed very thorough and numerous examinations, and found no absolutely no evidence of physical maltreatment. None whatsoever.

What about emotional abuse? Ridicule? Contempt? Disdain? Mockery?

Dr. Samuel Robida

I know of no research data to support the causal relationship you are suggesting.

A long, modern, one story beige brick and concrete building. A second story juts up abruptly above the entrance: the effect is Chinese. A sign is stenciled on the glass door, Bayside State Prison. Snow is falling heavily.

How well did you know John?
Roberto Salazar (47, prisoner)
He was my cellmate for two years.
Did he ever talk about what he was going to do when he got paroled?
Some.
What were his plans?
He was going to go to New York or LA.
Was he any more specific?
He was going to try to get work in a video store or something.
Were you surprised when he went back home? To Colorado?
Yes and no.
Can you elaborate?
Yes I was surprised in that he never talked about going back home. In fact, he gave me the impression that he hated it there. No, I wasn't surprised in that he told me his moms got sick, had a stroke or something. And I heard that he met some people here at Bayside who could provide him with meaningful employment.
So he met somebody in prison who got him a job? In Pueblo?
I don't know. You hear things here. Some true, some ain't.

A small brownstone on the corner of two busy streets. The street signs read 4th Street and 7th Avenue. Pedestrians in heavy coats, hats and gloves scurry quickly.

Were you surprised John returned to Pueblo?
Constance Collero (39, ex-wife)
I was shocked. He hated Pueblo. Always used to say to me "I have no hometown." He was close to his mother, but he's not exactly a caregiver. I don't know what he's doing there.
Did you ever meet his family?
I met them once, at the wedding. I liked the mother. His father never looked at me, never looked at me once. We went out to dinner at some Italian place. The mother tried to make conversation, asked me how we liked New York and about my studies, but I don't think the father said a single word to me. Although he did say, not to me but to the table, and I remember this well, that in the old country the family picked the wife for the son. He had no use for me. The mother told me later that "he was talking through his hat," that was the expression she used, that nobody picked wives for anybody in his family.
What did you think of Jerry?
I never met Jerry. He didn't come to the wedding.
Did you ever go to Pueblo?
I never went to Pueblo. When we were together Johnny went back once for his uncle's funeral. But no, I never went with him.
Why did you get divorced?
Johnny sold drugs and went to prison. He wanted to waste his life, that was fine: I wasn't going to let him waste my life too.
Have you kept in touch? Email or anything?
No. I signed the papers at my lawyer's and that was it. I heard from my sister that he went to Pueblo when he got out of Bayside, but we've had no contact since the divorce. That part of my life is over.

A slow left turn onto Driftwood, perhaps identical to one earlier. Modest bungalows on both sides of the street, some with snow-covered driveways, some with shoveled drives and sidewalks. The truck pulls into a drive that hasn't been shoveled, in front of a small red brick house, with black metal-rimmed windows. The sun is bright, and all of the shades are drawn tight.

You both served with Jerry in Desert Storm, is that correct?

Sean Rogers (35, former Sergeant First Class, US Army)

Yes sir, that's correct. First Squadron, 4th Cavalry.

Roberto Dominguez (41, Colonel, US Army)

Yes sir. There were six of us, Mace, Carlos, Sean, Jerry, Chrome and myself went through basic together at Fort Hood. We were in the same squad, and Mace, Jerry and Carlos were in the same RSTA team.

Was Kelly Light, also known as Glow, part of the squadron?

Roberto Dominguez

She came in later. Just before we bugged out.

Sean Rogers

She was shower-shoes all the way. Green. A rookie.

What can you tell me about Jerry?

Sean Rogers

Jerry was crackerjack sniper, an excellent shot. Expert rifle and pistol and Distinguished Rifleman, if I'm remembering. Not exactly a STRAC, by the book you know, but you could trust him. Couldn't say that for everybody.

What do you mean?

Roberto Dominguez

His buddies, Carlos and Mace. Both were real shitbags, especially Carlos. You didn't want to run with him.

Sean Rogers

You didn't want to cross him either. They both were always fucking high, excuse my French, and always looking for tail, both raghead and desert fox. Liked to take the ragheads behind the berm, if you catch my drift. Whether the rags wanted to go or not. Nasty pieces of work.

Roberto Dominguez

Motherfuckers and buddy-fuckers. Both got bad conduct discharges.

Sean Rogers

Big chicken dinners.

Are you suggesting that Carlos and Mace were involved in the rape of civilians?

Sean Rogers

Roberto Dominguez

I see. But Jerry wasn't like that?

Sean Rogers

No, Jerry was hooah. He owned a pair. Liked to party, but always had your back.

A small living room with a beige leather couch and loveseat, and a large dark wood console television against the wall in the center of the room. Above the television hangs an 8 by 10 photograph, framed in gilded wood. Jerry in his desert camouflage uniform with a matching baseball cap and an undefined outdoor background. His mouth is smiling but his eyes, partially shaded by the bill of the cap, are not. On the top of the television set sits another framed photograph, of Jerry in his dress blues, with a number of ribbons and medals on his chest and a US flag as background. If anything, his eyes are narrower and colder than in the other photo. Next to that photo is a black baseball cap with the words Desert Storm Veteran embroidered in gold blue thread.

Did you know if Jerry abused drugs while deployed?

Sean Rogers

Next question.

Roberto Dominguez
Sir, I do not know.
It sounds like you're trying to cover something up. Let me ask you again: did Jerry abuse recreational drugs while deployed during Operation Desert Storm?
Sean Rogers

Roberto Dominguez

A bright sunny day, spring or summer. The truck drives through a gate underneath an iron sign that reads Mountain View Cemetery. Past gravestones, crypts etc, the truck stops at a copse of green spruce trees. Birds chirp in the background. In the center of the trees a rectangular mausoleum of reddish stone, about the size of a small shed, with the word Bassetti in bas-relief, is visible. Smaller stones with first names and dates are arranged symmetrically around the crypt. In the distance, a large brick building rises to the west, with brown stucco apartment buildings behind.

Did you know Jerry in high school? Did you know John as well?
Angela Dipietro (39, ex-girlfriend)
I went out with Jerry for a year and half, sophomore to the end of my junior year. John was older, and was in a different group. He kept to himself more. Jerry was always partying.
You and Jerry went steady for a year and a half. Can you tell us about that?
(Laughs). I went steady, Jerry just went. Jerry was cute, he liked to party and a lot of girls wanted to be with him, and Jerry had a hard time saying no. I'm not bitching or anything: we had some laughs.
What was a typical night out with Jerry?
This was before they built the mall. We'd drive around for while, maybe smoke a joint, have a few beers. Then we'd go to

a party at somebody's house, or a keg by the river, or a football game or something. Sometimes the movies, the drive-in, get something to eat. We'd usually end up in the cemetery with his buddies, making out, some more smoke, a few more beers. Then we'd go to his truck, he had this foam pad in the back, and you know, have some more fun.

The small living room with the leather couch and matching loveseat on the right. The lighting is dim, and the grayish drapes on the left are closed tight. The magazine and newspapers are carefully arranged, two to three deep, on the loveseat.

Were you a good father?

Frank DeJoy (85, father)

What kind of question is that? Why don't you ask if my sons were good sons? I have a son who's a bum, he went to prison for selling drugs. An embarrassment he is, an embarrassment to me and my name. The other is veteran, was overseas in Desert Storm. 4th Cavalry. Why don't you ask if they were good to me? I can't say that they were. They've both been more trouble than they're worth my sons, more trouble than they're worth.

Did you want children? Were you happy they were born?

Of course I wanted children: what kind of man doesn't want children? That's why I got married, to have children. They were pretty good as kids, as little boys. They cried, and like that, but I didn't mind them too much when they were little.

At what age did they become a burden to you?

I don't know, maybe high school, maybe earlier. They always sided with their mother: they were both mama's boys. Especially John. Always playing that goddam trumpet. And reading, that mook. I thought he was going to be a pharmacist, like his cousin. Make some real money. I paid for most of his schooling to be a pharmacist, a pharmacist. Boy did he fool me. Film Studies. What is that, I ask you, what is that? He wanted to be a professor. A professor of movies. What kind of crap is that?

And Jerry was no better. Always with the girls, always with the girls. I could never find him to do anything, he was never home. I should have smacked them both around more. Taught them some respect. At least Jerry wasn't a drug pusher. Jesus Christ.

Do you consider yourself a good husband?

My wife, she had a stroke. That really messed me up. I didn't know what to do. Those nursing homes, they cost an arm and a leg, an arm and a leg. I'm an old man, how can I take care of her? How can I be a good husband when my wife is incapacitated? Can you tell me that?

Do you think you were a good husband before your wife became ill?

No. You want history, I'll give you history. I stepped out on her. I admit it, I stepped out. And she never said nothing. God, she never said nothing.

So you're saying that you had extramarital affairs? Why?

I never cared for her, that's why. And after a while, I couldn't stand her. She never said nothing. I never cared for nobody really.

If you didn't love her, why didn't you separate?

I don't know.

Did she realize how you felt for her?

I don't know. What's done is done. No use dragging up the past.

Snow covered streets and bright sunlight. A variety of playground equipment on the left, with a glass and brick building in the background. a stop sign and the Elmwood and Driftwood street signs. A turn onto Driftwood, and the red brick house in the middle of the block.

Were you close to your nephews?

Michael DeJoy

When they were younger, we were close. I took them to a few ballgames, to Elitch's in Denver once. When they got into high school, well, you know how teenagers are.

Virginia DeJoy

We took their mom sometimes too, when we had an extra ticket to something. We took them places because their dad never took them anywhere. We tried to make up for it. That man should have never had children. A wife neither.

Michael DeJoy

They were close to their cousins for a while. Our family just drifted apart.

What were they like as children?

Virginia DeJoy

They were cheerful boys: their mother's pride and joy. They both were happy-go-lucky. Johnny liked to read, even as a child, liked to go off by himself. He was happy by himself. Jerry was more social, wanted you to notice him. But when they were young they were both happy as clams. At least around the mother.

How did they get along with their father?

Virginia DeJoy

They knew what was going on, with the women and all. They knew. They didn't care for him.

Michael DeJoy

The boys never said anything, but they weren't close to their father. Not at all. I think it got a little rough when they were in high school.

Virginia DeJoy

This family, the men like to yell.

Michael DeJoy

Like I said, my brother was not a happy man.

Virginia DeJoy

You could tell by the way they looked at him. They didn't like him: it was obvious to everyone. And they way he treated them and their mother, no one could blame them.

The small living room with the loveseat and couch. In the corner between the couch on the loveseat sits a small wicker dog bed, a couple of rumpled blankets and towels, and a Mickey Mouse pet toy in the center.

Anything else you can tell me?
David Gomez
No, not really. They weren't the easiest neighbors, all that yelling. The father used to yell at the boys something terrible.
Melinda Gomez
And that poor woman. Wait, do you remember last year? Last May? The boys brought the mother to the house. I think it was her birthday or something. And the dad, the old man, he starts the pushing the mom, who's in her wheelchair, up and down Driftwood, up and down, three or four times, with the dog following behind, until finally the boys come out and take her inside. It was the oddest-looking thing.
David Gomez
It was hot, and the mom was holding the leash. I remember that. And the old man had the hateful look on his face. I thought maybe he was losing it.
Melinda Gomez
I think he just wanted to show the neighbors something. Maybe that she was still alive.

A snow covered street with bright winter sunlight. Modest bungalows on both sides of the street, some with shoveled walks and driveways, some with walks and driveways still covered. Vehicles inhabit many of the drives, mostly trucks and SUV's. A right onto Surfwood, and drive down for a block, then a left on Driftwood. The sun is bright. Slowing down. A split-level dark grey ranch with shoveled walks, then a small blonde brick ranch also shoveled, and then a red brick house with the driveway still covered in snow. The truck pulls into the driveway. The curtains are closed tight.

Tokyo Story

Yasujiro Ozu (1953)

A snowpacked road unplowed a background train racing beneath power lines.
The black truck in high contrast to the luminous brilliant white.
It was cold bright radiant the sunrays sparkling off the snow.
Everything too sharp too clear busted tools decrepit barns all threatened.
A brief slide nearly missed turn overcorrection wheels slipping finally catching.
No music a sunglassed face a three day beard slight grimace.
God it was depressing visiting his father he absolutely hated it.
That unkempt smell and commanding but weakening voice haunted for days.
It took him longer and longer to recover after each visit.
Recover to what his senile mother moron colleagues forever tweaking brother?
His exciting fulfilling life as a meth cook and dealer *extraordinaire*?

A foot or so of fenceposts dotting above the rolling drifts.
Snowcapped poles and power lines stretching to the horizon to infinity.
The road rough nearly unused he had followed Jerry's tracks out.
Who had driven to Gunnison and wouldn't be back until Thursday.
The Shelby problem would need to be solved before he returned.
Carlos would have to do it or Mace he simply couldn't.
He was Ransom Stoddard not the Duke he was no killer.
He'd insist they bury her near the pond someplace he'd remember.
Their gate where Dylan had stupidly turned and trespassed appeared suddenly.
He stopped the tiretracks turned left the road barely visible ahead.
Drive straight to the horizon never look back he turned left.

Some trouble climbing the hill he pulled up behind Liz's Trani.
Needed to do something about their mother getting worse and worse.
What was Kevin doing sitting on his step without a coat?
"Hey L'il Kevin what's up where's your coat aren't you cold?"
Kevin looked down around wouldn't meet his gaze that was strange.
"Carlos told me to stay out here be a watch out."
A vague suspicion "A watch out a watch out for what?"
"For you they told me to stay here watch for you."
A thought not yet believed "What's Carlos doing in my trailer?"
Kevin smiled raised his chin looked straight up in the air.
"Him and Mace are with that lady and making her cry."

The hallway to the bathroom separated his bedroom from his study.

Noises from the study scuffles and shrieks "No no you bastards."

Clenching hands cuffed above head Mace videotaping holding her legs apart.

Shirtless pants dropped Carlos looked up smiled directly into his eyes.

"Professor hope you don't mind sloppy seconds or thirds Mace's next.

Can't let this piece go to waste know what I'm saying?"

Drool dripped from his lips heaving belly undulating steadily in waves.

"I'm almost done but Mace likes *culo* we might need help."

She screamed Carlos slapped her "I told you to shut up.

Got any lotion or anything something we could use for lube?

Should thank me you're before L'il Kevin she'll still feel something."

He turned and walked to the living room the stereo cabinet.
Took out the Glock checked the magazine and racked the slide.
Walked back pointed it at Carlos' chest "Stop it right now."
Didn't look up or slow down "You ain't got the stones."
Much louder than expected echoing through the trailer one two three.
A stream of blood from Carlos' neck describing a dramatic parabola.
Shelby shrieked as Carlos fell sideways heavily over her right leg.
She screamed again "Jesus fucking Christ" scrambled back onto the couch.
Suddenly quiet the girl's sobs his breathing snow muffling outside sounds.
Smell of blood sex gunpowder and sweat *mort grande* not *petite*.
Now what dead meat fat pale ass pointing towards the sky.

Startled by another shot he twisted hard back into his room.

Something broke in the living room "Carlos I heard some noise?"

"Get the fuck outta here Kevin get the fuck out now.

You fucking bitch do that again I'll zip you right here."

Verticals his dresser's edge nearly closed door study's doorframe couch's edge.

Stupid shooting one of three no four grunts with Shelby prisoner.

Glow from outside in front "Carlos what's up I hear shots?"

"Carlos is meat the Professor killed him dead with his Glock."

"The Professor killed Carlos what the fuck where is he now?"

"Living room I think got off a round with my M9.

But this desert dime whore hit my arm and I missed."

"Christ what a clusterfuck Jerry's going to hit the friggin' roof.
Professor toss your weapon so Mace can see and come out."
He didn't want to die in a trailer of all places.
It was time to prove he could outsmart these country motherfuckers.
"We ain't going to hurt you or nothing you got protection.
Jerry and Rodriguez bros both skin us anything happen to you."
A plan would be useful here some sort of coherent strategy.
All Lee Marvin wanted was his ninetythree grand in hard cash.
All he wanted was to save the girl and walk away.
"It's freezing out here Professor whattya say Carlos not a problem.
Don't be a fool we ex-recon and we got the girl."

Ex-recon shit they thought he was somewhere in the living room.

"Let's avoid a firefight Mace can you bring the girl out?

Use her as a shield I'll cover Kevin go home now."

"She's cuffed but I'll shoot 'em off give me a second."

One shot floor creaking "Get up bitch Professor I'm coming out."

Waist down Shelby barefoot limping Mace's white Jordans followed hesitant stupid.

He aimed for the knees two shots quickly Mace crumpled back.

Two more shots one in the chest one in the forehead.

Shelby moaning from the hallway "Get back to the study now."

"Talk to me Mace" a spray of bullets to his left.

Tin trailer walls wouldn't stop a fly his futon might help.

"Mace you alright Mace shit Professor I need to hear you.
If Mace's dead I'll phosphor this whole fucking trailer to hell."
Didn't want to reveal his location Glow'd do what she promised.
If he didn't want his trailer baked he'd need her inside.
"Mace and I are hit and I think the girl's dead."
"You ain't lying to me Professor I didn't hear no M9!"
"You need a scorecard?" he dropped prone barricaded by the futon.
"I got Mace and accidentally plugged the girl you busted me."
"Mace's hit in the throat he needs help I need help.
"You blow us up now you kill Mace all I'm saying."
Silence now as the snow quickly swallowed all sound and reverberation.

A creak from the living room perhaps imagined four rounds left.

Glow'd soon see that Mace was dead where would she be?

Needed a bird's eye or crane not this POV low angle.

One maybe two shots she'd spray him good if he missed.

Another creak she was definitely in the living room but where?

Brief burst to his right "Mace ain't moving Professor you lied."

Another to his left closer plaster flying he ducked his head.

Four five how to stay alive six seven hell or heaven?

"It's all over Professor give up now I'll kill you quick."

Glow pitched forward into the room two holes in her chest.

Shelby limped into his doorway trembling slightly jeans bloody pistol pointed.

His living room his life shattered bloody discontinuous "Here's your backpack."

"So what do we do now killer wait for the cops?"

"Cops shit Rodriguez's and Jerry'll be on our asses soon enough.
And I'm not the only killer two of these are yours."

"Maybe I should have just let that bitch shoot you dead."

"Thank you for that but I don't think Lizzie was necessary."

""Y'all fucking cowboys how do I tell one tweaker from another?"

He shrugged "We should go drop off moms at a home."

"What about the big retard what do we do with him?"

"L'il Kevin he'll be okay until tomorrow when Jerry gets back.
I have money we should stay together at least for now."

Shame

Ingmar Bergman (1968)

*T*he air was thick with the smoke from the weapons and the floating particles of cheap trailer walls. She looked around the living room, then at me. Her face was pallid and dirty, with smudges on her forehead and matted hair sticking to her right cheek. Her lips were drawn into a thin grim line. Grim but strong. She held my gaze, as if she was trying to make some sort of decision about me.

"You okay?"

"Yeah. You?"

"I think so."

The smells of blood and gunpowder were beginning to stick in my throat. I looked down at the form that used to be Lizzie, and the room started to spin. I took a step forward to steady myself, and my sneaker stuck to the bloody carpet. I dropped my gun. My stomach contracted and I tasted bile. I needed to get out of the trailer, and as I stepped over the body, my other sneaker made a squishy sound, like I was walking in a swamp.

"This is a fucking dream. A bad fucking dream."

"Not my dream."

I looked at her, but she had turned away, her face obscured by her hair.

"Not mine either."

I made it to the door, opened it and stepped outside, gulping the fresh cold air. I put my hand over my brow, like a salute, to shield my eyes from the sun. It was clear and white and quiet, and I began to regain my equilibrium. The sky was deep Colorado blue, and the compound seemed serene, peaceful, idyllic. I looked around but couldn't see L'il Kevin: he could be in his trailer or the big house, hiding or just hanging out. Although if he wasn't around with everyone else, he was probably hiding. I'd need to find him to make sure he was ok, calm him down. And I'd need to take care of my mother.

I didn't do anything for a while. I just stood there, unthinking in the bright winter light, my breath visible in the cold air. I heard the door open behind me, but I stood still, watching the white mist of my breath curl and disappear against the blue sky.

After a while she spoke. "It's time to wake up." I turned to face her then. She had the same smudges on her forehead, and her mouth was set in the same firm line. She had put her sunglasses on, oversize Euro Wayfarers. I had never seen her in the daylight before, and noticed a few freckles dotting the bridge of her nose. Her hands were empty.

She looked away, repeated softly, "We need to wake up. It doesn't matter whose dream this is, we need to wake up."

We walked silently over to the main house. One of my sneakers left three or four bloody footprints in the white snow. She was limping badly, but didn't mention it. We made a cursory and unsuccessful search for L'il Kevin, and she went to Liz's bathroom to clean up. My mom was sleeping soundly in her chair in her bedroom, and I maneuvered her onto the bed, covered her lightly and left the door open. After putting my sneakers in a plastic bag, I sat at the kitchen table and wondered whether or not to pour myself a drink on an empty stomach. I still had that taste at the back of my throat, and even though nothing appealed, I thought I should try to wash that taste out, or at least replace it with another. But I didn't move.

I sat there for a while, and then closed my eyes. Glow's face appeared. It was the Glow from her birthday party, not the Glow with two holes in her chest. I wasn't frightened; it seemed natural somehow. I could make out individual strands of her long light brown, almost blonde hair, and could see tiny wrinkles on her thin lips and the pores of the skin covering her sharp chin. Of all my brother's girlfriends, I had liked Glow the best. I felt a little sad. Unlike the others, she wasn't cruel or stupid. Her image was remarkably vivid: it was almost as if she was in the room with me. The landline rang, the one we never used. I opened my eyes. I was alone. The phone rang again, and I got up to answer it. The line was dead. I replaced it in the cradle, and it rang again, a half ring, and then nothing. Silence. Weird. I sat back down and closed my eyes.

There was Carlos. Once more, the details were crystal clear, and I could see the scraggly black hair, the puffy red and hooded eyes, the grey and black stubble and the column of Chinese characters tattooed on his thick neck. He was smiling that mean, tweaked up smile, his two missing right premolars giving him this sadistic and stupid expression, a look that was a remarkably accurate representation of his essence.

"Fuck you," I said to him, "I'm glad you're dead."

"I didn't think you had the rocks, *bolillo*. Anyway, made the bitch come twice, she tell you that?"

"Once an asshole, always an asshole. And now you're a dead asshole."

"Whatya going to do now, killer? The Rodriguez brothers be after your shit. And Jerry, Jerry going to fuck you up."

"I wasn't a killer till I capped you."

"You wanna think your ice never iced no one, that's ok with me. You wanna believe no grade school *chiples* ever od'd on your product, that's your business. You wanna think no hardcore ever stabbed some *gringa* in a strong, well, what can I say? And they call you Professor. Shit. Yeah, I was the first one you ever killed."

That really pissed me off. Who was he to say anything about me? "I should have shot you sooner."

"Maybe you get lucky and the cops catch up with you first. Maybe reunite with your boyfriends in Jersey."

"Who are you talking to?"

I opened my eyes and saw Shelby standing in the doorway. She looked good: her skin tone was a bit pale (the carnage and the rape), but her eyes were bright and determined, and while she wasn't smiling, her face had shed that severe, forbidding expression around her mouth. She was wearing jeans and a flannel shirt, and it suited her. Her hair had lightened considerably into a strawberry platinum color. My mouth was dry.

"So who were you talking to?"

"Carlos."

She snorted. "Carlos? Carlos is dead." She sat down across from me and leaned forward. "I see dead people."

"What?"

She shook her head, a small smile on her face. "You're not feeling bad about Carlos are you? Guilty?"

"I feel bad for Glow, but nothing about Carlos and Mace. I hated both those motherfuckers. If I feel anything, it's anger. Rage."

"Yeah, they were raping me."

"Angry that they made me a killer. I never killed anyone before, and now I have. I'll never forgive them for that."

Her blue eyes turned toward me. After a while, "I never killed anyone either." My mother moaned quietly in the next room. I listened, but couldn't hear anything further.

"I never wanted to be a killer, and I kill two people. And cause two others to die. And my brother, he's not going to let this go. He's going to come after me. He was the one connection I have with the world. And now that's gone." I was beginning to comprehend my situation. I was beginning to lose my cool.

"Pull yourself together. I am."

"And why? All because some dumb-ass party boy needed some glass for his friends. And decided to crash a lab. How stupid was that?"

She turned away.

"No, seriously, how stupid was that? To drive into a big fucking meth lab at night, one of the biggest in North America, manned by ex-army recon soldiers, expecting to make a purchase. Like a fucking McDonald's drive-through. Let me tell you about Carlos and Mace. *Dis*honorably discharged from Iraq. For being too goddam vile. There was this Iraqi village, and this village didn't really want to give up their women and girl-children to a squad of American infidels. Didn't really see how that organized rape would be adding to Iraqi freedom. So they hid the woman in a small warehouse. Know what our brave Americans did? Called in an air-strike. On the whole village. According to Carlos, not a stick left standing. According to Mace, there was nothing left to fuck for miles and miles. He's got video. This is what your boyfriend drives into, and this is what fucks my life up for good."

"I told you he wasn't my boyfriend."

"This fucking unlucky, stupid move by this unlucky, stupid asshole and now I'm running for my life. Some ignorant whack decision by a total fucking stranger and now bam, welcome to a new reality. A moronic, asinine choice and five people dead, and my life fucked. Totally totally fucked."

"Dylan's dead and I've been raped. It's not only your life that has been ruined." That was true. How much was I responsible for?

She smiled a thin, tentative smile. "What are you afraid of?"

"I'm afraid of my brother tracking me down and killing me. Us."

"He's coming back tomorrow, right?"

I nodded.

"What if the cops were here when he came back?"

I still had that taste in my mouth. I swallowed and looked at her.

"I'm going to take a shower."

Before I took my clothes off, I checked myself in Lizzie's mirror. The bright florescent blanched out my skin tone so I looked ghastly. My forehead was sweaty and wrinkled, and my eyes were puffy. I turned my head, and noticed a long shallow scratch on my right cheek under my ear, near my jawline. I traced it with my index finger but it didn't hurt. I needed a shave. I looked like a killer. My scalp began to itch.

The shower cleared my head a bit, enough to think about survival. I was still angry, scared and confused, but I had a vague idea of what to do. I wasn't going to *Waterfront* my brother. I knew it was important to take Shelby with me—I didn't kill two scumbags just to have Jerry catch up with her and finish what Carlos and Mace had started. The Brothers would be pissed, but they'd be looking for me, not her, and I couldn't think of how they'd find out about her. Hopefully Jerry wouldn't tell, because if he knew what was good for him, he'd stay miles away from the Bros. I dressed quickly, glanced at my mother asleep on the bed, and returned to the kitchen.

She was looking down at the table, sliding the pepper mill back on forth between her hands. She looked up when I came in, and followed me with her gaze as I sat down.

We didn't say anything. I could hear the refrigerator humming. She stared down at the table.

Finally she asked quietly, "What do we do now?"

"We get out of here as soon as we can. I'm going to get my mom ready—we need to drop her off at a nursing home—then I'll get your clothes from downstairs. Dylan's shit is down there too, and we'll have to get rid of that. Then we'll both go to my place and you can get the rest of your stuff. You make sure you have *everything* with your name on it, *anything* that could be possibly traced to you. If you want to yell around for L'il Kevin, that would help. I think he likes you."

"Then you'll drop me off in town? After we settle your mom?"

"No. We're going to have Jerry and the Brothers after us soon. We need to get far away."

"*You* need to get far away."

"Jerry might know your name."

"So call the cops. From another town or something."

"I don't want to involve the cops. They have resources Jerry and the Rodriguez's don't. I don't want everyone in the world looking for us."

She stopped with the pepper grinder and looked at me.

Time passed.

"You said you had money."

I nodded, thought of *Ossessione* for a moment. I realize I'd passed the point of no return when I shot Carlos. Maybe even before that. The rest would all be falling action.

"I have one of those Swiss bank accounts. No shit."

"Just like Bourne." She looked at me.

I hesitated. "Come with me to pick it up."

"Where to?" She kept looking at me.

"Zurich, then Rome. You have your passport. I'll give you ten thousand dollars. For all your trouble."

She kept looking. "Make it twenty."

Double Indemnity flashed through my mind. Did Shelby have any Stanwyck in her? And then I thought about all those *In Cold*

Blood bodies in my trailer. Ten, twenty, what difference did it make? "Twenty it is." I got up abruptly.

I wasn't sure what to pack for my mother. I started in her bathroom, and placed her toothbrush, toothpaste, some med bottles and a couple of tubes of lotion into a makeup bag I found under the sink. Quietly and quickly, I put a few clothes into a suitcase—all the clean bras and panties I could find, two or three housedresses, some sweaters, a couple of pairs of slacks. It was unlikely that anyone would be able to return to collect anything she wanted, so this was it. If she still wanted. I looked down at her sleeping face. What do you want, mother? What do you want? She looked serene, her face undistorted by the struggles of consciousness. Was she dreaming? And of what? A peaceful visit by her two sons, the doctor and the lawyer, the successful progeny of her long and happy life? Or of the two meth cooks and assorted lowlifes she lived with in a ramshackle farmhouse outside of dying desert city? With rapists and tumbleweeds for friends. I bent down to stroke her face and smooth the thin hair off of her forehead. The skin on her face was dry and flaky. Dream on, mother. Dream on.

I stood up and turned to the closet, and noticed the two large boxes of Depends Underwear. Jesus. They must have those at the nursing home. I slid the front hangers to the side until I reached some of the dressier (and long unused) clothes in the back. The smell of dust and mothballs irritated my nose, and I sneezed quietly into an old woolen jacket. I took a couple of the nicer dresses: maybe someone would put one of them on for Easter or her birthday next or something like that. She'd likely be buried in one.

What else did she want or need? I had made arrangements with Nish to reserve a room for her in a pretty good nursing home and pay for it until she died. I'd ask him to contact my father. I could count on Nish. I looked on her nightstand:

someone, probably Lizzie, had arranged three photographs in small frames. There was me, in grad school, looking sullen and disappointed, my forehead and eyes on the way to settling into my current default expression of disappointed bitterness. And there was Jerry in his army uniform, likely stoned out of his mind, a sheepish smile conflicting with his hard, calculating gaze. And finally one of the both of us together in our swimming trunks, maybe middle school, all skinny limbs and ears and bad haircuts. Should I drop a dime on my bro? Was that the *Proposition*? I couldn't remember when or where the photo was taken. As I put them in the suitcase they reminded me that she had a couple of albums somewhere, books filled with photos of Jerry and me, as well as her parents and siblings. Maybe she could look at those sometime, maybe that would help. She needed her shoes too.

I quickly went through the drawers of her dresser, but couldn't find the albums. I did find the rosary from the Vatican I'd given her as a souvenir from my Italy trip, as well as an ancient key chain I'd woven from plastic laces when I was a kid in summer camp. That reminded me of the robe I'd given her a couple of Christmases ago, and her new slippers. The robe, the slippers, the keychain and rosary, all went into the suitcase, along with a couple pair of sneakers, the orthopedic kind with velcro. The suitcase was almost full. I wanted to find those albums, something of her life to take with her to the nursing home. I looked again in her closet. Nothing. There was no one (alive) to ask. I had to get going. I hadn't packed myself, nor made any arrangements to fly to Zurich. And I had no idea where L'il Kevin was. Careful not to wake her, I looked around again: under the bed, in her dresser, in her nightstand, in her closet. More nothing. This was her life now, a suitcase full of clothes and Vatican rosary. And photos of her two loser sons. I closed and latched the suitcase. It would have to do.

I carried my mom's suitcase out to the 150, then went downstairs for Dylan's. My mother's suitcase was small and light. I arranged the cases carefully in the truck bed. Shelby limped out and leaned on the hood of the Rover. She had put her sunglasses on.

"Why don't we take the Rover? There's more room."

"I don't want my fingerprints on a dead man's vehicle. I'm not going to drive this straight to the airport, too many surveillance cameras and shit. I'll abandon it somewhere and we'll take a cab"

"Jerry?"

"Jerry's the wild card. But he's not getting back until tomorrow. And by then we'll be in Zurich. Or at least on our way."

"You sure he's not getting back until tomorrow?"

"Pretty sure."

I put my gloves on, moved over to the Rover and fired it up, then put it into the garage. I closed up the garage and looked at the door of my trailer. I was not looking forward to going back in there.

"Your gun in there?"

"Not my gun."

"The gun you used."

"I guess."

I sighed. We went in.

The air had settled and the smell had condensed, but nothing else had changed. Lizzie's body was still near the door, and Mace's feet and torso still in the hallway, visible from the front door. I imagined (hoped) that Mace was still face down in my study, and Glow still sprawled in my bedroom. I looked on the floor for my Glock, and found it a couple of feet from Liz. I picked it up. "We don't want to be here very long, but make sure you get all of your stuff. Anything and everything that could possibly be traced to you. If you don't want to carry it, we can ditch whatever, but make sure you don't leave anything behind. Your bag is over there in the corner."

She slid her Wayfarers to the top of her head and moved quickly to the corner, where she kneeled to pick up her suitcase. Sun from a window illuminated her face and hair, and the contrast between her beauty and the surrounding carnage was breathtaking (Lee Miller at Buchenwald). I moved to the hallway, careful to avoid the darkened pools in the carpet. I saw Mace's camcorder and didn't know whether to leave it or not. All these fucking details. I'd need a bag for my things, which meant I'd have to go to me bedroom and confront Glow's corpse sooner rather than later.

Holding my Glock out in front of me like Peter Sellars, I checked my study (Carlos was still face down on the floor) and then quickly pivoted into my bedroom (Glow remained on her side, partially covered by my duvet). I put the gun down on my dresser, grabbed a nylon duffle off the floor of my closet and began to hurriedly throw clothes in from my closet and dresser, trying to think of what I'd need and what I could buy later. I reached for the strongbox on the top shelf of my closet, and flipped it open. I counted my cash, ten thousand, and took my bankbook. I had a fake passport tied to my bank account, as some countries don't welcome convicted felons. I wasn't sure how good the *fugazi* was: it looked legit but I had never used it. I could hear Shelby in my office. I looked around for a smaller bag to put this stuff in. I didn't want anything that had ever carried dope: the last thing I needed was to get *j'accused* by some airport Rin-Tin Tin. I found an old backpack, but I might have used it for deliveries. This shoe bag would be better than nothing. I jammed the cash and passport into it, and put my bankbook in my front pocket with my wallet. I wish I had some shit on the Rodriguez brothers, some *Where the Sidewalk Ends* folder or something to be opened on the event of my death that would ensure my survival, but I had squat.

I looked around my bedroom for the last time. I didn't feel much nostalgia, or much of anything. Glow's corpse had something to do with my indifference, but it wasn't like this room in a trailer was my childhood home. The only memories here were those of monotonous nights sleeping and (rarely) wanking: I couldn't remember another living creature ever being in this room. Fuck it. Before leaving I picked up my pistol and stuck it in the shoe bag, and stuck the shoe bag into the duffel.

I went into my study. I looked at Carlos, face down on the floor, and felt some satisfaction. I moved behind him to my desk and laptop. I never kept any info on my computer, never used it for anything except Netflix, Amazon and porn. I had transferred some of my grad work, a few papers and my dissertation, onto the hard drive for safekeeping. So it wouldn't get lost. My dissertation. The one thing I'd finished in my life. I left the computer there.

The one thing I cared about was my film collection. I stored it with my parents (not my wife) when I was in prison, and after had carefully packed and moved it from one shithole to another. It was really my only true possession. I had a red loose-leaf binder, cross-referenced and color coded, cataloguing over a two thousand DVD's, all alphabetized in bookcases on the wall. I even had some extremely rare VHS tapes, including Godard's *Numero Deux* and his Girbaud commercials. I glanced at the spines of my DVD's without reading or recognizing. And my fairly new 40 inch Elite Plasma. I wondered what would happen to my things, my TV and DVD's. Probably get seized as drug booty or whatever. Cops could watch the Bronco games in style, and maybe the shitty Pueblo university would get the films. I thought about putting a bullet into the flat screen. I thought about stuffing a couple of DVD's or some of the rarer tapes into my duffel. I thought about looking around for the hard copy of my dissertation. "Elektra tortured is still Elektra." I turned and walked carefully out of the room. I picked up Mace's camcorder before I walked outside.

It was nearly dark when I got to the driveway, the clouds

hanging thick and low and oppressive. I turned and locked the door to my trailer. I ripped open the camcorder, took out the disk and tossed the camera as far as I could into the snow. I'd try to fuck up the disk somehow after we left. Shelby was out by the Rover, her sunglasses pulled up on the top of her head, her pack swung over her shoulder. I avoided stepping in my previous footprints in the snow.

"Where'd these clouds come from?"

"I don't know. Looks like a storm."

I tossed my duffel bag in the back seat. "Did you get everything?"

"Yeah."

"Did you see L'il Kevin?"

"No." Her eyes were clear and unafraid.

"Are all of your credit cards maxed?" Her brow furrowed.

"I think so. Why?"

"We should make plane reservations."

"I thought you said you had money."

"I do, but I don't use credit cards. Can you get a, what do you call it, an extension? More credit? I'll give you the money. In addition to the twenty thousand. I just don't want to walk up to the airline counter and pay in cash."

She shrugged and looked at me. "I've got an American Express we could use."

"Great. We'll call from a payphone. We should get going. I'm going to get my mom."

"You need any help?"

"No. Thank you."

When I got back to my mother's room, she was still asleep, her face beatific. I smelled urine: she needed to be changed. I went to the closet and picked up the package of Depends. "If soiled adjustable underwear is being replaced, remove it and clean the groin and buttocks thoroughly." No way. I could shoot two people dead but changing my mother's diaper was beyond me.

Jerry could do it. He'd pop something or smoke something or drink something and then he'd get in here and do it. He'd look around, put some towels on the bed, get a washcloth or some wipes or something, and then effortlessly and impersonally remove the dirty diaper, clean her ass and vagina, and snap on the new, all without mom noticing or waking up. And before he'd brush past me he'd give me that look, that "what the fuck *can* you do?" look, that look our father initiated but he perfected.

Maybe when he came back here and saw all these bodies, he'd be impressed. And then he'd dedicate his life to finding and killing me. I tried to imagine his face when he bent down over Glow's body and put his fingertips on her neck to check her absent pulse, but couldn't. I could only see him with that mocking half-smile, his eyes narrow and grey.

I'd left him some mess to clean up. Four bodies including a dead girlfriend, a living halfwit cousin, a fully operational super meth lab that would get him life in the can, and some angry gangsters who'd be on his *culo* like brown on rice when they came for the pickup and *nadie*. I didn't want to add to troubles by calling the cops. I couldn't. I couldn't play that role, brother rat. Ever. Even to save my own *culo*.

I wondered what Jerry was going to do. WWJD? Would he bury the stiffs himself? Where? Not in this toxic dump. And he couldn't just drive Glow to a funeral home, pop her out of the trunk and expect full military honors. But he'd want something, at least for Glow. Maybe he'd call some army buddies. Maybe he'd call the cops . . . no, he'd never do that. And let's not forget L'il Kevin. Jerry was going to be pissed.

What to do about my mom? I could call Shelby in to help me, but changing my mother's dirty drawers was beyond the call of duty. I bent over the bed and looked down at her face, sleeping peacefully, serenely. Her eyes didn't have that twisted expression, as if she were constantly trying to focus, that shaped her face when conscious. Her skin was dry, I was sorry that I had already packed her lotion. I could hear a quiet snore. I tapped her on the shoulder. "Wake up, mother, wake up." She flinched, startled. Her mouth opened and she rolled her head to the right. Her teeth were yellow and had plaque near the gums. I couldn't remember the last time she had been to the dentist. Or the hairdresser. What had we become? The nursing home would be better for her. I stroked her cheek. "Mother, mother, it's time to wake up." She opened her lefty eye drowsily, and then closed it again. She hiccupped once, and her tongue rolled over her bottom teeth. I caught another whiff of her diaper.

I shook her shoulder a little harder. Her body felt so frail. "Mother, mother, we have to get up and get going." Both eyes opened and her tongue extended out of her mouth. I put my hand under her back and helped her sit up. She gave a little cough. I put a couple of pillows behind her to support her. She couldn't keep her eyes open, and her head fell quickly back. It really made no difference if she were awake or asleep. Thankfully, Lizzie had dressed her before in slacks and a thin sweater, so she'd just need a coat and some shoes. I went to her closet and took out a heavy brown wool coat, one I remember her wearing before she got sick. I kicked around her closet floor, and was sorry I'd already packed her velcro shoes. I found some old pink sneakers in the back, and hoped they would fit. She remained fast asleep as I removed her slippers and put her shoes on and laced them up. I didn't want to forget her new slippers. Her wheelchair was in the kitchen, and I hurried to fetch it. I didn't see Shelby, and I was grateful for that.

I positioned the chair next to the bed and swiveled her feet to the floor. She smelled pretty bad. I propped her up as best I could and wrapped her coat around her. I lifted her as carefully as I could by the armpits and sat her in the chair. Her eyes were open and blank, and she was breathing heavily through her nose. I brushed her hair from her face with my fingers, and caressed her cheek. She didn't respond. "Here we go mom, say goodbye." I put her slippers in her lap, and with some trouble wheeled her into the hallway, and then out into the cold.

"I don't know how to fold this fucking wheelchair." While I put my mother in the back seat, Shelby was wandering around the driveway. She was wearing a bright blue stocking cap and had put her sunglasses away. The clouds had thickened and darkened even more.

"I think I see that Kevin guy."

"Where?"

"Over there, by the hill."

"Where? Oh yeah, I see him. That's where he lives, across the road with Mace and Carlos. I'm going to see if I can talk to him." I tossed her the keys. "Start the car and warm it up. I'll be back in a few minutes."

"Kevin! Kevin! L'il Kevin." I ran heavily down the driveway. Kevin looked back at me, and started to run. "Kevin, wait up." He stopped.

I had this vague plan of getting him to the big house and locking him up somewhere. I didn't want him to go into my trailer, and I didn't want him wandering around the compound until the next day. I was out of breath when I caught up to him. He looked cold.

"I didn't have lunch."

"You're hungry, huh?"

"I didn't have lunch, Professor and I can't find Lizzie or Mace or anyone."

"Tell you what. We'll go to the big house, I'll make you some mac and cheese and you can watch the big TV. But you have to stay there, or else go to your own room. You can't go anywhere, else ok? Until tomorrow, when Jerry gets back. Stay away from my trailer. It's not good there. You promise me?"

"Where is everyone?"

"Promise me you'll not go near my trailer."

"Where's Mace? Where's my brother?"

"C'mon Kevin, let's go." I made to grab his arm, but I was too slow and he spun away.

"I don't want to watch no TV. I want to find Mace."

"Goddam it Kevin, you have to come to the house." Dealing with this fucking halfwit was the last thing I needed.

"Why? Why?" He looked like he was going to cry. He turned and started to run back to his trailer.

"Fucking Kevin, get the fuck back here." I followed, my legs heavy in the deep snow. "If I ever catch you I'll beat the fuck out of you. I'll give you something to cry about," I said, hopefully under my breath. "You want to see what's in my trailer? I'll show you what's in my trailer. Come on, let's go."

I was losing it. He made it to the door and ran inside. I stopped. I had to calm down. He was too big and strong for me to drag out, kicking and screaming. I closed my eyes and caught my breath. Fine. Goodbye, Li'l Kevin, goodbye. I turned and walked back toward my truck.

"How'd you get the wheelchair in?"

"There's a latch in the back."

"Thanks."

I looked in the rearview and saw my mother's and my face appeared juxtaposed in the frame. I couldn't see much resemblance. My mother's face was partly in shadow, and I could only make out the left side of her face. Her hair was sticking out, and I regretted not finding some sort of cap or hat for her. She was looking straight ahead, and her expression, while not blank, still seemed uncomprehending: she knew something was happening, but didn't know what. She began to form her mouth into an O and open and close it. What did she understand? What was she seeing? I looked tired and slightly shell-shocked, my eyes opened wider than normal, and my mouth cheerless and dour. She looked away to the right and then twisted her neck and back to look behind her. I positioned the mirror so I could see out of the back window.

Shelby climbed in the passenger seat and wrinkled her nose. "It stinks in here."

"My mom. I wasn't up to changing her."

"I'm going to keep a window open."

"I don't want to give her a cold."

"Ok."

About a quarter mile out of Avondale we began to see dark shirts and trousers, some in hay bale sized bundles and some scattered free, littering the road and shoulders. They were all the same color, a navy blue that looked almost black against the snow and in the fading grey of twilight. They looked like body parts from a weird explosion. Once or twice, a shirt and a pair of pants came to rest in a position that appeared eerily human, like one of the bodies we left behind in my trailer. The traffic ahead slowed and soon stalled, and we could see police lights ahead, in front of twelve or so cars and SUV's stopped in the road. We inched forward, and eventually came upon an overturned and opened van (evidently a laundry or uniform delivery truck of some kind), an ambulance and a tow truck, with a cop in an orange vest slowing traffic. Shelby and I looked at each other, and my mother made a noise behind. I turned quickly, but she didn't seem to be in any distress.

Fellini Satyricon

Federico Fellini (1969)

Scene 2

Professor, Shelby and Professor's mother in wheelchair facing wall. Nursing home, Int night.

11-17

The characters stand in front of an interior wall, every inch of which is covered with homemade valentines, layered two deep in places, in a riot of red and white cardboard and white and pink stiff doily lace. There are a few photographs scattered throughout the display—almost all depicting indistinguishable white-haired ladies—and candy hearts and cinnamon redhots are glued into patterns or letters to provide three-dimensional texture. The camera zooms in on a few: "Be Mine," "From Your Not So Secret Admirer," "Don't Sit Under the Apple Tree," "I Miss You So," and "Kiss Me." Some of the writing betrays a shaky hand and perhaps a fading grasp of the alphabet, while elsewhere Palmer method cursive is featured. The camera wanders. A no-nonsense block style handwriting appears and reappears, which, together with the generic quality of its messages ("Happy Valentine's Day," "You're Special!") signals a mediating presence, possibly a nurse or social worker. Some are from grand or great grandchildren ("Get Well Grandma"), and a patch originates from the local high school ("We Have the Valentine SPIRIT" and "Gimme an 'L,' Gimme an 'O,' Gimme a 'V,' Gimme an 'E'"). The mother begins to whimper in the wheelchair.

18
The Professor looks down at his mother, then kneels down and squeezes her hand.

19
Medium shot Shelby.

> SHELBY
> How much do you think she knows?

20
Medium shot Professor.

> PROFESSOR
> About what we just did? Or about what we're about to do? I don't know. Wish I did.

21
Medium shot Shelby.

> SHELBY
> Did she like that woman, the woman who took care of her?

22
Medium shot Professor.

PROFESSOR
(shrugs)
You mean Lizzie? I've no idea. I really didn't
pay enough attention.

23
Medium shot Shelby.

SHELBY
Look at all these. Look at this one: 'I want to
sex you up.' And this: 'Viva Viagra. Vinnie.'

24
Medium shot Professor.

PROFESSOR
(stands, wrinkles nose)
What's that smell? Smells worse than my mom.

25
Close shot Shelby.

SHELBY
Nursing home. I smelled it a soon as we walked
in the door.

26
Medium shot of Shelby walking in front of Professor and
mother, still staring at the wall. Can hear mother whimper.
Shelby has pronounced limp.

27
Close shot Professor.

28
Close shot Shelby.

SHELBY
These must be the pictures of the staff. Em-
ployee of the Month is Rogelio Lopez.

29-32
Medium shot from the rear. Professor pushes the wheelchair
slowly down the hall. Professor and Shelby continue to look at
the wall, until it ends. Then they move across the hall to the
last office in the corridor, where it stops and branches off into
a T shape. A closed door. Camera follows, then zooms on a
yellow post-it stuck on the door.

"I'll be in the Activities Room until 4:30, Janet."

33
Close shot Professor.
The Professor leans forward and looks left.

34
Professor's POV.
Vague figures, some standing and some sitting, at the end of a
long hallway.

35
Close shot Professor.
The Professor looks right.

36
Professor's POV.
Similar figures as to the left, but longer hallway, less defined.

37
Medium shot Professor.

PROFESSOR
Where the fuck is the activity room?
(he looks at Shelby)
What do you say, left or right?

38
Medium shot Shelby.

SHELBY
(she points to her left)
Left.

Scene 3
Professor, Shelby and Professor's mother in corridor. Nursing home, Int night.

39
Camera from the rear, tracking the three down a hallway, with doors on either side. Shelby limps to the right of the Professor, who's pushing his mother slowly, slowly. The corridor is peach colored, and illuminated not too harshly by overhead fluorescents. There's a thick blonde wooden railing on both walls. Ambient noise in deep background.

40
Tracking shot from Professor's left. A closed door.

41
Zoom in on door.
"Men's Bath"

Zoom back.
An orange "Occupied" sign visible above doorknob.

42
Tracking shot from Professor's right. Door opens as they pass.
An enormous woman, an extensive and extreme geography of
wrinkled white flesh and flower print robe, with loose egg-
plant colored knee socks pulled high, is wheeled out of the
steam. Her black hair is plastered to her forehead and exposed
right arm, and her mouth has a distressed expression, with the
lips pulled tight over the teeth.

43-45
Close up on her legs. We see purple flesh, impossibly bloated
and creased, with a thin, paper like skin covering the balloon-
like distension.

46
Camera zooms in on calves, stays.

> NURSE (O.S.)
> We'll get you to bed and then wrap them legs
> up tight.

> WOMAN (O.S.)
> But I'm tired, I'm tired.

> NURSE (O.S.)
> I'll bring you a snack, don't you worry.

47
Close shot Shelby.
Raises her eyebrow.

48
Tracking shot from left.
A flickering blue television light emanates from the next door
on the right. Professor peers in.

49
Professor POV.
Zoom in.
A bare bone-thin bluish leg raised slightly from bluish sheets
is visible in the background, with a dark curtain masking the
torso. A chalky face with bright red lipstick and a poison
green cloche appears suddenly waist high in the doorway
and then quickly disappears back into the blue shadows. The
ambient sounds become a little louder: an electronic music
undertone is audible.

50
Tracing shot from right. A thin man in a wheelchair, white
hair and yellow scarf wheels from door on left in front of
Shelby and takes both of her hands in his.

51
Close up of man's hands and arms. They are mottled and
bruised. A bandage with an ochre stain flaps from his left wrist.

MAN
Have you heard of me? Have you heard of me?

52
Medium shot of Shelby. She stiffens, leans back, looks around
for help. None is forthcoming.

53
Close shot of Shelby.

SHELBY
No, I'm sorry, I haven't.

54
Close shot of old man's face. His hair is wild, long and white, and his eyes look red-rimmed and panicked.

MAN
Have you heard of me?

55
Close shot of Shelby. Her face has softened.

SHELBY
No. Who are you?

56
Close shot of man. He looks as if he's about to cry.

MAN
Oh dear, oh dear. Can you help me? I want to go home. I just want to go home now.

YOUNG BLACK NURSE (O.S.)
C'mon Mr. Sanchez. Let's leave the poor lady alone and see if we can get you some food. When are you scheduled to eat?

57
Wide shot from the front. A young black nurse with long dreads, cheerful pink and orange scrubs, a thick brown leather hernia belt and red crocs materializes to fetch Mr. Sanchez.

58
Close shot of Professor.

PROFESSOR
Excuse me.

59
Close Shot of Nurse.

YOUNG BLACK NURSE   OLD MAN (O.S)
Yes?   Have you heard of me?
                            Have you heard of me?

60
Close shot of Professor.

PROFESSOR
Where is the Activities Room? We're looking
for Janet. Janet Donati.

61
Close shot of YBN.

YBN
All the way down the hall, straight in front.
Next to the cafeteria.

62
Medium shot of entire group from rear.

63
Close shot of old man.

OLD MAN
I want to go home now. Have you heard of me?

64

Medium shot from rear. The group disperses: Professor,
Shelby and mom down the hall, Nurse and Old Man back into
room on left.

YBN
Everyone's heard of you Mr. Sanchez, everyone's heard of you. Let's get back into your
room and see when you can eat.

65

Tracking shot from right. The camera looks into another
doorway, where we see the backs of two white-coated doctors
standing in front of the far bed, with a figure in a wheelchair
on the periphery to the left. One doctor turns as the camera
continues to track.

66

Close shot of the turned doctor's face. His grin is either stupid or lascivious.

67

Quick cut to figure sitting in an elaborate electric wheel chair.
A man, much younger that the other patients, maybe thirty
or thirty five. Both arms are cut off at the elbows, stumps are
bare. He's staring at the far wall.

68

Tracking shot from left. Another doorway. Shadowy, an ankle
high bed with dark blankets barely discernible in the gloom.
A sleeping face in the bed is brightly illuminated by light from
the door, contrasting strongly with the dark bedclothes.

69

Close up on three crisscrossed red nylon straps binding the blanketed figure to the bed.

70

Tracking shot from right. Another doorway. Three children between three years and six run around, jump up and down and laugh in the space between the door and a bed pushed against the far wall. A white Bichon Frise yaps and nips at their heels. A smaller child bounces at the foot on the bed on his knees. Their giggling, the dog's yapping and the sound of an off-screen television game show momentarily overwhelm the ambient noise.

71

Tracking shot from left. Sound from shot 70 abruptly stops and ambient noise grows louder. Close up of a homemade cardboard sign hanging above a doorway: "Manny's Room." Camera tracks down and zooms out to see Manny, a very dark-skinned Hispanic, sitting in a wheelchair in the doorway. He has a black moustache and is wearing a white cowboy hat, which he tips to Professor's mother and Shelby.

72

Tracking shot from right. A corner room. A clear glass wall that curves around to another hall. Room is full of smoke. Three figures can be seen through the glass and smoke, all sitting and all facing in different directions, all turned away from a small television playing in the upper right corner. A thin female in a white robe is hunched over, smoking greedily, a portable oxygen tank at her feet. Another thin female holds a cigarette to a dark space (balloon cuff) in her throat and inhales. Camera resists urge to zoom in, remains tracking slowly. Third figure is a large man in light blue scrubs, smoking quickly and nervously.

73
Tracking shot from left. Another room. An obese teenage boy with his ear pressed tightly against his left shoulder spins in tight circles in his motorized wheelchair in the center of an unfurnished, brightly illuminated space.

74
Medium shot from rear. The group has reached a more populated section of the hallway. Various figures, seated and standing, mill about. A female figure in light green moves quickly up on them from behind, maneuvers past Shelby on the right and disappears into a door on the right.

75
POV Professor. A bald man with severely crossed eyes shuffles past.

76
POV Professor. They approach a white haired woman in a beige nightgown parked in a wheelchair in front of the nurse's station on the left. As the camera tracks forward, we see that she's cradling a headless doll in her arms.

77
Close up of headless doll.

78
Medium shot from rear. We suddenly hear a 40's style romantic instrumental music. A trombone player, trumpet player and drummer appear from the foreground, all playing their

instruments, hesitate, and then file past toward the background between the Professor and the wall. The musicians are wearing matching powder blue tuxedoes. All have red paper Valentine party top-hats. The music fades into the dominant ambient noise.

79
POV Professor. Six or seven patients in wheelchairs are lined up on the left past the nurse's station. Two are accompanied by attendants in scrubs and hernia belts, and two more have drip bags attached to their chairs. The camera tracks the faces slowly, from the Professor's POV, which is slightly above the sitting figures. The figures face the right, and focus their attention exclusively to the back of the figure ahead. We see the waist and torso of the two attendants, but not their faces. They are both relaxing against the wall.

80
Medium shot from rear. They stop.

81
Close shot of Shelby.

                    SHELBY
        Jesus it stinks.

82
Close shot of Professor. He says nothing.

83
Close up of headless doll. Two or three seconds of the 40's music from the trio.

Scene 5

Professor, Shelby, Professor's Mother, Administrator and various patients. Nursing home cafeteria, Int night.

123

Slightly high angle shot (as from the top corner of the room looking down.) The room is made up of eight brown round tables surrounded by six chairs. Forty some patients sit around the tables in various states of disrepair, while four staff members in hairnets move back and forth between the tables and the serving window to the right, dispensing trays of food and pouring water or juice from plastic pitchers into plastic glasses. There is a great deal of noise of eating and loud nonsensical talking, which sometimes erupts into yelling.

124

Same angle, but now focused on one particular table, near the serving window and far from the door. The table is clear, nothing has yet been served. The Professor, his mother and Shelby sit around the table, and next to Shelby sits a woman who, although dressed in similar clothing to the attendants serving food (flower print scrubs on top and light blue pastel pants), is better groomed and coifed, and has an air of authority about her. Next to the Professor sits a very old balding woman in a neck brace and blue terry bathrobe, and next to her a thin old man in a worn oxford shirt with his head down on the table.

125

Close shot of older man with head on table.

126

Close shot of old lady. She's moving her tongue in and out slowly, rhythmically, NOT lasciviously or erotically.

127
Close shot of Professor's mother. Her eyes are bright, alert, excited. She's chewing, practicing her eating.

128
Close shot of Administrator.

ADMINISTRATOR
(speaking loudly)
This is our small dining room. We keep the numbers down here, so that the residents can receive more individualized attention. As you see, some of the residents here have cognitive or other difficulties that can make eating more challenging, and so we try to provide a slightly more supervised environment.

129
Close shot of Shelby.

SHELBY
Are these the most . . . uh . . . extreme patients you have here?

130
Close shot of administrator.

ADMINISTRATOR
(smiles condescendingly)
No. Some of the more challenged residents are fed individually in their rooms.
(turns to Professor and changes smile to encouraging)
I don't think your fiancé's mother is near that stage yet.

131
Medium shot of Professor staring at the table. He smiles
slightly to acknowledge Administrator's comments.

132
Close up of table. An orange tray with a beige industrial di-
vided plate appears. The plate holds four fish sticks in the
center, and, clockwise (from seven o'clock), tater tots, a dollop
of what is likely tartar sauce, a roll, and yellow corn. There are
glass of bright blue juice and white milk on the right, along
with a white paper napkin and a silver knife, fork and spoon.
A small white paper cup with three large red and white pills is
set next to the napkin. Steam rises from the plate.

133
Medium POV shot from Professor to old woman, who begins
clapping enthusiastically.

134
Medium POV shot from Professor to old man, who remains
face down on the table.

135
 Medium POV shot from Professor back to old woman. An
attendant stands behind her and ties a paper bib around her
neck. The old woman leans forward excitedly toward her food.

136
Slightly high angle shot (see # 123) of room. A large black
male attendant wheels in a frail looking old woman wearing a
silver paper crown and what looks like a blood red cape. He
begins to direct her to a table next the Professor's.

137

Medium POV shot from Professor. An attendant, with an orange tray in his hand, stands behind the old man and gently shakes his shoulder.

138

Close shot of attendant over the old man.

> ATTENDANT
> C'mon Roman, you gotta sit up. C'mon Roman, it's time to eat. Roman, I know you're awake.

139

Close shot of Administrator.

> ADMINSTRATOR
> (smiles stiffly)
> Gently Robert, gently.

> FEMALE VOICE
> (O.S., loudly, suddenly)
> This is my goddam seat!

140

Medium POV shot from Professor. Camera tracks from attendant over old man to table next to him. View of large black attendant's back, and not much else.

141

Medium POV shot from Professor, camera tracks left, as if Professor leans. The old lady with the crown is visible to the right, as is a table surrounded by various elderly residents sitting around.

DEEP MALE VOICE
(from the attendant pushing the lady with the crown)
It's Mrs. Valardi's birthday, Mrs. Hochaver. I'm
just asking you to move over one space.

FEMALE VOICE (O.S)
I ain't moving nowhere. This is my seat.

142
Medium POV shot from Professor, camera searches for face
of FEMALE VOICE.

FEMALE VOICE
I always sit here. I ain't moving nowhere.

143
Close shot of Administrator. She's standing, facing the next
table.

ADMINISTRATOR
Now Mrs. Hochaver, wouldn't you like Mrs.
Valardi to have a nice birthday?

144
Close shot of lady with the crown (Mrs. Valardi). She smiles,
and it's impossible to tell if her smile is smug or confused.

FEMALE VOICE (O. S.)
I don't give a good goddam whose birthday it is.
I always sit here.

145
Camera moves in and around, trying to locate the face of the
speaker.

146
Close shot of Administrator.

ADMINSTRATOR
(sighs)
Sometimes our residents are not cooperative.
(She motions to the attendant)
Samuel, move Mrs. Valardi to table number six.
There should be room there.
(She turns)
Robert, can you please give Samuel a hand?

147
Medium shot of attendant and old man from Professor's POV.
Attendant places tray on table near old man's head and moves
off-screen camera left.

148
Close up of table, similar to shot #132. An orange tray and
beige plate is set in front of the Professor's mother, identical
to the previous tray except for the pill container.

149
Close shot of Professor's mother. Her eyes shine as she opens
her mouth and keeps it open.

ATTENDANT (O. S.)
Does she need a bib?

150
Close shot of Professor.

PROFESSOR
Yeah. She might need someone to feed her as

well.
>   (hesitates)
>   She does, she will need someone to feed her.

151
Close shot of Professor's mother. A paper bib is tied around her. Her mouth is still agape.

152
Close shot of Administrator.

>   ADMINSTRATOR
>   Thank you, Jonathan. I believe can manage.
>   (she turns to the Professor)
>   Would you like to help feed your mother?

153
Close shot of Professor. His face is drawn.

154
Close shot of Professor from another angle. Shot's #'s 153 and 154 are long shots, about a minute each.

155
Close shot of Professor from angle in #153.

>   PROFESSOR
>   (finally)
>   No.

156
Close shot of Administrator.

ADMINISTRATOR
Yes, of course.
(pause)
I understand completely.

157
Close shot of Administrator as she leans to the left and begins
to cut the food in front of Professor's mother. The random
sounds of eating etc have coalesced into something like a wild,
embryonic rhythm, still in the background. The administrator
smiles kindly at the Professor's mother.

158
POV from Professor to close shot of Shelby. She smiles and
crinkles her nose.

159
Close shot of Administrator. The rhythm has returned to the
chaos of noise and the underlying electronics.

ADMINISTRATOR
(smiling gently, slowly feeding Professor's mother)
There. Isn't that good? Do you like fish? Open
up.

160
Close shot of Professor's mother being fed. Her chin is shiny
with some sort of fluid.

ADMINISTRATOR
(to Professor)
She's hungry.

162
Close shot of old woman at table. She's eating quickly, chewing with her mouth open, her face covered with pieces of half-chewed food. Her forehead and cheeks are shiny and moist, and her lips and surrounding skin are stained purple.

163
Close up of old woman's tray. She takes her full glass of milk and pours it into her half filled glass of juice. It overflows rapidly down onto the tray.

164
Close shot of Administrator. Still feeding the Professor's mother, she turns to face him.

> ADMINISTRATOR
> Would you like a plate? I know it's not The Marriot but our dieticians make sure it's wholesome and nutritious. And we encourage guests, when they visit, to eat with the residents.

164
Close shot of Professor.

> PROFESSOR.
> No, no thank you. We had a late lunch.

165
Professor POV shot of old man face down on table with tray beside head.

166
Close shot of Shelby. Her brow furrows. She looks around.

167
Close shot of Professor. He frowns, as if he's smelled something bad.

168
Close shot of Shelby.

> SHELBY
> Did someone have an accident?

169
Close shot of Administrator.

> ADMINISTRATOR
> (wrinkles her nose)
> It seems so. Sometimes our residents get over-
> excited during dinner.

170-179
Various medium close shots (NOT close ups) of the residents'
faces while eating. All are shiny with moisture, even those
who chew disinterestedly or with full cheeks stare off into
a distance. The background sound coalesces at times into a
vague and vaguely threatening rhythm, but just as quickly disperses into chaos with low frequency electronics. Hair-netted
and hernia-belted attendants add and remove trays, stop and
cut up food, clean spills and wipe tables. Sometimes a resi-
dent is wheeled out.

180
Close shot of Professor's mother being fed.

181
Close shot of Shelby from Professor's POV. She mouths the words Let's go.

182
Close shot of Professor from Shelby's POV. He shrugs, turns away toward his mother.

Scene 8
Professor in truck. Nursing Home Parking Lot. Truck Int night.

37²
Close shot of Professor from inside the F-150. He sits in the driver's seat, in the dark, staring straight ahead. Half of his face is illuminated by a raised offscreen streetlight from the driver's side. There is some weak ambient light from the rear: his silhouette is always visible. He looks utterly despondent. Car headlights pass and reflect from off of the various glass surfaces of the Ford. All quiet except for the noise accompanying the headlights of the passing cars.

373
He slumps forward and places his forehead into his right hand.

374
We hear what might be a sob and perhaps see his shoulders shaking ever so slightly. It's difficult to tell in the dark.

375
External crane shot of Ford in a nearly empty parking lot. The truck sits near the edge of a circle of light surrounding a streetlight.

376
Back to interior shot (#372). He suddenly leans forward.

377
Close up of glove compartment. It's very dark, and so we can't see much. We hear, rather than see, him open the glove compartment. He removes something and sits back.

378
POV Professor. We see the glint of his pistol as he turns it over in his hand.

379
Close shot Professor. He stares down at the pistol in his lap.

380
Close shot Professor. A car passes by (headlights and sound).

PROFESSOR
(softly)

     Fuck.

381
POV Professor, looking down at the gun. If we can see anything, we can see only vague outlines of his legs, etc, illuminated by reflected and ambient light.

382
Close shot Professor. He raises the gun. We can see the outline clearly from the backlight.

383
External crane shot of truck in the parking lot.

384
Close shot Professor. He holds the Glock in midair, pointed straight up. It begins to move.

385
POV Professor, looking straight ahead through windshield to a brightly lit door (nursing home).

386
We see a shadow extreme camera right and hear a knock on the window.

387
Close shot Professor, who lowers the pistol as he twists to his left. We catch a glimpse of the shadow moving around the back window.

388
POV Professor. After a couple of beats the passenger door opens and light goes on, illuminating the interior. Shelby, holding a paper bag, begins to climb in.

> SHELBY
> I found a 7-11 and got us some beers. You could use something harder. You and me both. That whole scene pretty much sucked.

389
Close shot of Shelby from Professor's POV. She closes the car door, light goes off. She fumbles around in the bag.

> SHELBY
> I was going to get Heineken, but I wasn't sure if we have an opener. So I got Tecate cans.

390

Medium shot front of both Professor and Shelby. Professor is still, and Shelby takes out a can from the bag, opens it and hands it to him. He doesn't move.

391

Close shot Shelby, from the front. She shrugs, takes a sip.

> SHELBY
> (cheerfully)
> That was seriously fucked up. Could you believe the smell in there? And when somebody took a dump at the table . . .

392

Medium shot both Professor and Shelby.

> SHELBY
> We haven't eaten all day. We should get some-thing, although I wasn't going to touch that muck. This is your town, so where should we go? I don't feel like Mexican. Italian would be good. They have sushi here? Nevermind, after the smell of that fish I'm not sure my stomach could even handle a hamachi roll.

391

Close shot Shelby from front. Hesitation.

> SHELBY
> So, what's with the gun?

392

Reverse shot Professor from Shelby POV. He stares straight ahead.

393
Reverse shot Shelby from Professor POV.

> SHELBY
> You planning on going postal in the nursing
> home? Who you going to cap first, that creepy
> lady with the headless doll? Or that bitchy nurse
> with the flame red hair? 'You've had plenty to
> eat Mr. Phelps, plenty to eat.' Fuck you, give
> him another tater tot. Jesus.

394
Reverse shot Professor, who's now looking at Shelby.

> PROFESSOR
> You look pale.

395
Reverse Shelby from Professor's POV. She leans forward and
grasps the rearview mirror, twisting it around to look at herself.

> SHELBY
> I look pale? You think so? OMG. I look pale.
> (she turns toward Professor)
> I wonder why I'm missing my usual healthy
> glow. Could it be because I was raped? Or
> maybe because I killed two people? Or maybe
> because I've been held hostage by a tweaker
> family from hell.

395

Medium shot both in the car. Shelby turns away, looks out the passenger window.

> SHELBY
> (softly)
> Anyway, I'm not the one with the pistol in his hand.

396

Close shot Professor from front. He guffaws, and stares straight ahead.

> PROFESSOR
> Me, personally, I've had a terrific day. First, I visited my dear old dad. I always have a great time with daddy, he always makes me feel A number one. Then I came home and killed a couple of my coworkers. That was ok, because I didn't really like them anyway. One was my brother's girlfriend, but, you know, my bro and I were never that close. And to top it all off, I got to put my mom in a nursing home. They'll probably cure her, and she'll be good as new in six months, tops. So all in all, it's been a fucking great ten hours or so.

397

Close up gun at Professor's side.

398
Close shot Professor from Shelby's POV. He's still staring
straight ahead.

PROFESSOR
I lost my entire family today. My entire life.
(he turns toward Shelby, then looks down)
I wish you'd stayed away. Ten more minutes.
(hesitates)
Ten more minutes.

399
Reverse shot Shelby. She's looking directly at the camera.

SHELBY
(very softly)
I want that money.

A *Man and a Woman*

Claude Lelouch (1966)

A MAN AND A WOMAN
(Un homme et une femme)
from A MAN AND A WOMAN

Original Words by PIERRE BAROUH
English Words by JERRY KELLER
Music by FRANCIS LAI

"There's Frontage Road, Eagleridge, La Quinta, The Ra-mada, Cracker Barrel . . . I am officially out of Pueblo. Good-bye."

"You might not ever go back."

"I will never go back. Not even to be buried."

"You're from here, right? Your parents and family are from here?"

"I was born here, yeah. I left when I went to college. And it was the worst mistake I ever made coming back."

"I take it this is not your favorite town."

"I hate this fucking place. I only like it when I'm leaving. And now I'm leaving for the last time. Goodbye."

You weren't supposed to hate your own hometown so much that you could only breathe when you left.

This was going to be a long trip.

"It took you a while."

"I'm not very punctual. Jesus it's cold. What time is it?"

"A little after six. The thermometer says it's twenty two."

"Where are we?"

"Fountain. Outside of Colorado Springs. We got another two and a half to the airport. So you tossed everything? My key, the suitcase, my gun?"

"I tossed everything. Just like you said."

He wasn't bad looking, she thought, not really. He had kind of a sweet face, thin, but not mean or unhealthy looking. He did look more like a teacher than a gangster, and reminded her of a couple of professors she'd had. Not the ones who tried too hard to be hip, telling lame jokes and coming on to all the sophomores in sight. No, he was more like Mr. Allison, her Contemporary Lit teacher last year, 45-50, nice clothes and bad posture, but the sweetest eyes, and she loved the way he talked; long, beautiful sentences that she sometimes got lost in. She thought he was gross at first, but at the end of the third week she put on her canary yellow dress, the short one, and stopped by his office in the late afternoon. She didn't have a definite plan, wasn't sure what she would do, but didn't rule anything out either. He wasn't there. No note, nothing. Two weeks later she started hooking up with Joshua. She never went back to his office, but she never missed a class either. Heaven knows what might have happened. She'd not been tempted by a prof before.

This was cozy, driving at night, surrounded by snow. It was like they were completely alone in the world, just the two of them, hurtling through the darkness toward some unknown destination. It was almost enough to allow him to put the day's events out of his thoughts. He wondered if she had a boyfriend, and wondered how he could find out.

He couldn't remember the last time he had shared such an intimate space with a woman. He had once driven up to Steamboat with Glow, but their conversation petered out before they got to Springs, and she had napped from Monument, her shades down and her mouth open, a gentle snore sometimes audible in the gaps between the songs he played quietly. Not exactly *Children of Paradise* ("Garance is a flower"), or even *Lovers on the Bridge*. More like *Wages of Fear*.

He continued to steal glances at her. She had tucked her right foot under her, and had turned her hips toward him, while her shoulders and gaze faced forward. She seemed smaller than before, like she was finally settling into her true size. He wondered what she was thinking.

"Can I turn some music on?"
"Go ahead."
Dig if you will this picture

"What's so funny?"
"Nothing."
"That's a good song. People dug that song back then. This was sexy."
"Oh was it?"
"Do do do do, when the doves cry."
"How old were you back then?"
"When was this, 84-85? I was 23. In grad school. You weren't born yet, were you?"

He needed the conversation, needed the words to envelope them and take their minds of their shared past. They had been through a lot together, but what they had been through wasn't exactly something they could dwell on, something they could reminisce about and smile, à la Ekberg's villa in *Intervista*. They had left five corpses behind them in an old ranchhouse/meth-amphetamine lab, and were driving to the airport to leave the country forever. At least he was. She would return to school, a little richer and perhaps wiser, while he attempted to, to what? Live out his life in some remote corner of the world, constantly looking over his shoulder and listening for the creak of a door or the crack of a twig? Maybe he should contact the Rodriguez brothers, try to arrange some deal, try to buy himself out of the contract. But it wasn't them he was afraid of . . . it was his own brother. And he couldn't buy himself out of that.

He kept sneaking glances at her: her face sometimes illuminated by the oncoming traffic and intermittent highway lights, sometimes by the dim console glow. She was beautiful. Her hair seemed darker than in the day, as did her eyes. Her cheekbones were higher, her eyebrows thicker and better defined: they contrasted nicely against her pale skin. Her lips were thin and her nose was long and aristocratic. Aquiline was the word. The snow was getting thicker. He had better keep his eyes on the road.

So Europe would be fun. All expenses paid, plus the twenty grand. She didn't think she'd rat him off. Unless things got way weird. No one knew she'd left with Dylan, and no one really knew she was planning to go to Aspen. She'd give her moms a call from Europe, tell her she met some guy or something, she'd be back at school at the end of the week. Same story to Jenny and Kelly, although she might tell Kelly what really happened. Leaving out the manky rape part of course. A shiver ran down her spine.

She wasted two chicks. Truth be told, she didn't feel that differently. One was in self-defense and the other, well the other was probably self-defense as well. None of these tweakers were innocent: they killed Dylan, tried to rape her and were eventually going to kill her. No doubt. And this guy, the Professor, or whatever his name was, was he any different? Well, he had capped those two nasty greasers who were bumping her without permission. So he wasn't all bad. She'd go to Switzerland or whatever with him, collect her dough, hang for a few days and then say goodbye. They'd be more than square. Maybe she'd hit Paris on the way home.

"So what are you going to do after you get your money?"

"I hadn't thought about it."

"You haven't thought about it? You don't know where you're going? You don't have some sort of elaborate plan?"

"No, not really. I thought I'd go to Zurich, get my money, and try to go somewhere where my brother won't find me. Disappear."

"You should go someplace you always wanted to go. For at least a couple of days. And then decide where to disappear to. That's what I would do."

"Oh yeah? Where would you go?"

"Paris. Definitely Paris. Hey, does your brother know about your Swiss bank account?"

"I don't think so."

"Does he know about your fake passport?"

"No."

"So you're cool."

"I guess so."

Can you keep a secret

"This is another great song. Must be a college station or something, 80's night."

She felt a yawn coming on, and put her hand over her mouth and to swallow it. She was exhausted all of a sudden: it had been a day. A nice warm bath and nice clean sheets in a nice hotel . . . she could sleep for days. She'd definitely conk out on the plane. If they made their flight. They were flying coach. It was funny, how shocked he had looked when she quoted the Business Class price. She guessed meth cooks didn't get to Europe much. He looked like he didn't get out much at all. She wondered where all his money went: certainly not into clothes or cribs. And this truck, while nice enough, was nothing special. Not only did he not have any bling, he needed some new shoes. Maybe cooking didn't pay all that well. But he had already given her twenty-two hundred for the tickets. And he did have his Swiss account. So at least he wasn't shining her on. Not yet anyway.

She felt another yawn and turned toward the window. Her ankle was starting to hurt her again, so she leaned down to rub it. She wondered if he had brought his magic bag along, because she'd probably need something before the night was through, although if she took something now she'd be asleep before the next exit. He must be as tired as she was. She'd try to stay awake, to be polite, but no promises.

This song was beat. She had brought her iPod, with some Timbaland and Jay-Z, but she didn't know where it was. It was funny how psyched he got about these tunes. Why not, he had partied in college just like she did, only twenty years earlier. Like the parents. Before iPods right?

She wondered what he was like twenty years ago. He wasn't born an ice cook, and he did have some smarts, so riddle me this: what the fuck happened? We all need money and shit, and jobs are not easy to find, but not many of us white people, when we dream about what we're going to be when we grow up, have the picture of ourselves as a meth cook in a little house on the prairie of Colorado, surrounded by some mean-ass clowns, a half-wit farm boy and a drooling-in-her-soup mom. She'd heard of folks fucking up, but that must have been some huge my bad to end up hiding behind that mattress with his bro's girlfriend stepping over stiffs trying to cap his ass. Maybe she'd ask him what happened, about his past. They had a ways to go and these tunes were getting on her nerves.

Where should he go? To Zurich sure, but where after that? That was a good question. Where did he want to go? Why not Italy? They could take the train to Rome. Maybe he could check out CinaCittà. And those weird fascist buildings in *The Conformist*. That would be cool.

Capri. That's where he wanted to go. To the villa at the end of *Le Mépris*. They could go there for a couple of days, hang out, then he could figure out what to do. Jerry wouldn't follow him that quickly. . . there was no way. All he needed was a few days, until he had a plan about when and how to disappear. Pick up his money in Zurich, a couple days in Roma, then head down to Capri. And then, well, who knows? This could be his new life. He looked next to him at the girl's face. And maybe she'd come along for the ride. At least some of it.

He thought about James Mason and Sue Lyons. He didn't want to be that guy. She was a little more than half his age, and yes, could be his daughter. And yet.

They were in Springs now, just past Motor City. He was free. He had about a million, a beautiful girl at his side, and two plane tickets to Europe. How long would she stay at his side, that was the question. What was she like, what was her story? He needed more information, like if she was involved with someone and how heavily. This was crazy.

"So, what do you like to do?" "How did you get into that business anyway?"

"Go ahead." "No you first."

"How did I get into this business anyway? You want the long or the short answer?"

She shrugged.

"Let's see. I was pre-pharm as an undergrad, and then I switched to film studies, which annoyed my parents to no end, especially my father. Then I went to grad school. Collected some debt, finished my dissertation, got married and couldn't find a job. Or found really shitty ones. My wife was getting a little impatient, and I was tired of being poor. Some guys wanted me to sell some coke and ice for them, and so I did. I got caught and sent to prison. Five years no parole. Where I met some other guys. And with my particular skill set, well, short version, one thing led to another, and here I am, driving in this car with you."

"So some guys set this lab up for you?

"No, it was pure coincidence. They had built this lab and it was already to go, but their crew got pinched at some *la migra* sweep. They needed a new crew and a manager who knew what he was doing. I was getting out in a month, was from the area, knew the chemistry, and *voilá*, a meth chef was born. I got in touch with Jerry, who was being rotated back and discharged, and there you go."

"What about your mom?"

"She started getting sick just before I came back. Too much for my dad to handle. So we took her in."

"What happened to your wife?"

"I don't know. Never saw or spoke to her after the trial. Her lawyer served the papers when I was inside. I signed and that was it."

"That must have sucked."

"It sucked being in prison. I had a girlfriend here for a while, but my current career makes having a stable relationship difficult."

"I'll bet."

He turned to look at her. "Former career I meant. Former career."

Why did he lie? About the girlfriend? What was he trying to do, make her jealous? Shit, it was like he was still in high school. Maybe he could write her a note: Did you see me with Mary-Lou? Yes. No. Maybe. Do you like me? Yes. No. Maybe. Will you come to Capri with me? Yes. No. Maybe. What a tool.

It did feel good to talk to her. She was probably just being polite, asking him these questions, but it was nice to have some sort of genuine conversation. Other than Nish, he didn't really talk to anyone. And with Nish, it was always about films or about Nish. Even when Nish asked him questions about his personal life, he got the feeling that Nish was only trying to collect his experiences for some sort of vicarious thrill. He really never had the chance to explain himself: his ex-wife was incommunicado, his mother senile, his father furious and his brother indifferent. And there was no one else to give a fuck. Not that there was that much to explain. He sold drugs, got sent to prison, and now was a meth cook. But that was in the past.

They were already to Chapel Hills Mall. Monument was coming up. The snow would probably get a little worse, but it didn't seem bad enough to close I-25. With any luck they'd be in Denver in a couple of hours, by seven-thirty. Their flight was at nine. They should have time to ditch the truck, catch a cab and check in. That is if the snow didn't get too bad. He could try to find some weather on the radio, but he liked the music too much. *Shoot that poison arrow through my heart.* He wondered where he should ditch the truck. Downtown somewhere where it wouldn't be found for a while. Maybe a Park-n-Ride. It was registered to his father, and his father didn't know anything about where they lived or what they did. Didn't want to know.

Maybe he could just vanish into thin air.

She yawned again. Jesus. So he wasn't born a low-life drug dealer, like the skinny-ass creepers on *Cops*, with the mullet, crusty wifebeaters and whole body tattoos. And he did have some smarts, she had been right about that. Pre-pharm was tough: her recent hookup Josh was pre-pharm, and he was always studying, or almost always. Had a great body and was good in the sack . . . too bad he was dull as dirt. Kinda sexist too, didn't like condoms and expected her to always take care of the baby prevention. She was on the patch but he didn't know that from the get-go. He wanted her to clean his place up, too, whenever she spent the night. She didn't miss Josh. Well, maybe his hard ass. And his tongue that knew its way around her pussy. But talking to him was like talking to an adobe wall. When she got back to school maybe she'd see what Marco was doing. Or maybe she'd take a break, hang out with the girls for a couple of months, let the world come to her.

Paris would be cool. The last time she had been there she had gone for a week with her cousin Claire, to drop her off for study abroad. They had hit the tango bars hard the first couple of nights, and Claire had hooked up with Rodrigo, this Argentinean dude she was still seeing. The last two days she was pretty much by herself, which she didn't mind at all, exploring Montparnasse and having her breakfast at this hip little café near the Moulin Rouge, where she flirted with a couple of Greek tourists one morning and got her breakfast for free. Her parents had taken her and her two brothers for ten days three summers before, for her high school graduation. She hadn't hit the bars then, had mostly shopped and seen the sights, and hung out with her little brother in the Luxembourg Gardens, playing with those creaky boats (which she liked) and riding that old carousel (which she didn't). She had played the family gal then, the good daughter. Paris would be pretty fun without the rents and some coin. She could call Kelly and fly her out. That would be a blast.

His ear lobe fell in the deep

"You have to like this song."

"It's kind of fun."

"Rock Lobster, huh huh. Rock Loooobster, huh huh. I used to have an eighties haircut. You know? Long on one side, short on the other. Flock of Seagulls? Thompson Twins? Nothing, huh. 'You're killing me. I'm dying here Leon.'"

"Who's Leon?"

"You ever see *Dog Day Afternoon*? 'I'm dying here Leon, I'm dying?' No?"

"I'm not trying to be a total asshat, but can we turn this down a little?"

"Sorry."

"No worries."

"How's that?"

"Good."

"So what about you? What's your story?"

"Me? I'm boring. No prison, pregnancies, divorces or drug running. I'm just a plain old student."

"You're neither plain nor old. What are you studying?"

"I'm going to declare Communications. I might want to go to J-School, I don't know. The news biz doesn't seem all that lucrative right now."

"You married?"

"Hah. No, I'm not married. Nor engaged. I am seeing someone, I guess. We've been together for a couple of years now. He's in the architecture school."

Why'd she tell him that? The architecture school? For a couple of years? What the fuck? She just didn't want him to get any ideas. She'd go with him to get her money, a couple of days in Switzerland, and that was it. Separate hotel rooms all the way. He and his posse had basically kidnapped her, and almost raped her (she didn't want to think about that), and she wasn't going to fall for any Swedish syndrome or whatever. Purely platonic. No friends with benefits. Not even friends.

That wasn't quite fair. She looked over at his profile. He looked bummed, like he had just killed his brother's girlfriend and had put his mom in a nursing home. Ice cooks have feelings too. He was ok looking. A little shopworn, a little grey around the temples, his lips a bit thin. He was probably at least forty. But he had those smiling eyes, when he did smile, and that she liked. He had nice skin, although he could use a shave. He had done some living, but he still looked kind. She had been with worse, that was for sure.

And he had saved her life. But they were even on that score (see the brother's girlfriend). But he could have very easily just walked away when that fat pig was trying to fuck her. But she didn't ask to be locked up in a trailer with a sprained ankle. But he didn't invite them to come crashing into their compound at two in the morning. All this thinking was giving her a headache. She'd like to turn that damn music off. The fake boyfriend was a good idea. Avoid all complications. Get her money and get to Paris.

So she had a boyfriend. What did he expect? A good-looking girl like her, of course she'd be coupled. It was madness to think anything else. To think anything at all. He felt tired all of a sudden. Exhausted. He hoped this wasn't all a mistake. He considered turning the music off, but it helped him keep alert. Truth be told, although he almost never touched the stuff, he could use a little tweak. But he had left everything back at the compound. He chuckled. Ice, ice everywhere, and not a quarter to smoke. Speaking of ice, even though they were approaching Monument, the snow was actually starting to let up a bit. Thank God for small favors.

Maybe he wouldn't go to Italy after all. Maybe he would go someplace truly foreign to him, someplace where his preconceptions wouldn't already color his experience. Italy, France, England, Sweden and Germany were immediately out. Russia too with Eisenstein, Tarkovsky and Vertov. Poland, no, with Wajda, Kiéslowski and Holland. Spain had Buñuel and Bardem (he had never dug Almódovar). And Romania had all the Draculas and other vampires, and Denmark had Dreyer and Von Trier and was probably like a cross between *Ordet* and *The Perfect Human*. He was frightened of Africa (*Burn!*, *Battle of Algiers* and *Cobra Verde*), and besides, it would probably be too much like Pueblo; hot, dry and alienating. Except with worse food. Serbia maybe, or Albania. Not attractive. Maybe Iceland.

"So what are we going to do?"

"You know we're flying to London, and they'll we get tickets to Zurich. I think I'm going to take your advice and go to Italy for a few days. That's one place I really like. What about you?"

"Paris. I think I'll go to Paris."

"Paris, Paris is nice. Have you ever been to Italy?"

"No."

"Would you like to come?"

What the hell, might as well get it out in the open. Abrupt maybe, uncalled for, but there it was. She'd say no, and then he'd get on with things.

She was afraid of this. Last couple of days, lonely ice cooks seemed to have a thing for her. At least he asked.

Although Italy might be fun.

"Where in Italy?"

"Rome for a while. And then maybe Capri."

"Where's Capri?"

"It's an island off the coast of Naples."

"Have you been there before? Is it special to you?"

"I've been to Rome four or five times. But not to Capri. I like Rome, all the old buildings, all the ancient history. I'm half Italian. There are some buildings I'd like to see, from a movie I really like. Do you know Bertolucci's *Il Conformista*, *The Conformist*?

"No."

"The beginning of the movie takes place in this suburb that Mussolini had built that's this great example of fascist modern architecture: the *Esposizione Universale Roma*. Your architecture boyfriend probably knows about this. And for Capri, there's a villa that's in another movie I like. It's a pretty amazing house, with stairs built into a wall and this gorgeous view. It's called the Casa Malaparte. Your architecture boyfriend probably knows about it too. You can telephone him once we land in London."

Yeah, her architecture boyfriend. She would have to pretend to call him.

It might be cool to chill out on an Italian island for a couple of days. A little swimming, lounging by the pool, padding around in those thick white robes. Nice. And then at night, a little hardcore clubbing with the Eurotrash. All on someone else's coin. Jenny had been to Ibiza and dug the hell out of it. Hmmm.

So he lied about being to Rome four or five times. So what? She wasn't coming with him anyway.

"You really like films don't you?"

"Yeah, I do. With my life, there's not much else to like."

If I wait for just a second more

"This is another cool song. Sorry. I don't mean to get maudlin on you. You like cinema?"

"The word cinema reminds me of French class. *Allons-y au cinéma*."

"Movies, then."

"Sure I like movies. Who doesn't like movies?"

"Who do you like? What actors or directors?"

"I dunno. I liked *Pulp Fiction*. And those Bourne movies. Jason Bourne."

"I've seen *Pulp Fiction*. I haven't seen Jason Bourne."

Going for the pity fuck, huh? That never worked. There wasn't much else to like. Jesus. Although in some ways it was true: the only way he could hang with Carlos, Mace, L'il Kevin and his psycho brother and not put a bullet in his head was to lose himself in film. Not to mention his life in Pueblo as a lonely teen. Without movies, without cinema, he'd be dead. Or, same thing, teaching high school at Pueblo County. And not that recent crap either, but *nouvelle vague*, noir, *neue deutsche* and Italian *neorealismo*. Was that as pretentious as it sounded?

He felt old. Even Bonnaire of *A Nos Amours* fucked her age, didn't she? This was hopeless.

He liked what he liked. *Allons-y au cinéma*.

Dude was a fanboy, a film geek. That was ok. She liked folks who were really *in* to things, who really felt passion about their interests. As long as they weren't stupid about it. And she wasn't going to marry him, she wasn't going to even fuck him. She just might go to Italy with him. She could see how much it would mean. She'd think about it.

"Why do you like movies so much?"

"Probably for the same reason most people like them, to escape. I guess my life hasn't been all that great, and so I usually need something to get me out of my current reality. Some people do drugs, some do sex, some find Jesus. I found Fassbinder."

"So you went to the movies a lot when you were a kid?"

"Not so much, no. I went to the library. I used to go to movies theaters when I was in junior high, but I soon realized that I really didn't like the films they were showing, the *Star Wars* and *Jaws* and *Close Encounters*. Blockbusters. I liked the stuff I saw in French class. So I went to the library instead. They wouldn't let me check stuff out, and I didn't have as machine to play anything on anyway, so I'd sit for hours in this small windowless room, no bigger than a walk-in closet, and watch two or three films on videotape straight every Saturday. VHS and Betamax. I did that pretty much every weekend until I went away to college."

"Did you have any girlfriends then?"

"I had plenty of girlfriends. I played shuffleboard on the floor with Monica Vitti, chased Kim Novak all around San Francisco, came *this* close to a Vegas wedding with Gloria Graham, danced with Anna Karina in a slinky blue dress trimmed in white fur, had Hanna Schygulla dance for me in a German officer's cap and nothing else, and let's not even mention Harriet and Bibi Anderson. They weren't twins, but close enough."

"I don't get it."

"These are all famous film actresses. I had huge crushes on all of them."

"Oh."

"I had a couple of real girlfriends too. But these actresses were much more interesting."

Now he was sounding a little creepy, a little Dungeons and Dragons.

He'd never told anyone that story before. His mom knew, and maybe his brother. But he never mentioned it in grad school. And certainly not in prison. And he never told his (ex) wife. She never asked. He hoped he wasn't coming off as creepy.

"Look, I'm not crazy. I know the difference between film and life. It's just that too often, my life sucked and film, well, the films I watched never sucked. They might be sad and even extremely painful, but they were always beautiful. This director I admire, the one who directed the film on Capri, said that 'Everything is Cinema.' I think I believe that."

"I'm not sure I do."

"Do you remember watching the World Trade Center collapse on TV? 9/11? Everyone said it was just like a movie, right? Just like a disaster movie? And don't we try to act like the famous actors and actresses we saw on screen, like Bogart and Eastwood and Belmondo? At least we used to."

"I don't know who those people are. But anyway, that's just for some things. I know what you mean by 9/11: it did seem like a cheesy movie. But other things, like what happened back at the house, or with your mom, and here, now, they don't seem like movies to me. Any movies I've ever seen."

He started to say 'Well maybe you haven't seen enough movies' but stopped himself.

One of her freshmen slams, her main one really, when she was living in Hassayampa, always said his life was like a movie. He was way smart but a real slacker. Loved his X and his TV and hated getting out of bed, whether she was with him or not. Some weekends, she'd leave his dorm on Saturday morning, come back Sunday night and she swore he hadn't moved, maybe to take a piss or fill his bowl or something, but nothing else. Obviously not the best hygiene, but was fun to talk to. Always had these crazy ideas about the two of them going to Africa or Central America or something, growing killer weed and living *la vida loca*. She could work on her photography and he'd play his music, and life would be sweet. His dad would give them some money to start out with, and then they could sell some of their dope, but they wouldn't need much dollar. Fucker was smart, could roll out of bed and ace his tests without cracking a book. Any time he actually got out of bed and did something, like going out to eat or playing Frisbee or walking over to her dorm he'd say 'My life is like a goddam movie, Shelby. Exactly like a goddam movie.' They tired of each other by the middle of the Spring semester, and when she stopped going over and he never called, well, that was it. The end of her freshman romance.

"Who's your favorite actress?
"I don't know. Uma Thurman. Angelina Jolie. Nicole Kidman. I like Nicole Kidman."
"They are all very beautiful. Did you ever want to be like them? Behave like them?"
"I used to do that Uma Thurman dance. The one where she's twisting with John Travolta and puts her hands in front of her face. I liked her in *Kill Bill* too."
"Did you ever dress like her? Or say anything she said?"
"Like what?"

She yawned.

He yawned.

"I'm sorry. This must be terribly boring."
"No, no, not at all. I'm just exhausted, and my ankle's starting to hurt. It's been a day, huh?"
"Hey, this is a great song."
I feel shot right through with a bolt of blue
"This was the greatest song of the '80's. You have to like this."
"Yeah, yeah, this is a good song. By the way, you didn't bring anything for pain, did you?"

"No, no, I'm sorry. I can't remember if those scrips are kosher, and with the airport security and everything, I left everything back home. I'm really sorry. I think we have time to stop at a gas station in Springs for some ibuprofen."

That was too bad about her ankle. In all of this turmoil, he'd forgotten about it. This was a great song though, probably one of his all time favorites. He had danced to this song many times with his now ex-wife at Freddy's, this little bar in Williamsburg that didn't have, strictly speaking, a dance floor. Connie. She had wanted him as much as he had wanted her, back then. He felt less tired, suddenly. The song always seemed to be about possibilities, about different lives that were (still) viable.

She hadn't said yes or no to Italy. He thought again about *The Misfits*, about Gable in his high-rise jeans fighting the stallion, and Monroe looking on screaming.

There was a gas station on the left.

She was beginning to feel this zone approaching, this space of quiet indifference. It was a fuzzy mood where she just sort of chillaxed and went with the flow. She was usually such a control freak, but sometimes she found it nice to let someone else drive for a change, and these moods were often welcome, and often came at a time when her life was most stressful. She could resist, of course, by canceling dates, refusing invitations and going to the gym manically, sometimes twice a day. But she often welcomed it. It was like a small vacation.

She could use a small vacation.

"There's a gas station. I'll try to find you something strong. You want anything else?"

"No, thanks."

The Professor and the student. A mismatch. A mis-fit. Fuck it: if Gable didn't care, why should he?

"You never answered my question about Italy."

She smiled and closed her eyes.

He waited.

"Sure. Why not?"

A MAN AND A WOMAN
(Un homme et une femme)
from A MAN AND A WOMAN

Original Words by PIERRE BAROUH
English Words by JERRY KELLER
Music by FRANCIS LAI

The Conformist

Bernardo Bertolucci (1970)

About ten minutes after the hydrofoil left the dock he spotted the sun piercing through heavy clouds, reaching the opposite side of the large island in the distance. It was the first time he had even a glimpse of the sun since just after the ~~gunfight~~ incident ~~days, weeks, years, lifetimes ago.~~ The rain was pelting down on the window, and the shape in front was largely indistinct, grey and dark green, but there were low shafts of yellow sunlight streaking through the leaden sky, backlighting the outline which now filled the entire horizon over the bow. Soon they'd land on Capri.

The twenty-foot ceilings were impressive. He sat in a private office before a large Art Nouveau desk, flanked by two detailed pythons carved into the dark mahogany columns. Two table lamps graced either side of the empty desktop. On the wall to his left, thin rectangular windows, stained blue, green and white in an ornate floral pattern, began about five feet up from the floor and rose nearly to the ceiling. The walls and ceiling were paneled in light brown oak. Four rectangular Jugendstile prints of four different cats hung on the wall behind the desk. A beautiful serpentine vitrine cabinet, about eight foot wide and twelve feet tall, dominated the right wall. He was sitting in one of the two bent wood and leather chairs, a matched set as the left chair-back curved up to the right and the right to the left. A thick oriental rug matched the pattern of the windows, although in dark green, red and black, and covered the entire floor. He had never been in a space so painstakingly decorated. This was *not* what he expected, although he didn't know where his expectations originated, as he couldn't think of a specific movie where a character went inside a Swiss bank.

The tall thin young man with the tall thin haircut re-entered. He was carrying a small duffel bag, which he set down on the desk in front of him. "Are you sure you wouldn't like some coffee. We Swiss are good very good at coffee."

"No, no thank you."

"You will want to count that. I hope hundred-euro notes are satisfactory. I apologise for the carrier."

"That's fine. Thank you." He unzipped the bag. So this was eight hundred thousand euros. All he owned in the world. He probably should give Shelby her money, but the sooner she got it the sooner she'd be gone. He'd wait until Rome at least. "I see you like cats."

"What? Oh. No, I'm afraid I don't much care for them. Not at all. I collect art prints, and these are by Theophile Steinlen, who is Swiss. If this amount is satisfactory, please sign here. And I'll need to see your passport again." He hoped he hadn't offended him.

The rain had stopped completely and the sky had cleared to a deep purplish blue. The sun had dropped behind the crest of the island, and he could see a few lights from houses rising as they hugged the hill between the outlines of rocky cliffs that flanked both sides of the harbor. The hydrofoil cleared the jetty and slid sideways next to the quay, docking with a gentle bump. They were on Capri.

He rose quickly. Shelby looked up at him and, removing her earbuds from her ears, began to gather her things. He waited, and then hurried to the rear of the boat, where he took his suitcase, helped Shelby with hers, and walked (Shelby limping) down the ramp to the dock. It was surprisingly warm, almost spring-like, and the air was moist and sweet. He stopped when he reached the dock and breathed in heavily. He could hear music coming from someplace near the docks, and as they began to walk down the dock towards the town, he searched out Shelby's hand. He began to feel better.

The train compartment was certainly cramped, but for all that, still kind of nice, with rounded, Streamline Moderne curves, sleek horizontal lines with undecorated but stylish surfaces, and a drinks cabinet in the middle with an embossed ocean liner image in silver that folded up against the wall opposite the beds. He liked the way every inch of space was utilized, from the tiny folding sink in the corner to the folding bench creating the bottom bunk. He also liked the light green metallic walls, and the black cargo nets at the foot of each bunk. Shelby did care for any of this. There was only a single sleeping car available, which she found suspicious, and her dark doubt accompanied them, occupying half of the top bunk and much of the bottom, spilling out into the corner by the mirror and sink. She was "exhausted": didn't want to be touched fucked, talked to or even acknowledged. Without speaking, she had immediately climbed into the top bunk—where she quickly burrowed beneath the covers—undressed, placed her earbuds into her ears and one of the airplane sleep masks over her eyes, and turned to face the wall. He could see this in the mirror as he washed his face in the sink. He had purchased two small bottles of Chianti in the bar car, but recognized that any offer or other remark would be readily and completely absorbed and ignored by the nearly palpable mass of Shelby's bad mood and the armor of her headphones. After a quick flashback to another train trip with another relationship ~~although this wasn't really a relationship~~, he turned out the lights, sat back on the bottom bunk, opened one of the bottle of wine and waited for the train *~~Strangers On~~* rather than *~~Closely Watched~~* or *~~Brief Encounter~~* to start. They'd be in Rome in the morning.

A small electric flat-bed vehicle appeared, not quite the size of a golf cart. A man tipped his cap, climbed off and began to take Shelby's suitcase. "*Prego.*"

"Is this from the Hotel Scalinatella?"

"*Si, si, Hotel Scalinatella.*" He shrugged as the man loaded first Shelby's then his suitcase onto the back, then his duffel and Shelby's backpack. The man looked at Shelby and motioned to the folding chair next to the driver's seat. She laughed a little and climbed in and sat down. There were no other seats. "*Prego signore, prego.*" Through gestures and shrugs, he was made to understand that he was to sit in the back with the baggage. He shrugged and climbed aboard, facing the back. He held his duffle on his lap. The cart lurched forward, up a steep hill.

The ride up the hill was a bit harrowing. He felt lucky that the cart was underpowered, given the winding turns, abrupt switchbacks and frightening vertical drops. They passed three well-dressed middle aged women in tight slacks and high-heeled boots a couple of turns before the main road which ran along the top of a high ridge above the marina far down below. After hurrying through the main square they entered a narrow alley, with tiny shuttered boutiques and closed gelaterie on either side. A quick right down another small alley and in front of a darkened luxury hotel, he felt the sun, low over the horizon, on his face. The sun. ~~He turned and looked at Shelby, who, eyes closed, was letting the sun wash over her long blonde~~

~~hair.~~ He looked down from the ridge out to the sea and actually had to shield his eyes. The color was fantastic. The sky was a deep bluish purple, with pink smears against grey clouds floating above the muted slate-blue sea. A golden haze at the horizon hugged the horizon. Brown cliffs dominated the scene to his right, and in the center he could see numerous bright white structures, likely houses and hotels, along with a low terra cotta church. They hadn't seen anything except off-white, grey and dark blue since they'd arrived in Zurich. The sun felt good on his face.

The cart stopped abruptly and the driver began to unload the bags from the back of the cart. The lobby of the Hotel Scalinatella was the structure's top floor, with the guest floors, restaurant and pool descending the mountain beneath. The main floor was a white Moroccan riad, with a low crenellated roof, a wide keyhole arched door and a large medersa window trimmed in blue. Vacant patios with keyhole doors flanked either side of the entrance, and to his right he could see a staircase descending to the covered pool with stacks of lounge chairs, tables and umbrellas arranged neatly beneath the roof of the shuttered outdoor bar. Two three-foot Venetian stone lions guarded the entrance, and the words Hotel Scalinatella were spelled out in foot high iron letters above the keyhole. He hopped down, and they followed the driver through the arched entrance.

The lobby was luxurious and inviting. The floor was composed of deep white and Mediterranean blue marble tile. The walls were white, and sail vaults rose and fell gracefully overhead. A dark blue and deep crimson oriental runner led them directly to the white reception desk, with a thick blue curtain screening a small office niche behind. Round gold-framed bust portraits of Italian nobility decorated the walls, adding both color and variety. Two half tables, with marble tops and bases of gold painted wood carved into thin roman female figurines, flanked a white fabric couch with painted gold legs. Two matching chairs were arranged around a glass-topped table with a golden base in front of the couch, and two more matching chairs occupied another corner of the lobby, leading to the dark wooden bar, with its three accompanying dark wooden barstools.

"So this is Rome." These weren't the very first words she'd spoken since they'd gotten on the plane, but close. They were pulling their suitcases down a Termini platform, beneath a concrete awning, trying to avoid the ever-present rain. The platform was crowded, with various porters (with their red carts), carabinieri and just plain travelers moving at different speeds in both directions.

"I thought we'd stay at a nice hotel for a couple of days, see the sights, and then head down to Capri. Does that sound okay to you?"

"What hotel? Do they have a W here?"

"I don't know. I don't think so."

"I thought we'd go to the Hotel Excelsior ~~where Anita Eckberg got slapped around~~. It's four or five star, and right on the Via Veneto, *La Dolce Vita*. We'll stay there for a couple of nights, do some sight seeing, and then head south to Capri. Okay?"

She shrugged. "Sure. I could use some breakfast. That bread they gave us on train was beat."

"How does room service sound?"

A man in a nice dark suit approached. "Welcome Madame, welcome Sir, please welcome. We hope your stay at the Hotel Scalinatella will be most pleasant. My name is Michelangelo, and I am the concierge. If there is anything, anything at all I can provide for you, please do not hesitate to let me know. Unfortunately, only one of your rooms is presently prepared. We will certainly, as soon as possible, have both rooms ready for your occupancy. This is early, very early, really before the season starts, months before the season actually begins, a least two months before, and we still have not labored out all of the kinks, the bugs, the problems. when it comes to staffing. And arranging. So please accept my apologies. Apologies from the heart. I assume Madame will want the room that is currently prepared. Would you like to freshen up, Madame? And sir, would you like a drink? While Madame freshens? I would be happy to offer you a drink, free of charge, to make up for this difficulty. Madame, if you follow Davide here, he will show you to your room. And sir, if you step this way, I would be more than happy to provide you with a beverage. Maybe a glass of wine? We have some very nice wine local wine, and by local I mean from Napoli. The Napoli area, *il Campania*. Not the city itself of course, there are no vines in the city. An old proverb. We have an excellent *rosso*. Very nice, very nice. Please please. Sit at the bar and tell me your wish."

Shelby stayed in her room at the *Westin* Excelsior while he went for a walk. He started north and turned around at Harry's Bar. He passed the *Café Strega, Ristornate Antonello, Asador* and *Café Veneto,* and, arriving at the Excelsior again, continued down the hill past some nameless hotel, until he reached the Boscolo Palace and the Hard Rock Café. This was the Via Veneto? It was unrecognizable. He knew that Fellini had built a model at Cinecittà, but still. It had been a while since had had seen the film, but he always considered *La Dolce Vita* one of his favorites. This was a scene that could be in Denver, or San Francisco anyway. Except for the weaponry. First of all, the street was nearly fucking abandoned. It was a cold and rainy evening, but only six thirty, and the only people he could see were various soldiers and policemen in assorted colored uniforms, crouching in the doorways or gathered under awning, smoking silently, their submachine guns visible beneath their capes or coats. One or two black-jacketed waiters made appearances in doorways, but seemed too tired or hopeless to offer welcoming smiles or any sort of acknowledgement or invitation. The outdoor tables and chairs of the cafés, which had seemed so exotic and wonderful in the film, belonging to an age and culture that the Pueblo boy could only dream of, were all enclosed in thick terrariums of glass, and were dark and deserted. He peered into the glass of the cube in front of the *Café de Paris*. There was no light, and the chairs were stacked on top of one another like the unused corner of a high school cafeteria.

A couple of those tiny little Smart cars zoomed by, as well as one or two scooters decked out in elaborate rain gear, but the street itself was merely a conduit, a way of getting from one place to another. No one was trolling, no one was slowing down, peering out of windows wanting to see and be seen. There were no convertibles, and no one was wearing sunglasses.

He sat at the bar, duffle in his lap, and watched Shelby disappear through a small doorway to his right. She looked back at him and smiled. Michelangelo appeared before him on the other side of the bar. He had forgotten to tip the driver. "Please, please, what would you like? American whisky? Heineken beer? Anything you see. On the house, on the house. It is my pleasure. To show how honestly sorry I am for the inexcusable delay. Please, sit."

"It's ok, it's ok. What's in those bottles there? The ones with the long necks?"

"Grappa. It is Italian brandy. But earthier. More *terroir* as the French say. Some like the taste very much. Others do not. It is produced from the emptied skins and other pieces of the grapes that remain after they are crushed for wine. These pieces are distilled, and the type of grape determines the taste of the grappa. As I've have said, some like this very much, while others find the taste too vigorous." He shrugged and looked around. "We do not drink it before dinner. Perhaps some wine, or whisky?"

The grappa looked inviting, but he certainly didn't want to be some hick from the sticks, so he'd wait until after dinner. "I'll try the local red."

Michelangelo produced a large red burgundy glass from nowhere, placed in front of him, and poured a healthy drink of beautiful deep claret liquid. "This is a very nice *rosso*. It tastes something like strawberries. Subtle, yes, and not sweet, but nice. I will pour you a nice glass. See if you like it. A drink can relax one, no? It is important to relax, especially while on Capri. Islands are made for relaxation. Please."

It was good, ~~but it didn't taste like strawberries~~. "This is very nice. Thank you."

"*Si, si*, I'm glad you like it. Yes, islands are made for relaxation. You will see that about Capri. Although you have arrived months before the season, and months before the relaxation can truly begin. The island is nearly deserted until Easter. But no, we are not like Napoli. We are made for relaxing. In Napoli, it is impossible to relax. Roma and Milano are very active as well, but Napoli is crazy. In Napoli, no one can relax, not even a saint. I lived in Napoli for three years, and now, do you know how many times I've been back? Do you have a guess?"

He took another sip and shook his head.

"Never. I have never been back. And I don't want to go back to Napoli. You know, when I take the boat, I take it to Sorrento. I do not like Napoli."

"Would you like to join me?"

He shook his head and looked down. "No, I am very sorry, but I cannot." He stood straight, his arms folded in front of him. The resemblance to Buster Keaton was remarkable.

He sat in the corner of the opulent dining room, all gray walls, white chandeliers and parquet floors, with a plate full of prosciutto, melon and small delicate pastries filled with custard. He was alone, except for an older waiter who appeared every ten minutes or so to straighten out one of the chafing dishes of the buffet. The melon and prosciutto were delicious ~~as well they should be, given how much the two rooms of the hotel were costing him~~. The table linen was a light grey, as was the wood of the Queen Ann chairs, and the seats and backs, as well as the cushions of the scattered *méridienne* and *récamier* strewn about, were upholstered the color of blood oranges. The setting dwarfed him: the long rectangular room boasted thirty foot ceilings, and on each of the long sides a faux peristyle balcony appeared twenty or so feet above. On one of the long walls, full-size bas-relief classical figures cut from the plaster enjoyed wine and grapes, while the opposite wall was made up entirely of eight large panes of plate glass, against which rain was pelting heavily.

He felt self-conscious eating alone, and although they hadn't been getting along, he wished Shelby would come down to join him, or at least that he had a newspaper or something to study. Like magic ~~on cue~~ she appeared across the room near the grand piano. She walked in few steps toward the buffet and hesitated. He half stood and waved, and she waved and moved toward him. He stood and pulled out the chair to his right.

"Good morning."

"Hello. I couldn't see you in this crowd."

She had her golden hair pulled back, and she looked good, refreshed, the skin on her face smooth and her brown eyes bright. He wondered what mood she was in. "Did you sleep well?"

"I slept ok." She smiled and they both sat down.

"Do you want coffee? They brought me a whole carafe."

"Love some. Need some." She lifted her cup to him and he poured.

"They'll also make cappuccino for you. Anything you want, I imagine."

"Is this cream?"

"Yes." She poured, stirred and sipped. "This is good."

He watched her drink her coffee. "Do you want to walk down to the Trevi Fountain? It's not too far from here, and it's beautiful and famous. We can play tourists."

"Have you seen it before?"

"Yeah, when I was here earlier. ~~With my wife.~~"

"Sure."

"We could go to the Coliseum and the Forum too. I don't know how interested you are in ancient monuments. Or we could go to some art museums. Or even the Vatican."

"Where is the stuff you wanted to see?"

"A suburb called EUR. We can get there by subway."

"Let's go to the Fountain, and then I might head out on my own for a few hours." She smiled, took a sip of her coffee, and then rose from her chair. "I think I'll hit the buffet. If the waiter comes out, ask him for more coffee. Do you want anything else?"

"No, I'll probably go back to the buffet." He leaned forward and lowered his voice. "When we finish breakfast I'll give you your money."

"What brings you to the island, Sir? Do you mind me asking? I hope I am not intrusive. Perhaps you are here on business. Or as a tourist? Capri is very beautiful, always, but especially in the spring. Winter, not as beautiful, but today is a very nice day. It is usually very cold and with lots of wind, and the sea is not smooth, not smooth at all. But today, a strange day, a day with strange, calm weather. You are lucky. Days like this are very rare, almost as rare as snow. And we never have snow. I have, of course, seen snow. I have been skiing in the Italian Alps. Very nice. But this weather, it is as strange as snow."

"We're here to see the Casa Malaparte."

"You are a writer? An architect? It is a beautiful house, very stylish and intelligent. It fits Capri well. Casa Malaparte. *Casa comme mi.* Did you know that the owner of the house, Curzio Malaparte, changed his name? No, he was not born Malaparte: he had a German name, Kurt Suckert, and he changed his name as a joke against Napoleon. Bonaparte, from good parts, Malaparte, from the bad. Have you read his books? They are grim, but strangely beautiful, this man from the bad parts. He designed the house himself. Yes, it is true. He had the famous architect, Adalberto Librera, draw a few ideas down, sketch some ideas for the house, but *Signore* Malaparte made the actual design, with all the distances, the details and measurements, himself. I do not know how much of the idea for the shape was Librera's and how much Malaparte's, but Malaparte drew all of the details, all of the lengths and the widths and the heights, as well as the materials. Librera was more famous, so he received all of the applause. But if you are an architect, you know this already. "

They entered the square from the church side, having walked down Via Veneto and through the small alley-like tourist streets, their large Excelsior umbrellas protecting them from the cold winter rain. The square was crowded: the terrace surrounding the fountain ringed with large and small umbrellas, thick down jackets and raincoats two or three deep. A group of forty or so ten-year old schoolchildren lined the steps in the center, all in lime green ponchos with matching lime green hats. One of the children's minders, who sported the green hat but not the poncho, was shouting Italian into a cell phone over the roar of the fountain and the chattering of the crowd. They walked quickly to the railing where the crowd had thinned, just to the right of the children. The rain continued.

He looked at Shelby. She was bareheaded and ponytailed, and the rain glistened in her hair. He turned his gaze back to the fountain, to the four large Corinthian columns with unfluted shafts defining the structure of the façade. He focused on the center exedra housing the main statue of Neptune, standing on a shell chariot, glancing down to his right, to one of the two tritons with accompanying winged seahorses pulling his *bigae* along. He thought of Anita Ekberg and her kitty, and poor Marcello searching for milk in the deserted early morning. What did Marcello want? Sex? It had to be more than that. Didn't it?

The roar of the water cascading from the base of Neptune's chariot was more than matched by the giggles and shouts of the schoolchildren, the culinary and logistical questions of the tourists who spoke English and the general murmurs and mutterings of the tourists who did not. A group of high school kids had positioned a boombox under the outcropping of rocks on the far left, and appeared to be breakdancing on a wet piece of cardboard. What did Marcello want? It was hard to concentrate. He turned to look at Shelby.

"We should get in."

"What?"

"We should get into the fountain. You first, and I'll follow."

"What are you talking about?"

"It would be great. You go in, under the waterfall there in the center, and I'll come in after you." She looked at him for a moment, her eyes searching for something in his face. Suddenly she smiled, and turned to carefully make her down the stairs, stopping once to look back at him. She collapsed the umbrella and placed it behind her, then slowly removed her coat. He started to walk down the steps as she turned back and hung her coat over the railing. He was a foot or so away when she stepped over the rim into the water.

"So, what do you think?"

"I can't hear you."

He leaned toward her. "What did you think?"

She shrugged. "It's beautiful."

"Yeah, Roman fountains are amazing. Did you ever see *La Dolce Vita*?"

"~~Of course. I adore that film.~~ No."

"There's a tradition that if you throw coins into the fountain, you're guaranteed to return to Rome"

"I'm getting cold."

"Should we throw some coins in?"

"No, I'm not an architect. I'm a professor." He grinned to himself. "Of film."

"Oh yes, Jean-Luc Godard. Jack Palance. Fritz Lang. Brigitte Bardot. Ooh la la. Bellissima." He began to make that up and down curving motion with both of his hands and then abruptly stopped. "Yes yes, a fine film, a very fine film. My father met Mr. Godard. And Miss Bardot as well. He was the caretaker of the house when they arrived, sometime in 1962. It was a big time, yes it was a very big time for Capri. I was a small child, and I remember all of the men crowding around the dock, trying to see a glance of BB, trying to make BB see them and smile at them. Even the old men, crowding around, yelling 'BB, BB' and smiling, showing their muscles."

"So it's close by?"

He stopped and shook his head sadly. "The Casa, *signore*, it is difficult to see. The foundation who owns it, they keep it locked tight. They don't want visitors. They open it up once or twice a year for students. But no more." He continued shaking his head, then reached down and poured him another drink. "There are iron gates to block off the paths. You can see it from a distance: you walk right down the *Via Tragare*, the path in front of the hotel. This will narrow into a smaller pathway, the *Pizzolungo*. You keep walking, past the big rocks, The *Faraglione*, and ten, fifteen minutes later you look down toward the sea and you will see it. I hope you have not come to Capri for nothing." He looked down at his watch. "If you begin very soon, you will still have the light to see it from the pathway."

"Is that all? I can't get in? Are you sure?" ~~Another wild goose chase.~~

"*Si si*, I am very sure. My father was caretaker for fifteen years. The foundation is very secretive: they want to keep it out of the eyes of the public."

He had an idea. "Does your father still caretake?"

"No. My father is no longer living," he made the sign of the cross with his right hand. He face looked even sadder than before.

"I am sorry." ~~Fucking A.~~

"Yes. Yes."

He walked up the subway stairs and found himself facing a sheep pasture. Well, not directly a sheep pasture: he faced a small BP gas station and then a rolling pasture of sixty or so well tended black and white sheep, grazing stolidly in the rain. This was the last subway stop, but he hadn't expected sheep. To the right he noticed a huge concrete office building, and some sort of low barracks toward the horizon. Nothing here but the sticks. He turned around to face the road.

Cinecittà. The rose stucco H-shaped entrance building glistened in the rain, its ruby metallic letters standing out like neon. Cinema City. City of Dreams.

How the fuck was he going to cross the street? Small cars and trucks zoomed by without respite, along with various scooters and motorcycles. He saw the red metro sign to the left of the entrance: he'd taken the wrong exit from the station. He quickly descended the stairs, crossed under and ascended to the front of the entrance. The rain seemed harder on this side of the street. He hesitated, and peered in around the corner. He recognized it from *Intervista*. He could see two driveways leading to dropgates with occupied glass and metal guard shacks, and a full parking lot behind. Behind the lot were tress, and he could see buildings of the lot further back. That was the soundstage of *Cleopatra*, perhaps, or *Satyricon*, or even the construction of the *Via Venuto fugazi*. Fellini and Ganni di Venanzo must have walked through the gates, arguing film speed for *8½*. Or maybe Venanzo and Antonioni, discussing the lighting of the scene of Mastroianni and Moreau rolling around in the dirt. Maybe that near building was the script office, where Cesare Zavettini worked on *The Garden of the Fitzi-Continis*, or Marco Ferreri on *La Grande Bouffe*. He crept further in, under the roof, and folded up his umbrella.

He wondered if they'd let him in. What would he say? Maybe if he just walked purposively, head up and eyes straight ahead, he'd seem like he was somebody and the gates would magically open. Yeah right. For some reason he thought of *The Great Escape*. Or maybe if he talked to the guards, explained who he was. But who was he? He had no ID and no credentials, and he didn't speak Italian. He could try a bribe, but only had about a hundred euros on him, and he didn't want to insult anyone. He wasn't sure he had the balls to pull off a bribe anyway.

Hugging the wall, he inched forward. He could see a pedestrian gate to the far left, with a turnstile and an unoccupied booth. Maybe he could hop it and run into the building behind, although it would probably be wise to avoid an Italian arrest, what with extradition being what it was. Keeping his umbrella to his side, he leaned forward out from underneath the top of the passageway. A limousine passed him from the street, stopped at the gate closest to him, and was quickly waved through.

Who was in the back of that limo? Was Carlo Ponti still alive? Those black bushy eyebrows and that bald head, Sophia Loren on his arm. Or Georges de Beauregard: dead for years now, and more French than Italian. Maybe one of the di Larentiis's, maybe all of them, packed into the limo's back seat, although Dino must be eighty by now. *Barbarella* wasn't bad, but everything else was schlocky crap. Maybe Mankiewicz, with his pipe. Alberto Grimaldi, that would be cool. He liked *Salò*, and *The Decameron*. "Why create a work of art, when dreaming about it is so much sweeter?" Indeed. Ah, mama Roma. He hoped that it was Grimaldi in that limo.

"*Scusi, scusi signore.*"

Fuck. A guard had spotted him and was walking toward him, motioning to him to leave.

"*Scusi signore, scusi.*"

"Okay, okay."

No joy. He unfurled his umbrella and turned quickly to go.

Maybe they could take that walk now. There might be same way to climb a fence or something, although a Capri arrest was probably no better than a Roman. He looked at the doorway through which Shelby had disappeared. ~~Hurry up.~~ He looked down at the bag in his lap. "Can I put this in the hotel safe?" He finished his wine and started to stand up.

The subway ride was quicker than he expected, and he soon found himself walking up the steps of the *EUR Palasport* subway station. *The Illustrated Man* rain continued, and the sky was low and dark. He bounded up the marble stairs and looked out upon a small lake, surrounded by grass and bare trees, with square office building in the background. This was the lake that the car thief drove into in Antonioni's *L'Eclisse*. If he had time, he'd see if he could find Monica Vitti's house.

He looked around and checked his map. Lots of office buildings and lots and lots of cars. He was searching for the *Palazzo dei Congressi*, where Bertolucci had filmed much of *The Conformist*, and where some of *La Dolce Vita* had been shot. The concierge told him to walk away from the lake on *Via Cristofo Colombo*, and so he turned and walked toward what appeared to be a main road, then crossed the street left. He walked against the rain for a couple of blocks, and then spied an odalisque a couple of blocks away. The palazzo should be further down to his right. Soon he stood in front of a large white rectangular building, with a colonnade of fourteen Tuscan columns supporting an entablature into which the words PALAZZO DEI CONGRESSI were carved clearly. A smaller half-domed rectangle rose above the flat roof, featuring a balcony jutting uselessly from the center of its sheer white wall. The colonnade was fronted by ten concrete steps running the entire length, and a small square, protected by a ring of soup-can sized traffic barriers, defined the approach to the steps. It didn't ring any bells, but it was pretty cool. He decided to explore.

He walked up the stairs quickly until he reached the shelter of the portico, where ten more steps led to the glass doors of the entrance. Without folding his umbrella, he walked up and tried one of the locked doors. He cupped his hands and looked through the glass, and saw a severe cuboid foyer, with ten carrera marble doorways on the opposite wall and two rectangular balustrades surrounding staircase openings on either side of the foyer. The ceiling was high, rising at least forty feet. The floor was made up of black marble tile and the end walls were white carrera. The opposite wall featured a large fresco of a woman in a red robe and big eyes with various Roman buildings (he recognized St. Peter's and The Coliseum) in the background. He tried a couple of doors, and the third swung open. He hesitated, closed his umbrella and walked inside.

He moved over to one of the balustrades and looked around the room. He thought he recognized the atmosphere of *The Conformist*, the feeling of being eclipsed by the setting, rendered insignificant by the cold marble, geometric lines and inhuman scale. But he couldn't recall anything specifically being filmed in that foyer. He felt he was getting close, but there was nothing he had experienced yet that he could match to definite images he could recollect from Bertolucci's film. He wished he could take a picture of the foyer to maybe later compare when he watched the film again. But he didn't have a camera. ~~Nor did he have any photographs of his family or his friends. He'd left everything back at the Colorado ranch. He had nothing left to conform to.~~

He'd definitely need to pick up a camera somewhere. He looked down and noticed a puddle on the black floor from his dripping umbrella. He didn't know if this was a public building or not, didn't know if he should be there. He moved quickly to the door opposite the glass entrance directly below the woman in the red robe.

It was almost dark, and they were following Michelangelo and his large flashlight down a gently sloping, paved path. The path was smooth and well marked, with a short brick and stone guard fence on their right. He could hear the deep rumble of the Mediterranean below. They had passed the silhouettes of two large looming outcrops of rock (The *Faraglione*) about ten minutes ago. A seagull screamed, and when he looked down, he could see the contrast of the grey rocks with the black water. The air smelled woodsy, with a salty underscent. Michelangelo was muttering to himself in ~~what sounded like~~ Italian in a small but excited whisper, a whisper continuous since they had left the hotel. They had to move slowly, as Shelby's ankle still bothered. They came to a stop beneath a pine tree. "This is it. The Casa Malaparte. We will go down these stairs until we come to an iron gate. The house is further on, just over that line of rocks." They walked down twelve or so stairs, and made a hairpin turn to their left. The path narrowed, forcing them into single file. And there it was, the house, nestled into the *punta*, its outlines unmistakable even in the fading light. His heart skipped a beat. There was the little bay where BB dived naked into the water, her body mysterious and beautiful, but forever inaccessible to Piccoli's sorrowful gaze. He remembered it as a medium shot, Bardot's body more suggested than detailed, inaccessible to all.

He entered a large, empty cube, with a high, cross-vaulted dome rising about a hundred and twenty five feet from the floor. All four sides of the cube were ringed by three floors of open arcades, in grey carrera marble with black metal railings around the top two. X's of slanted staircases, grey marble with accompanying black railings, three to each side of the cube, were placed symmetrically above each other on all three floors. Above the marble, perforated gold-orange metallic walls ascended until they met the windows of the arch that supported the dome. Dark grey clouds obscured much of the natural light, and the cube was filled with a murky, abandoned air.

He looked up, and walked to the very center of the cube, directly underneath the point of the dome. He stood there for a moment, and then looked around. He liked the angles and design of the marble arcades, with the geometry of the staircases and the severity of the railings. The symmetry, the scale and some of the materials, they did remind him of *The Conformist*. It was close, but still, there was nothing specific here, nothing present or real that he could definitely attach to an image from the film.

~~It was weird. Film gave the illusion of travel, or being somewhere else, while architecture *was* that somewhere else. Movies put him in a different place: in a black marble office of fascist Italy, in the streets of Rome after a coup, in the covered passageways of the Coliseum hiding for his life. But architecture brought him back to the present, to the here and now, and made such travel impossible. Visiting a place in real life didn't ruin the experience of seeing it in a movie, just as seeing a place in a movie didn't ruin the experience of seeing it in real life. But the two things were difficult to reconcile.~~ He walked over to the one of the sides of the cube and put his hand on the cool marble. ~~No, architecture didn't ruin film, or visa versa, but the two experiences were incompatible: one was the negation of the other. Film was representation, was transformation, was flight, while architecture was presentation, was formation, was stasis. To visit a place after seeing it in a film was bound to be disappointing, as the film naturally transformed the place into someplace else. There was never room for both presentation (architecture) and representation (film) in the same location: one or the other had to withdraw. Another name for this withdrawal, either by the architecture or by the film, was disappointment.~~

~~Substitute the word "life" for the word "architecture," and for "film," the word "imagination." Maybe.~~ It was time to go.

They stopped again. A large semicircular iron gate barred the path. Michelangelo rattled some keys from his pocket, examined them under the flashlight's beam, and and tried one, then two. "The lock is sure, but small." He finally unlocked the padlock, swung the gate open, motioned for them to proceed, and closed it behind them. He scurried out in front of them, and they followed. They were still high above the house. They followed a set of switchbacks as the descent grew a little steeper. His excitement was building with every step. Godard walked down this path, Lang walked down this path, Bardot walked down this path, Jack Palance, Michel Piccoli. Through the trees he caught a glimpse of the famous staircase to the roof, just to his right and below. After the fiascos of Rome ~~The Hard Rock Café~~, he'd never thought he'd actually get to visit a place like this, a place so important to his imagination. And yet in five minutes he'd be bounding up those steps, or walking through that small side door and into the salon with the long low furniture and large picture windows. Maybe it all had been worth it. Not the killing ~~necessarily~~, although except for Glow, the bodies in the Pueblo ranchhouse weren't the remains of productive or even potentially valuable human beings: they were the lives of bad, stupid, greedy and destructive animals. No, the only life he wasted was his own. But being here, at the Casa Malaparte, well, maybe his life wasn't so worthless after all. Maybe he still had hope. He hoped that little window underneath the mantle near the floor was still there: he imagined bending down and showing it to Shelby.

He wondered what she was thinking, if she was having a good time or was just humoring him, counting the minutes until she could split, to Paris and shopping and then back to Arizona, where she'd have some cash and a good story to tell. Or not. This hadn't been exactly easy for her, and like she had said, she hadn't asked to be kidnapped and raped. Still, she wasn't completely innocent, as Lizzie's corpse with that hole in her cheek would attest. He had no idea if she would recover quickly or not, or even if recover was the right word. The money would help, and she seemed resilient enough, but he didn't think she would exactly profit from the experience. He thought again of the porter he hadn't tipped.

The trees suddenly parted, and they were about thirty feet above the house. The sea's low tone was louder, but still benign, soothing almost. The salt scent was much stronger. He noticed a small chicken coop to his left. He had to stop himself from running. Michelangelo turned to face them. "Would you like to go to the terrace? You must be careful, the wind can be strong. And there are no railings."

"Sure."

"Let's go inside."

Her ankle. He'd go up there tomorrow, where he could see the staircase and the surroundings more clearly. He nodded.

"Inside it is."

They moved quickly down a few stairs to the small landing on their right. He placed his left hand on the rough plaster wall and then leaned his back against it. Just like that translator in the film, what was her name, the one who followed Palance around? The brunette? She was no Bardot but wasn't bad either. Michelangelo quickly scampered up the porch stairs, unlocked the iron gate and the wooden door and stood, waiting for them to go inside. He hesitated, then followed. As he passed Michelangelo he could see his mouth moving, and could just make out a stream of language above the low and now stronger rhythm of the sea.

"The salon is upstairs. There are bedrooms downstairs, something like a dormitory. I believe art students stay here rarely. Would you like to have a glance downstairs?"

"The salon."

Michelangelo opened the door and flicked on a lamp.

It hadn't changed. It was a long rectangular space, severe and angular, but familiar, comfortable, welcoming. Some of the furniture had been rearranged, of course, and the couches and chairs were no longer bright blue but covered in white, but the four large picture windows were still there, and the fireplace with its low stone bench in front, and that concrete bench opposite against the wall. And the walls were still museum white, and floor, made up of large, irregular stones, was only slightly darker. He walked quickly to sit on the bench in front of the fireplace, in part to test the reality, and in part to see if that small window still existed. The bench was hard, solid, present, and as he bent down, he could see the darkness outside through the small square glass, and the sea below, the faint lines of grey waves on the dark water. He got up and walked over to the far left window, the one furthest out on the point. He could see his reflection in the glass as he approached, and smiled to himself and he touched the window with the fingertips of both hands. He stared out: the dark water surrounded him, with the rocky coastline off in the distance to his right. He stepped back, and again saw his reflection in the middle of the salon of the Casa Malaparte, with the stone bench and the fireplace in the background.

The concierge informed him that Signora Shelby had gone out to the Hard Rock Café, and started to give him directions, but he turned on his heels and walked out before he could finish. The Hard Rock Café. Fucking perfect.

The place was packed. He was greeted by a table of eight twenty-something Germans, faces beefy and red, who sat in front of large plates of brown food and big glasses of beer, laughing and talking loudly with greasy chins and wide mouths. Three middle-aged men with hard Australian accents hovered near the hostess station, laughing and talking about "Sheila's," "a map of Tassie" and "a frostie and a feature." A group of young boys, sixteen to eighteen he guessed, ate pizza, drank soda, and watched a soccer match on TV. He quickly scanned the room: the last thing he wanted to do was to have to walk around like a lost puppy looking for his mistress. ~~Fuck her. If she wanted to hang with the United Asshole Nations, she could be his guest. He'd go to the hotel or someplace a little more authentic to get his drunk.~~ He considered leaving, but gave the place another quick scan. To his left, a long room was filled with assorted tee shirts, wall clocks, jackets and other paraphernalia. Somehow, he didn't think Shelby the type for a forty euro Willie Nelson do rag. Was that "More Than a Feeling" in the background?

He turned to the bar side. There was a passageway to his left, but he decided to check out the bar more carefully first. And there she was, shot glasses and a large plate in front of her, chatting up the bartender. He was too old for this. He plowed his way to the bar.

She was sitting next to the waitress station, with a thin hippie guy with long straggly blonde hair chewing on a hamburger to the other side. The bartender gave him a dirty look as he sidled up next to her on the waitress station side.

"Hello."

She turned to him and smiled. "Hey. How'd did your sight-seeing go?"

"It was all right. I didn't get into the movie studio, and it was raining everywhere. We can go to Capri tomorrow."

"Lemme you introduce you to the bartender. Gio, this is the Professor. Professor, Gio."

Gio looked daggers at him. "Giovanni. You want drink? Budweiser?"

Could this get any worse? "~~Sorry to break up your party, pal.~~ No, I don't want a Budweiser. What's that Italian beer?"

"Peroni."

"I'll take a Perini. A big one."

"Peroni. You want Peroni, which is not so strong, or Nastro, which is stronger?"

"The stronger."

"You want a menu?"

He looked down at Shelby's half-eaten salad. "Do you want to go someplace else?"

"No, I'm still working on my salad. Why don't you grab a burger or something, and then we'll see." She leaned toward him and stage whispered in his ear. "Do you want a shot or something? Gio's been buying me shots of Patrón." Her breath smelled like lemons and peppers. All of a sudden he was back in Pueblo.

The perfect ending to a perfect day.

"Yeah, sure I'll have a shot. But I'll buy it. Couple shots of Patrón please, and one for yourself. And a menu."

He heard a door close and turned around. Shelby sat alone on the windowsill of the picture window kitty corner from him. She shrugged. "He said to lock the door when we leave and bring him the key."

She took a drink from a glass in her hand. He walked across the stone floor to the table near the door, took the wine bottle and poured himself a glass. He then sat down next to her on the windowsill.

"You look pretty happy."

He took a sip of his wine.

"I guess I am."

~~She leaned over to kiss him. He could feel her lips brush against his, and again, and then her mouth opened and her tongue gently explored his as she put her arms around his neck.~~

She leaned over to kiss him. He could feel her lips brush against his, and again, and then her mouth opened and her tongue gently explored his as she put her arms around his neck.

~~She leaned over to kiss him. He could feel her lips brush against his, and again, and then her mouth opened and her tongue gently explored his as she put her arms around his neck.~~

Contempt

Jean-Luc Godard (1963)

"And my knees, too?"
"I really like your knees."
"And my thighs?"
"Your thighs, too."
"Do you think I have a cute ass?"
"Really."
"Shall I get on my knees?"
"No need to."
"And my breasts. You like them?"
"Yes, tremendously."
"Gently, Professor. Not so hard."
"Sorry."
"Which do you like better, my breasts, or my nipples?"
"I don't know. I like them the same."
"You like my shoulders?"
"I don't think they're round enough."
"And my face?"
"Your face, too."
"All of it? My mouth, my eyes, my nose, my ears?"
"Yes, everything."

When he woke on the couch in the cold light, a sheet wrapped around his body, he knew immediately that Shelby had left for good. He could dress quickly, try to catch her at the ferry, but that would be awkward and ridiculous, and likely useless. The sex notwithstanding, and he was grateful for the sex, he had no arguments for why she should stay with him. She had a life that she had to return to, a life of partying, studying, whatever else coeds did these days. She possessed a future, a career, relationships, maybe babies or whatever with that architect. And what did he have? Eight hundred thousand euros, a fake passport and at least one person trying to kill him.

"Sentiment is a luxury few women allow themselves."

He stood up, shivered, and wrapped the sheet tighter around him. He walked to the nearest picture window, the one across from the fireplace closest to the entrance door. Clouds had arrived overnight, and the sky was low, thick and grey, with a few scattered streaks of gold and pink. The sea had changed too, and roiled violently against the sharp rocks across the small bay to the north, the spray rising high into the grey morning air. He noticed his vague outline in the window glass, sheet wrapped around his body. He thought of Bardot and Piccoli, walking around in towels and robes, ready to fuck or fight. But that was in Paris, not Capri. He wondered what Piccoli did after Bardot left him and crashed. Maybe he opened up a factory in Switzerland, married Hanna Schygulla, and allowed a Polish film director to stage living reenactments of Rembrandt's *Nightwatch* in his factory to the strains of a late Beethoven quartet. He needed to get dressed, as he wanted to climb the stairs to the roof, and hoped the wind wasn't too strong and it wasn't too cold. He was in no hurry to do anything else.

It was strange that he felt so at home in the large white rectangular salon with the covered furniture and picture windows staring out into the now turbulent sea. He hadn't felt so peaceful in such a long time: not in Pueblo, certainly, what with the drug lab, the gang and his parents. And not in prison, no, not prison. And when he was with Connie, there was always that pressure to get a job, establish his career and bring some money in somehow. In grad school it was all about getting out trying to get things published and go to conferences, and as an undergrad, it was the grades and going to pharmacy school. In high school it was about trying to protect his mother while getting the fuck out of Dodge. Always someplace else. It was only in that little TV room in the library, smelling slightly of the sour apple Jolly Ranchers he'd smuggled in, sitting in the dark and watching Peter Lorre tug at the corners of his mouth, Susan Hayward dance at a party and Jean Belmondo smoke—*that* was the only place he felt safe, at ease, comfortable, like the immediate world wasn't arrayed, either by design or chance, against him. That small dark room in the Pueblo library, and here.

That was pretty pathetic, wasn't it? Where would he be without movies, *sans le cinéma*? He wouldn't be here, that was for sure. Without *Contempt*, he'd never have heard of the Casa Malaparte. He'd be working at a drug store somewhere, maybe even in Pueblo, earning a good living, married with a couple of kids, taking care of his mom. No tragic career path, no disastrous marriage, no prison term, no meth lab and no multiple homicides. He'd have some authentic connection with other people, some genuine relationship with the real world.

"Ok, But when do we get the real things?"
"When we want. These are the deeds."
"I want everything now."

Instead of having every thing, every feeling and every experience filtered through the lens of film. And sometimes, often, he wasn't sure there was a real world. Or, to be more precise, the world of film was infinitely more interesting and comfortable than the factual situations in which he found himself. It would be nice just to live in the world, immediate and free, and able to enjoy his wife, his children and his surroundings. It wouldn't be much of a story, this happy Colorado pharmacist. But this wasn't much of a story either. Or it was a story without an audience. An audience of one.

"Cinema does not cry, does not cry over us. It does not comfort us, because it is with us, because it is us."

But he couldn't even imagine such a life. It was impossible to forget, to erase, to unlearn, to *not see*. Once he had the combination of image, music, action and character that film was in his head he couldn't shed it if he wanted to. How could anyone forget anything?

How was it possible to forget Anna Karina, Franz and Arthur doing the café dance?

"Parenthetically, now's the time to describe their feelings. Arthur watches his feet, but thinks of Odile's mouth and her romantic kisses. Odile wonders if the boys notice her breasts moving as she dances. Franz thinks of everything and nothing."

Or the *High and Low* killer in the mirror shades, staggering through Dope Alley? Or Widmark's giggle? Or Dorothy Malone's hands caressing that miniature oil derrick? Kinski in a white suit surrounded by brown jungle Indians? How could he erase the image of the young boy's hand on the blurry projected image of Ullmann's face? Deborah Kerr's voice? Gleason's embarrassed eyes? Marcello's shrug on the beach, Veronika Voss' song? These were more authentic to him than any geographical home.

Nish had asked him once, "Why you such a hater on Pueblo? It's your hometown." *This* was his home, as much as any place else. He looked around at the sea spray rising above the rocks. This was real: he could feel the cool tile under his feet and the cool glass on his fingertips, where his breath fogged the window in front of him. This was real, but reality wasn't enough.

He padded through the salon to the bedroom, and then into the bathroom. The walls were made of beautiful vertically striped grey and white marble, rising six feet from the marble floor, topped with two feet of white plaster and a white plaster ceiling. The tub was of the same striped marble, and was set off in a small recess with a showerhead set into the plaster, centered. The sink was just to the left of the tub, and was carved into the crown of a two-foot white stub of a fluted marble column. He didn't see this in *Contempt*. He moved over to the mirror and looked at himself, letting the sheet fall off his shoulders to the floor. As he turned to take a piss, he heard a telephone ring somewhere below.

"At the cinema, we do not think, we are thought."

He shrugged, washed his hands in the sink, and went back to the salon, where he gathered his things and dressed quickly. His mind was a bit muddled from the *rosso* and jet lag: he could use some coffee and something to eat. He'd noticed a small kitchen last night near the stairs to the door, but didn't want to go rooting around. He wondered what time it was. He wondered who'd phoned. Shelby? Probably Michelangelo. He didn't want to leave.

He hurried out the down the stairs and out the door, then down the five steps to the landing, where he stood and faced the large rocks, the *Faraglioni*. The waves were battering this seaward side of the *punta* as well, and he could just feel a fine mist on his face from the crashing below. The air smelled heavily of saltwater, and was thick and moist. A deep, visceral rhythm dominated the morning, drowning out the birdsong and other superficial noises. The metal gate swung sharply against the plaster: the wind was strong but not impossible, although he would have to watch his step on the roof. He looked out to the sea, past the waves breaking violently on the rocks, and noticed the horizon darkening. He'd better hurry.

He scurried up the patio stairs to the base of the grand staircase to the roof. He looked up, and then began his ascent. He climbed the steps slowly, one at a time, moving toward the center as the staircase fanned. The wind was picking up a little, and he shivered. Thirty-two steps, more than he imagined.

He finally reached the top, and moved quickly to the left of the white plaster screen. He stopped and looked to his right: that was where BB lay naked on the towel, but he didn't want to think about that now. Instead, he walked rapidly to the far edge of the terrace. He could make out the outlines of the Sorrento peninsula to his left, and in front and to his right the Mediterranean opened out. If he remembered correctly, this was the final shot of the film, the tranquil sky blue sea, and then the word "Silence," followed by its translation, "*Silenzio.*" The sea wasn't sky blue: it was dark purple, and it certainly wasn't placid, it was agitated with whitecaps. Nor was it silent, as the violent meeting of water on rock reverberated from his left, his right and below. Lang described the scene as Ulysses gazing upon Ithaca as he returned home, but the film portrayed neither the gaze not the homeland, but simply the water. He stared out.

He walked out to the very edge. He thought about the conversation Piccoli and Lang had about Ulysses as they walked down the path to the house, about how Ulysses didn't really want to return home to Penelope, about how he used the war to get away from his wife. No way. No, Ulysses understood that the place he was returning to was no longer his home: Telemachus had grown up, Penelope had grown lonely and Ithaca had changed in twenty years. Home was no home. *Unheimlich.* Ulysses understood he should have stayed away, remained with Circe in Aeaea. But that was fate, his fate, to return to a place that was temporally far away from his home. Geographical origin was overrated. Origin was no origin. He was living proof of that.

"Europe has memories, America has t-shirts."

He stepped back, and turned around and walked back to the screen. He sat down on the brick, his back resting near the center of the curved wall. He was sheltered here from the wind. He rubbed his arms to warm himself up. The red brick roof (floor) was heavily dappled in birdshit. He didn't see that in the movie either.

He ran his right hand against the rough surface of the brick. This was real, concrete and brick, he had no illusions about that. He remembered his thinking about forgetting in the salon. This landscape, this scene wasn't unfamiliar to him, he had been up on the terrace of the Casa Malaparte in Capri before. He might have been in the darkened Pueblo library closet, or sitting in some screening in New York, or in front of his wide-screen plasma at the meth lab, but he had been *here* before, with Lang, Godard, Bardot and the rest. There was no denying it, no forgetting it, no pretending it hadn't actually happened. But that "actually," what did it mean?

The architecture, the reality, the bricks and mortar existed before the film. *Malaparte avant Godard.* All cinema was documentary, in that it was the record of objects, scenery, figures that pre-existed the act of filming. Film transported you to a different place because it was the documentation of a different place that really existed. Film per se didn't create from nothing: it recorded what was already there, whether there was the recreation of a Parisian street on a soundstage, a bombed Vietnamese village near Hanoi or a house on Capri. Which came first, film or reality? That was the question he was asking: which came first *for him*?

"All you need for a movie is a girl and a gun."

Just to his right, only a couple of feet away, was the spot where BB lay naked on the towel. She was never his dream girl—he much preferred the brunette slimness of an Anouk or Slim Hepburn to the topheavy robustness of BB or Ekberg—although it was true that Godard didn't give her much to do besides pout. He liked her better in *And God Created Women*, especially the dance on the table. Although she did look good in the black wig on the floccari rug. And the beginning scene, the red white and blue. Which the evil American producers forced Godard to include. If we're going to pay all that money we want to see her ass. They were right.

Contempt was an odd choice for an urtext. There was no happy ending, and none of the characters learned anything. He couldn't relate directly to the plot—even when he was in the bad stage of his marriage he didn't feel contempt from or for his wife—nor could he identify with any of the characters. Piccoli was a drip, Bardot a cipher and Lang, well Lang was Lang. Prokosch was the only round character, maybe, the ugly American who wants to buy everything: culture, histories, narratives, love. But Piccoli, and everyone else, even Lang, was willing to sell. And sell and sell. No, Bardot and Prokosch die, Piccoli goes on to write his shitty play (and then marry Schygulla) and Lang finishes his film.

He had eight hundred thousand euros to buy the rest of his life.

And Godard in general, what was the attraction there? All that bullshit agitprop, and the absolute tedium of that Dziga Vertov Marxist crap. People fucked, talked too much and then usually died at the end. Sometimes they didn't fuck and sometimes they didn't die. Lots of times, things didn't make sense: sometimes you felt like Godard was so much smarter than you, and sometimes you were sure he was fucking overrated, throwing his shit on the wall to see what'd stick. There was nothing there to teach anybody anything. So why was Godard, especially *Contempt*, so significant to him? What was so absolutely vital, so all out goddam important that of all the places he could go in the world, he travelled thousands of miles, planes and trains and boats and carts, to sit alone on the terrace of the Casa Malaparte on the island of Capri, in the middle of February, waiting for a storm to hit?

"Every thought should recall the debris of a smile."

Maybe it wasn't so important which came first. Maybe what was important was that the experiences he'd had completely outside of film were inconsequential, unremarkable, easily forgotten. Prison, for example, where no movie had prepared him for the utter soul- and intellect-crushing dreariness and terror of day-to-day life. Or his days in the meth lab. They were really almost blanks, marked only by a few fragments of bodily memory: smells of the prison cafeteria and the odor of boiling meth, the metallic drip at the back of his throat after cooking Shamu, the sound of the guard's shoes at night in the utter darkness. These were clichés really, impersonal, unowned. His childhood, however, as painful as it was, was colored by his viewing of many films, from *The 400 Blows* to *Eldorado* to *My Fair Lady*, which he saw with his mother and brother at the drive in. Most were screened after the fact, and few dealt with a childhood he could identify with, or childhood in general, but they all did help shape his reality and his memory in some real and significant ways. Grad school was nothing but cinema, two or three movies a day sometimes, and afterward drunken conversations lasting well into the night: everything ranging from to *L'Avventura* to *Zabriskie Point*, from *Greed* to *Jeanne Dielman*. And his marriage, although going from Nick and Nora and *Woman in the Dunes* to *La Notte* and Cassavetes, was also marked by his Vincent Minnelli obsession (*Ziegfeld Follies*, *Kismet*, *The Bad and the Beautiful* and *Some Came Running*), which spurred his second Dean Martin phase (the first three Matt Helms, *Kiss Me Stupid* and even *Airport*): in other words, his marriage was defined by films that had very little to do with his factual life circumstances. So if it wasn't a direct relationship, a coincidence of character, plot or tone, then what was it? What was the relationship between the films he watched and the life he led?

The temperature dropped, and the sky darkened to a color he wasn't used to seeing. He probably should get back to his hotel, but he wasn't ready yet. He felt at home here at the Casa Malaparte, a place he had only visited before in a film. Why was this place more like home than his real home, the place he was from?

He was beginning to understand that it had to do with the way film and architecture merged together, the way reality and art combined to form a site where his imagination could flourish and remember. It wasn't so much a question of which came first, but a question of synthesis. The places he felt alive and connected to were the places where films provided a context or environment in which he could perceptively and sympathetically experience his surroundings. And the surroundings, the architecture, in turn provided a sensory, concrete atmosphere where his imagination could breathe.

There existed many places; prison and Pueblo for example, where the concrete reality didn't allow the cinematic context, and these places were flat to him, almost impossible to remember, dead. Conversely, there were many films that remained mute to him, voiceless, that didn't actualize themselves in his

living in the world. Most films made after 1980 fit into this cat-
egory. And almost everything made in the US after 1970. With
the exception of Coppola and Scorcese. Some of Scorcese. And
he did like that Turkish dude, what was his name?

"A tracking shot is a moral act."

But what exactly was it about film that allowed his imagination to exist? If it wasn't characters, plot, or tone, then what
was it? Technique didn't make any sense, nor did vision, for he
loved disparate directors and films, from 20's silent comedies
to 80's tragedies. He'd never been ashamed to talk about "aesthetic quality," but what the fuck did that mean?

He stood up. The wind was fierce now, and it was getting
too cold for his sweater. The rain would come soon. He looked
around at the sea, which was whitecapping continuously now,
and he could hear the tempo of the surf begin to increase in
both frequency and volume.

On some level, it had to do with choice. That's what you
learned from art, how to make choices. You watched a film and
saw the director, actor, DP make decisions, or rather you saw
the product of the those decisions, the end result, and if those
decisions were successful, if they were integral to the creation
of that work, then you learned from that. You learned how to
make similar, artistic decisions about your own life. Godard's
decisions, to film that first tracking shot with the voiceover at
Cinecittà, that was a decision. To include Lang as the director
of the film inside the film, that was a decision. To give Bardot
a black wig, a decision. All those decisions adding up, all those
choices where something could have gone wrong but didn't, all
those almost endless possibilities together formed something
that was just correct, and (gulp) true. Beautiful. Maybe that
was what great art was about. And with Godard, the fact that he
didn't always make the right choices underlined the difficulty,

the near impossibility of the process. Artistic choices were seldom easy, and it was a miracle that any good film (or painting, or novel or symphony) ever happened at all. What Godard showed, probably more than anyone else, was the impossibility of making good decisions every time. Godard first, then Fassbinder, they were the real highwire artists. Easy choices were attractive, but seldom right. It was nearly impossible to make good art, just as it was nearly impossible to live well.

This wasn't making any sense. If he had learned anything from film, it *wasn't* how to make good decisions. Look at his life. He decided to quit the pharm school track and go to Film History grad school. And then he decided to get married. And then he decided to sell drugs because he couldn't find a teaching job. And then he decided not to rat off his suppliers and do his full sentence. And then he decided to return home and supervise a meth lab. And then he decided to kill his coworkers. And then he decided to come here. No, his life had been a litany of terrible choices, one after another, with the exception of coming to Capri. His life was anything but beautifil: it was barely even a life.

He felt a drop of rain on his face, and stood up. The wind blew hard against his head and upper torso. The only thing that cinema had done for him was to help ease some of the pain and to help him escape the lowest points of his shitty existence. It was like heroin, helping him blot out the painful memories of his wasted life. It even determined his happier moments, like hanging out with Shelby. Film had come between him and his life.

"Loneliness isn't a cause of death."

Not that his life was any great shakes anyway. His mom was in a nursing home, he was dead to his father and his brother was out to kill him.

He wondered what Shelby was doing. He wished she had stayed. A week, a month, at least until he settled somewhere. Too much of a *Moontide* fantasy, true.

He walked again to the edge of the terrace. The wind picked up when he cleared the screen, and he could feel a few more raindrops on his head and face. He stopped at the edge, looked out at the rolling waves, and blew into his hands.

"Terrified to find myself in front of a mirror without any images."

He did have eight hundred thousand euros.

He leaned out.

"To be or not to be. That's not really a question."

"What I wanted to say is . . . Oh, what's the point. What an idiot. Shit . . . a glorious death . . . shit."

"The

End

of

Cinema."

Berlin Alexanderplatz

Rainer Werner Fassbinder (1980)

A pair of black John Lobb men's shoes lands loudly on the terrace. As the camera reverse zooms, the shoes (and now ankles, surrounded by black pinstriped silk) begin to stride purposively forward. The frame expands from the ankles to include the knees, then the waist and torso, until finally the complete form of Buster Keaton (Michelangelo) is visible in a long shot profile. He stops a couple of feet in front of the curve of the white screen on the roof. It's cloudy, but not nearly as dark as it was earlier, and the wind, while still evident, has lost much of its bluster and force.

"Franz, that was a very nice catch. How is he?"

"My name's not Franz, but thank you. He's fine, fine, sleeping like the proverbial baby. He's actually heavier than I imagined, and I was forced to utilize one of the local motorized carts. Which I just returned."

The camera tracks slowly to the right, and focusing on the midpoint between Buster and the second voice. "What will he remember?

"I'm assuming he'll be able to recall much of his time here, up until the end and his slapstick exit. He'll awaken in his bed puzzled about his transit from the Villa to his hotel bed, unable to piece together how he moved from the edge of this terrace to The Scalinatella, but for him it will likely remain forever a mystery, a lacuna in his life, an existential gap in the fabric of his consciousness. A jump cut."

"That's good, that's good, Franz. Excellent work."

"My name is not Franz."

Maria Falconetti stands with her back against the screen, typing into an iPhone. She's wearing a brilliant fuschia short elephant jacket, a tight black semi-sheer silk tank top and a slightly higher than cocktail-length white satin skirt with black silk leggings, all from Christian Lacroix. Shiny black leather Louboutin stiletto boots reach up to her knees. She has good legs, and a hint of left nipple peeks out from under the folds of her jacket. She sports the bristly shaved heard of the prisoner Jeanne, with a small diamond stud in her left ear. She looks up.

"I know it's not Franz."

"When he wakes up we could take him for a walk, perhaps find him some supper. Some time has passed since he partook of nourishment, notwithstanding the wine I provided last night. A substance designed to whet his appetite rather than sate it. And the poor bloke looks like he could use a good meal. We should be able to find a half-respectable trattoria or such on this island, even given the fact most establishments for dining and lodging are shuttered for another month at least. We haven't even reached Ash Wednesday yet. I mean who in his right mind comes to Capri in February? Not even Nicholas Cage and his extended *famiglia* show their pampered faces until at least after the Feast of the Sacred Heart. *Is quisnam adveho mane sino valde.* EVERYTHING'S boarded up, all the Pradas, the Ferragamos, the Versaces, the Lido del Faro, and the Quisi, everything. But people have to eat. There must be something open, something where one can get a nice *totani e patate* or some good ravioli. The harbor doesn't tempt, doesn't tempt at all. We might have to go to Anacapri. The Palace is open, if I'm not mistaken, and their kitchen, the name is presently escaping, is reputed to be quite decent, quite decent indeed. We could go there, enjoy a refreshing and tasty repast, and then our hero would be ready again to face the world. I think this an excellent plan. Do you agree?"

"I'm writing."

"Oh, I see, I'm sorry. You're writing the report. Would you like my assistance?"

She strides forward and hands the phone over. "Please."

Meth, Mister Meth (Mister Meth), Mister Meth
Mister M E T Hhhhhh (that sure spells Meth),
You will wind up soulless, close to death, if you mess with Mister Meth
(Don't mess with Mister Meth, don't mess with Mister Meth)
Don't mess with M E T Hhhhhhhhhh (that sure spells Meth).
You'll feel better once you testify (testify, testify)
[I want to testify, I want to testify]
Well, then, cleanse yourself my child, cleanse yourself
Brothers and sisters, I happen to now this poor unfortunate soul
And the fight she is waging against sin
That old Devil Meth has changed her
Into the unsightly person you see before you
Give us your testimony, my child.
[Well it all began with Dylan] (Yeah?)
[He said he needed ice to score] (Yeah?)
[But the tweakers killed him dead as can be] (No)
[That's why now I have to come clean] (Why?)

[Because if I didn't shoot and run] (Oh my)
[They would have murdered me!]
Who's to blame? (Who's to blame?) What's his name?
(We know his name, his name is)
Mister Meth, Mister Meth, Mister M E T Hhhhhhh
Don't ever mess, with Mister Meth, unless you want to meet
your death

If your head feels like it's an inch wide
You'll feel better once you testify (testify, testify, testify)
[I want to testify, I want to testify]
Well come forward, dear brother, come forward.
You see here, ladies and gentleman, a man who a mere five
years ago
Was fighting overseas for this great country
In the Armed Forces of the United States
Here he is now, a shadow of his former self
Oh give us your testimony, dear brother
[I was cruel and I was mean] (he was mean!)
[I was a fool, an asshole] (he was a fool an asshole)
[Meth got me in its clutches] (Meth got him in its clutches)
[And that's why I need forgiving] (Why?)
[Cause all I want to do is kill my brother]
That's a shame (what a shame), who's to blame (who's to
blame?)
(Mister Meth, Mister Meth, Mister M E T Hhhhhh, that
sure spells Meth)

(You'll feel better when you testify, testify, oh yeah, testify,
oh yeah testify)
[I wanna testify, I wanna testify.]
Ah, but you don't have to. [Oh, but I wanna, I wanna] (Let
the bum testify)

Okay, then put down that duffle bag and come forward here,

And let us lead you on the path of righteousness, not long ago, brother and sisters, this helpless soul was a PhD in Film Studies, with a beautiful and intelligent wife

Living in the great city of New York

He had his entire future in front of him

Possibilities endless the world his oyster,

Now go ahead and tell us your story

Don't be shy

[You see, I couldn't find a job and I needed money] (We've been there)

[So I got in with some bad characters] (Oh no)

[Long story short I started making drugs] (Your poor parents)

[And now I'm a killer on the run] (that's right)

Amphetamine is a whacked out scene it'll make you deaf and dumb

Ice ain't nice please think twice else you'll end up low as scum

It's so not cool to be such a fool and fly to the candle flame

Try some meth take your last breath there's only one guy to blame

(Oh Mister Meth, Mister Meth, Mister M E T Hhhhhh, don't ever dooooo)

Don't you think that you can cope if in you're in down with Nazi Dope

(Oh Mister Meth, don't mess with Mister Meth)

Your teeth will rot, you'll lose the plot if you mess with Mister Meth

Don't mess with M E T Hhhh and that spells meth

(And you'll meet your death with Mister Meth)

(Your last breath with Mister Meth)

Don't mess with Mister Meth

Don't mess with Mister Meth

Buster and Maria are sitting across from each other at a wooden table in a garden beneath an evergreen tree. A bottle of red wine and two glasses sit on the table between them, along with a pack of cigarettes, matches and an ashtray. Buster is writing quickly (miraculously) on the iPhone. *Haydn String Quartet Number Four* plays softly in the background. Buster leans forward and reads, "Carlos Gutierrez. Born 1976 in Durango, Mexico. Died 2006 outside of Pueblo, Colorado, of three gunshot wounds to the neck, severing the carotid artery. Mother, Mercedes Gutierrez, born Jimenez, deceased. Father unknown. Enlisted United States Army in May 1999, deployed Operation Desert Shield October 1999, dishonorably discharged April 2001. Discharge papers read: 'Private Gutierrez continues to show blatant disregard for the safety and welfare of the Kuwaiti civilians he comes into contact with. Allegations of rape and unlawful civilian fraternization continue and persist, and given the current investigations, have proven credible enough to warrant a DISHONORABLE DISCHARGE from the United States Army, effective forthwith.'"

Maria lights a cigarette and takes a drink from her glass of wine. "Write instead that 'Cruelty and hate made his face ugly and his posture grotesque, twisting the very muscles, bones and tendons into a misshapen mass of stupidity and violence. Seldom showered, and was reliable only to engage in whatever activity necessary to achieve his extremely limited interests. Possibly evil.'" She leans back in her chair, pauses, then says, "Write 'Deserved to die.'"

Buster nods, pours wine into a glass, sips, then reads, "Mackay 'Mace' Sotterfield. Born 1974 in Salina, Kansas, died 2006 outside of Pueblo, Colorado. Four gunshots, one in each knee, one penetrating right lung and one penetrating prefrontal cortex. Mother, Karen Sotterfield, nee Smithson, age 78, of Salina

Kansas. Father James 'Jimbo' Sotterfield, 85, also of Salina. Also enlisted United States Army in May 1999, also deployed Operation Desert Shield October 1999, also dishonorably discharged April 2001. Discharge papers read . . ."

Maria leans forward. "No, no. Write instead 'A natural follower, with few if any original thoughts. Technologically adept but socially insensate, bordering on autism or Asperger's. His limited or non-existent creative intelligence generated strong feelings of loyalty and dependence. His eyes were blank and vacant, and his mouth often open. Shoulders rounded and thin hipped.' Write 'He's much happier dead.'"

"Elizabeth DelPino. Born 1982 in La Junta, Colorado. Died 2006 outside of Pueblo, Colorado of three gunshot wounds to the face and upper chest. Mother, Jennifer Montoya, 50, of La Junta. Father, Leroy Gerrard, age and whereabouts unknown. Married Robert DelPino, 30 of Pueblo, in 2001, separated in 2003. Employed as an RN, St Mary Corwin Hospital, Jan of 2000, discharged (unspecified cause) May 2001. Employed Pueblo State Hospital as RN October 2001, discharged (unspecified cause) August 2003. Employed Sangre de Cristo Hospice November 2003, discharged January 2004."

"Write 'A born loser, with the intelligence to realize it. A drug addict and a sneak-thief who liked fast cars and felt the world owed her something. Facial expression reflected her perpetual disappointment, body reflected periodic bouts of bulimia. Would and did steal from everyone. Self-pity the defining characteristic.' Then write, 'Missed by no one.'"

Buster stands, shakes his legs. He leans over and takes a cigarette from the pack, taps it three times on the back of his hand, and inserts it into his mouth. He lights it with matches from the table, and then exhales. He begins to circle the table slowly, his eyes on the iPhone. "Jennifer 'Glow' Deveraux. Born in New Orleans, Louisiana 1982. Died in Pueblo, Colorado, from two gunshot wounds to the back, penetrating and collapsing both of her lungs. Mother, Virginia 'Virg' Devereaux, born Giscombe, age 46, of Baton Rouge, Louisiana. Father Clinton Deveraux of New Orleans, age 45. Enlisted in United States Army January of 2000, deployed Operation Desert Shield April of that year, redeployed to Fort Carson, Colorado November 2000. Retired from active duty United States Armed Forces in January 2003. Enrolled University of Colorado at Colorado Springs in August of 2003, dropped out after two semesters. Shall I continue in this vein?"

Buster hesitated to the right of Maria's chair. She looked up at him and exhaled. "No. Write 'Always ran with the wrong crowd. Unusual intelligence masked chronic self-doubt. Prone to fits of melancholia and depression. Facial expression often hopeful. Body had a forward lean. Felt trapped by previous decisions. Amateur oenologist.'"

The compound is overrun with various uniformed and plainclothes men and women, scurrying busily around, searching, measuring, inspecting, detecting. There are three men in bright orange hazmat suits, their hoods off, talking near the garage. Various vehicles, including ambulances, police cars, a blue and white SWAT stepvan and a white unmarked van are parked willy-nilly in the snow. A couple of uniformed cops shuffle out of the Professor's trailer, followed two white-jacketed ambulance attendants carrying out a white-sheeted body on a gurney. A few blotches of red blood are conspicuous on the white sheet. A middle aged balding man in a brown suit follows, and then another uniformed cop.

"Gang war?" the uniformed cop asks.

The suit shakes his head. "Doubtful. Most likely, one guy got fed up, decided to rip the rest of the gang off. That's my preliminary guess anyhow."

"I recently had a dream... that capitalism invented terrorism, to force the state to protect it better."

"Oh no. You're not one of those 9-11 conspiracy nuts, are you?"

"Same with drugs and gangs. It was all part of my dream. Very funny, isn't it?"

"What the fuck are you talking about?"

"Failure of CINEMA. Ludicrous disproportion between immense possibilities and result."

The light is dim, murky, with only the faintest yellow glow coming from the full-sized windows covered in brown butcher paper. A match illuminates Maria's face as she stands and surveys the small, square space. The match goes out and the murk returns. Then another match, and she looks to her right, stumbles forward. The light goes out again. Her outline moves to the wall, and she places her hands against it. She eventually finds the light switch. A single recessed weak florescent tube flickers on, off, then on, illuminating the shuttered shoe store, with the word PRADA in foot high letters in black stencil above the wall farthest from the windows. A multitude of knee-to-foot manikin legs lie in scattered two or three deep in piles on the floor, akimbo on shelves and against the walls, taking up nearly every inch of the space. Each leg features a shoe or boot. Maria sits on a cushioned chair and takes her left boot off. She then sifts through the scattered legs, removing some shoes and trying them on. Buster appears from the left, whistling a familiar tune.

"Please, Franz, please."

He stops. "My name's not Franz. You don't like my piping?"

"I don't like that inane song, nor that inane film. Lelouche and his Gallic sentimentality make me gag."

Buster leans against a counter, and pulls out a book from his suit jacket pocket. "Listen to this: 'Of course my language does not kill anyone. And yet, when I say 'This woman,' real death has been announced and is already present in my language; my language means that this person, who is here right now, can be detached from herself, removed from her existence and her presence, and suddenly plunged into a nothingness in which there is no existence or presence; my language essentially signifies the possibility of this destruction; it is a constant, bold illusion to such an event.'"

Maria tries on a poison green lizard-skin Mary Jane, and turns her ankle this way and that to evaluate it.

"'My language does not kill anyone. But if this woman were not really capable of dying, if she were not threatened by death at every moment of her life, bound and joined to death by an essential bond, I would not be able to carry out that ideal negation, that deferred assassination which is what my language is.'"

"Is he still asleep?"

"I believe so. This isn't about him, is it?"

"Franz, do you like these?"

"My name is not Franz. No, not really. I meant to say that this isn't a dream."

"Of course not. This isn't about his subconscious, or his psychology at all."

"But it's difficult to have narrative without psychology, don't you agree?"

"Difficult, but not impossible. How about these? I sort of like the beading."

Something definitely was amiss. When I walked into the trailer, I heard shrieks coming from the study. "No, no you bastards. Leave me alone. Please." I knew immediately what was happening. I walked slowly down the hall, afraid of what I was about to see. I turned into the doorway.

I saw Mace first, one hand on his video camera, the other holding the girl's left foot and ankle. He was hopping around from foot to foot with this stupid smile on his face. As I moved further into the doorway, Carlos' bulk dominated the scene. He had his shirt off, and his flesh rippled and swelled in rhythm. A string of thick saliva dripped down from his lips. I looked at his eyes, his face, wondered what a creature like that could be thinking. I didn't look down at the girl. I noticed the faint smell of salt. It took him a while to notice me. He was otherwise occupied, but finally he looked up. Didn't stop or modify his cadence.

"Hey Professor, what's up? You can be next. Mace'll wait, he likes the *culo* anyway. Don't you Mace?"

The girl screamed, and he slapped her hard with his backhand. I continued looking into his eyes. How much were we alike?

"You got any lube or anything? She's dry, and tight. Maybe we give L'il Kevin a turn. Need lots of lube for that."

Fucking pig. Fat fucking pig. I had to get out of there. I turned and walked quickly out of my trailer to the truck. I got in and drove for miles, trying to get that image of the thick string of Carlos' drool out of my head. When I got back, five or six hours later, there was no sign of the girl.

Buster and Maria are sitting on a bench in front of *L'Arco Naturale*. Buster stands, moves to the railing, and gazes out, through the rock arch and down to the sea far below. "I've never cared for heights," he says, loud enough for Maria to hear. "I don't like being above the birds." He turns, sees some painted graffiti on the ridge of rock behind the fence.

He nods with his head. "Look at this. 'Nostalgia is just another form of depression.' Who said that? Was it Wim Wenders?"

Maria twists around. "No Franz, Wenders never said anything that intelligent. Some American I think." Maria turns again, looks down at her shoes, a pair of rainbow beaded lipthroated Chanel pumps. "I'm not sure about these shoes."

"Whomever said it has a point, don't you think? And why don't you like Wim Wenders? And why do you insist on calling me Franz?'"

"Which question would you have me answer?"

"The first, definitely the first."

"He does have a point. Nostalgia is a cheap escape, an abdication of thought, an abandonment of character. There is, however, a huge difference between nostalgia and a suspicion of progress. Those who insist on believing their own generation the best and the brightest are doomed to remain children. Look at America, for example. In culture, as in life, there does exist progress, as well as decadence: some things are better than others and some things really aren't as good as they used to be."

"*Der Engel der Geschichte*. Americans have their faith in progress, but they have their nostalgia too. Look at the Professor, who can't watch a film made after 1985."

"The Professor misses a past he never had."

"The very definition of nostalgia. To be fair, he never had much of a present, either."

"I'm not sure that's true. And what does he miss, exactly? I don't think it's primarily a recreation of the feeling he got when he watched all those movies in the tiny darkened library room. He doesn't want to relive his childhood, not even his childhood in that room. It's not a longing for a lost self."

"What is it a longing for then? Love?"

"A longing for longing? A desire for desire? I don't fucking know."

395
Medium shot of Professor and Shelby in the car. Shelby turns away, looks out the passenger window.

SHELBY (softly)
Anyway, I'm not the one with the pistol in his hand.

396
Close shot of Professor from front. He guffaws, and stares straight ahead.

PROFESSOR
We're all in a fucking nursing home: we just don't know it. All we do is eat and shit, and sometimes manage to fuck. And the important thing is not to eat where you shit. That's all life is. That's all life fucking is.

398
Reverse shot of Shelby. She's looking directly at the camera.

SHELBY
I want that money.

The background is unimportant: a few easels and the backs of stretched canvases are visible before they fade into the darkness. She sits on a blanket-covered stool, bended into a near right angle <TAH, where T is the big toe of her left foot (resting on a cushion), A is a point just beyond the curve of her ass and H the tip of her head. Her right thigh juts out parallel to the floor, and forms two near forty-five degree angles, <KAH and <KAT, where K is her knee. Her right elbow rests on her right knee, and her arm runs upward, nearly parallel with her spine. She rests her chin in her right hand. Her left arm is tucked inside her right, her left elbow rests on her right thigh and her left forearm separates her breasts, her hand grasping her right shoulder. Her left breast curves out from her torso, brushing against her left forearm, her nipple pointing out parallel to her right thigh. Her shoulder length brown hair is tucked behind

her left ear. She rests in perfect profile, her eyes open and her mouth slightly curved downward in a thin line. Her head and neck will sometimes break the pose: she'll swivel the top of her head around, or dip the tip of her head, her eyes staring down at the cushion floor, the hair falling down on both sides. But she always returns to profile, always recovers stasis.

The skin tone varies from a light Bisque or Moccasin color on the top of her back and her left hip and thigh, where the light hits most directly, to a darker Peru Brown where her flesh is in shadow, to the deep shaded Saddle Brown of her right thigh and torso to the near black outlines of the crook of her right arm and the distorted triangle of her pubis.

The scratching of pen on paper, brush on paper, and the quiet clattering of pen and brush on inkpot remains constant, but out of frame. Sometimes it will be silent for a few moments, but the scratching and clattering inevitably return.

Buster and Maria walk side by side down one of Capri's narrow, twisting, alley-like streets. They hear a young child's voice on a radio, playing loud. Buster slows, then stops. He places his hand on Maria's elbow to stop her. "Listen."

"The art of existing against the facts, says Oehler, is the most difficult, the art that is the most difficult. To exist against the facts means existing against what is unbearable and horrible, says Oehler. If we do not constantly exist *against*, but only constantly *with* the facts, says Oehler, we shall go under in the shortest possible space of time."

The radio abruptly goes silent.

"These shoes don't really fit with these tights, do they? I should have kept my boots."

Buster looks down and Maria's shoes. "No, I agree. You should have kept your boots."

"I'll put them back on before we go to dinner."

They walk for a few steps, and then Buster says, "We haven't really touched on the women question."

Maria turns to him but continues walking. "What's the women question?"

"There aren't that many women here."

"Here in Capri?"

"No, you know what I mean. All the women here are objects, symbols, flat characters to be loved or killed. The women are all mere images, actresses: there are no female directors, not even any women DP's."

"We could have followed Shelby. But she certainly doesn't need our help."

"No, Shelby can definitely take care of herself." They turn into an even narrower incline that is mere steep passageway. Maria walks in front of Buster.

"I mean there are not that many women directors anyway."

"There are a few. Ackerman, Varda, Lupino, Rainer, Holland. Don't forget Riefenstahl."

"Ha, Riefenstahl."

"I don't think we can privilege directors over actors anyway. That's tired. This isn't the 60's or 70's." Maria turns back and looks over her shoulder. "What can I say? He's a character and he has a story. This was part of it."

A muppet-faced Russian partisan stands over a portrait of Adolf Hitler in the mud. He brings his tattered rifle up his shoulder and fires, once, twice, three times, four, five, six, seven . . . After each shot, the reels of history rewind: corpses rise from graves, soldiers depart battlescarred fields, units march back into their homes, houses reassemble, bombs lift upward into bellies of warplanes, shells fly backward to their barrels, borders are uncrossed, tears return to eyes, flags fall, speeches go back into throats, documents are unsigned. Baby Hitler in the arms of his mother.

Cinema's dream?

Eight, nine.

Or cinema's nightmare?

The Russian's face is splattered with mud. His unit awaits. He turns.

She sat in the truck and rubbed her ankle while he hurried into the Stop-N-Go. She was glad the radio was off: those songs were beginning to get on her nerves big time. It was important to pick your soundtrack, and not live in someone else's story. And if you were going to live in a movie, it had better be a good one, not some weak black and white subtitled shit. Whatever. She wished he'd hurry up with that ibuprofen.

Buster and Maria sit supine on two blue and white striped lounge chairs on a hotel balcony, drinking from large martini glasses and smoking cigarettes. Maria is wearing her knee high boots, which she admires from time to time. A brilliant white tablecloth has been placed on a table behind them, upon which an elaborate bar has been arranged, as if for a party. Buster is playing with the iPhone. Maria leans back over her shoulder at the sliding glass doors. "Is he awake yet?"

"No, I don't think so. This is quite the device. Did you know you can obtain films and watch them on the screen."

"Those aren't films, Franz."

"My name is not Franz. But look, yes you can: *Superman, Superman II, Superman III, Superman Returns, Batman, Batman Returns, Batman Forever, Batman and Robin, Batman Begins, The Dark Knight, Spiderman, Spiderman 2, Spiderman 3, Darkman, Iron Man, Iron Man 2, Watchman, The Transformers, The Transformers 2, Hellboy, Hellboy 2, Hulk, The Incredible Hulk, The Fantastic Four, The Rise of the Silver Surfer, X-Men, X2, X-Men: The Last Stand, X-Men Origins: Wolverine . . .*"

"Franz."

"You can even download *La Passion de Jeanne D'Arc*, for example, and view it anytime you like. A couple of clicks, a credit card, and wait, wait, and then look, there you are." The Voices of Light soundtrack plays faintly from the phone.

"That's not me."

Buster moves the iPhone closer and then further from his face. "It is difficult to read the intertitles. Not that we need them: the story is fairly obvious. Look, look at you." He leans over and shows the phone to Maria. "Such tears."

She looks away. "That's not me."

Buster leans back on his lounge. He looks at the screen, then at Maria. "You're right, it's not you." He takes a big drink from his martini glass. "This isn't about film, is it?"

"Yes and no."